Freefoot

Also by Allen L. Wold

The Planet Masters

Star God

Jewels of the Dragon

Crown of the Serpent

Lair of the Cyclops

The Eye in the Stone

V: The Pursuit of Diana

V: The Crivit Experiment

V: Below the Threshold

Cat Tales

A Closet for a Dragon and Other Early Tales

Stroad's Cross

Freefoot

Stories from Blood of Ten Chiefs

by

Allen L. Wold

Ogden House

The original stories were published in this order:

"The Deer Hunters" *Blood of Ten Chiefs* v.1, 1986
"Summer Tag" *Wolfsong: Blood of Ten Chiefs* v.2, 1988
"The Flood" *Winds of Change: Blood of Ten Chiefs* v.3, 1990
"First Born" *Against the Wind: Blood of Ten Chiefs* v.4, 1992
"The Naming of Stonefist" *Dark Hours: Blood of Ten Chiefs* v5, 1993
"Howling Time" *[untitled]: Blood of Ten Chiefs* v.6, unpublished.

Some of the characters mentioned, but not appearing in the stories, were created by other Participants (as we were called) in the Blood of Ten Chiefs anthologies. All others, except Freefoot, who was created by Wendy Pini, are mine.

Thank you to Richard and Wendy Pini, for creating ElfQuest, and for allowing me to publish this collection of my stories from the *Blood of Ten Chiefs* anthologies.

Thank you to all the fans who have showed a continuing interest in ElfQuest, and who have on occasion asked for my autograph.

A special thank you to the late Robert Lynn Asprin, for inviting me to the party.

And, of course, thank you to my wife Diane, who has always supported me in every way, and to my daughter, Darcy, who has always been an ElfQuest fan.

Contents

These stories are presented, not in the order in which they were published, but in the order in which they occurred.

Halfhill was called that because it was just half a hill, a steep clay cliff cut by Small River, which ran from west to east a few eights of paces south of its base. The cliff was taller than two elves, and long enough for every family to have its own den dug into it. Between the bank and the stream was the common yard, a treeless stretch of short grass where the elves spent most of their time with each other when not hunting, sleeping, or working on special projects. There were more trees and a waist-high fern brake across the stream, where the cublings frequently played in the mornings, or when it was hot, or whenever they felt like it. Trees and bushes crowned the top of the cliff, which sloped gently down upstream to the west and downstream to the east. The forest closed in at either end. This was home.

Summer Tag

There was still morning mist in the forest as Raindance, Suretrail, and Sunset moved quietly and quickly from tree to tree. Their eyes searched in all directions, their ears were tuned for any sound of pursuers, or of their quarry who, since the trail was not that fresh, might be anywhere. In spite of this, they carried no weapons, other than their knives, and they tracked their quarry without the aid of their wolves.

Raindance, tense as a bowstring, was in the lead. Her rather short amber hair was damp with more than mist. Though it was still early in the day, she and the others with her had already seen some action, and she knew that one misstep could cost her and her companions. The trail was faint, but she spotted a bent leaf ahead, a sure sign that she was leading them right. She raised one hand briefly to signify that she'd found the way.

Suretrail, two paces behind her, and responsible for making sure no one came at them from the sides, had seen the leaf before Raindance had, but he had said nothing, as this was her lead. Two paces behind him Sunset, as brilliantly dressed as if this were a normal day, kept watch at their back. She tried not to breathe too loudly in the near stillness, struggled to identify each of the small noises she did hear, to make sure none of them was someone on their trail, even as they pursued another.

Though the elves did not have any weapons, they each carried an elaborately carved taal-stick, as long as an arm, in special slings at their belts. That was part of the risk of the day, since the sticks were no defense against any agressive animal they might run across inadvertently.

They came to the edge of a shallow ravine, where more firs than maples grew. The slope was steep, and they looked down together. It was a good place for an ambush, but there seemed to be nobody there.

"Which way," Sunset asked as she scanned the tree limbs overhead. She was nervous, though no stranger to this kind of hunt.

Suretrail glanced up the ravine, then down, then across again. There, on the far side, was the mark of elvin passage, but he said nothing, waiting for Raindance to report it.

"Straight across," she said. Her voice was only a whisper. "But it looks like they doubled back." Around them, except for the normal chatter of squirrels and birds, the forest was silent. "How many?" she asked Suretrail.

"Three, I think." He, too, was whispering. "We're gaining on them."

"Quiet," Sunset hissed, and they all crouched lower as they listened.

The birds off to their left had stopped calling. They held their breaths as they tried to sink into the all too scanty cover on the edge of the bank. But whatever had disturbed the birds must also have stopped moving, for after a moment the chirps and other bird sounds returned to normal.

Suretrail breathed more easily now. It had been hard for him not to take the lead from Raindance, as good as she was. He wished Sunset had not been so intent on living up to her name and had worn something less brilliantly colored this morning.

"Let's move," Raindance said softly, "and see if we can't shorten their lead."

"And," said Sunset, "leave whoever is following us behind."

With one more glance around, in case of ambush, and specially careful of a dense tangle of wine-berry vines hanging from a pair of gigantic cedars on the far slope of the ravine, they left their resting place and descended the steep but shallow slope, then hurried up the other side.

Lonebriar, as he was known then, high in that very tangle of vines, kept still as he watched the three elves cross the ravine. He had had a tense moment when it had seemed that Suretrail had looked straight into his eyes, but apparently the older elf had not seen him after all. Lonebriar had never intended to ambush them from here anyway, he would make too much noise coming down through the vines, and would lose all surprise. He was willing to be patient, to wait for just the right place before making his move.

He did not stir until the three elves on the ground below had disappeared from sight, and almost from hearing, and even then kept to the treetops as well as he could as he left his hiding place and moved to intercept them. He did not follow them directly, but paralleled their line of travel. It wasn't his trail they were following — those others had gone by some time before. And besides, it was Raindance he wanted.

He moved quickly, being as quiet as he could, away from the three below in an arc, and then back again, hoping to cross their path some distance ahead of them. But even as he chose his place he heard them turn aside. What for? He dropped down to the ground to look for the trail they had been following and couldn't find it. He hadn't followed that other trail far enough, and had missed a turning.

By now he could no longer hear the all but unnoticeable sounds of their passage. He feared that he had lost them and started off in pursuit. The forest floor was more open here, which gave him less cover, but it allowed him to be as quiet as he wanted to be. When he saw a slight movement maybe fifty paces ahead, he took to the trees again, and ran along the higher branches — oaks here — hoping for a good place to make his move, and in his hurry almost revealed himself to the three elves. He stopped and ducked back behind the high trunk and listened.

There was no sound of movement below. He peeked around the trunk, barely wide enough this high up to conceal him, and saw the three, crouched in some tall weeds, barely visible from his vantage point. They must have heard him, since they were glancing almost directly at him. He very slowly moved back out of sight and waited, listening as hard as he could, until he heard the subtlest of rustles from below.

But if he let them get away from him again, he might not have another opportunity for a long time. He had to take a bold chance. Once again he moved on in a direction which he hoped would take him ahead of their line of travel, until he came to a single smooth snake vine dangling down. He looked at it for a moment, weighing the possibilities in his mind. Its lower loop ended only three elf-heights from the ground. Yes, this would serve him very well indeed. Especially since he was rather well concealed by the foliage of the branch on which he crouched. He gripped the vine and waited. It was a tricky move, and a risky one. If he didn't make a count this time, he would have lost his only chance. And it seemed that his plan was going to be tested, for there they were, coming toward his tree, with Raindance still in the lead.

It was all he could do to wait until they passed — marvelous luck — directly beneath him. He gripped the vine with one hand, took his taal-stick from its sling with the other, then stepped off the branch and slid, a bit too fast perhaps, down the vine to land just two paces behind Sunset.

The three heard him as his feet hit the ground, and startled, started to turn, but he leaped, swung his taal, and struck Sunset a glancing blow on the head. Without a pause he spun and even as Surtrail turned to face him, struck him on the shoulder. Raindance was just beyond Suretrail, and Lonebriar leaped for her too, but she was already standing in a face-off crouch. He pulled up short.

"Where did you come from?" Suretrail exclaimed as he burst into laughter.

"Owl pellets," Lonebriar said with a frustrated jerk of his taal-stick. "I could have gotten you two any time, it was Raindance I wanted to count."

Raindance was laughing too as she straightened from her crouch, but Sunset was rubbing her head ruefully.

"A bit rough, there," she said. "Were you in those wineberry vines back there by the ravine?"

"Way up high," Lonebriar said, "but that was just to spy you out."

Suretrail was looking up at the snake vine from which Lonebriar had descended. "If you'd come down just a moment earlier," he said, "you'd have gotten her."

"I know," Lonebriar said, "but I got greedy at the last minute. Sorry I hurt you, Sunset."

"Not the worst I've been hurt today," she said. "That was a real good move."

"Who are you following?" Lonebriar asked his three friends.

"Hornbird and Puckernut, I think," Raindance said, "and Grazer."

"I havent' seen them all morning," Lonebriar said.

"I got Grazer once," Suretrail said, "when he had to stop and send Smoke back to the holt. The poor wolf just didn't understand that he couldn't play with us today."

"Can I join you?" Lonebriar asked.

"Sure," Sunset said.

But Raindance shook her head. "I think I'd like to go off on my own for a while," she said.

So she left them, and Lonebriar, Sunset, and Suretrail went on, skirting the far edge of the part of the forest they'd designated for counting taal.

Faun was not old enough to go out with the elders that day. She felt old enough, but she didn't yet have her adult name. She was he oldest of the cubs, but still her parents, Grazer and Dreamsnake, had told her she had to stay near the holt. It was little comfort that her mother, too, had to stay behind to take care of the children. Her father was out there having fun, while Faun had to make do, playing with the younger cubs.

Of course, once she started the game she forgot about the elders. Right now she was sneaking through the fern brake, across the stream from the holt. Beyond the edge of the head-high ferns she saw Sundrop, just about to take refuge in the same place. Faun leaped out with a shout and tagged her, fair and square. Sundrop, surprised, burst into a scream of laughter. Faun laughed too.

Then the two stood back to back for a moment. Faun yelled "Now!" and they ran away from each other as hard as they could. Faun counted two eights of paces, then ducked behind a tree, hoping to get out of sight before Sundrop could turn around and start chasing her, but Clamshell, quite a bit younger than she, was already there and waiting for her. He tagged her with both hands, and laughed at her surprise.

He's going going to be good when he gets a little older, Faun thought as they stood back to back. That was an important part of the game, as was racing away from each other a counted two eights of steps when the winner of the last tag gave the word.

This time Faun kept running until she got to the white rock, a large outcropping of massive stone, and ran around behind it, almost afraid she'd find somebody there waiting for her. But luck was with her, there was nobody there this time. She stopped a moment, looked quickly over her shoulder, then climbed up the rough, white face toward the rock's flat top. She kept low, in case anybody was watching, and paused on top to catch her breath.

From up here she could see Greentwig, almost as old as she, come sneaking around the rock from the willow wood right next to it. This would be an easy tag, she thought, but before she could make a move, Sundrop dropped down from an overhanging branch and got him.

Poor Greentwig, Faun thought, he's tagged nobody so far this morning. But he seemed to be having fun in spite of that.

Faun watched as Sundrop and Greentwig stood back to back and raced away from each other. Greentwig went right back into the willow wood, but Sundrop ran away from the white rock through clear forest, so Faun dropped down from her hiding place to chase after her. She ran so fast that she caught up with Sundrop before she finished her count of paces and tagged her as she ran past. But Sundrop must have heard her coming because she turned just then and tagged Faun in return. Both were surprised.

"I thought you were Greentwig," Sundrop said, laughing.

"He's in the willows," Faun told her as they put their backs together.

But before they could race away from each other, Greentwig came screaming out from behind a tree and got them both.

"Good score!" Faun told him. She was very surprised, Greentwig was hardly ever clever enough to think of doing something like that.

"I heard you chase Sundrop," he said. His smile was as broad as if he had actually accomplished something. "It's my first tag, and a double, too."

They all three put their backs together and, on Greentwig's word, raced away in different directions. Faun ducked into a clump of berry bushes, where the foliage was so thick she couldn't possibly be seen by anyone outside the bush. She crawled through the low, clear space near the stems, then felt someone tag her hard on the ankle.

She turned in utter surprise, nearly scratching her face on the low branches, and saw that it was Sprig, the youngest of the cubs.

"I was waiting here all the time," Sprig said, laughing so hard he couldn't crawl out of the bushes. They laughed together, then worked their way clear of the berry bushes and stood back to back. Sprig's head barely came up to Faun's shoulder blades. He gave the word and they raced away.

This time Faun kept running until she was far away from everybody else, then she circled around the outside of the area they'd marked as the territory of the game, until she heard a squeal coming from the hollow in the bend of the stream. She approached carefully and saw Clamshell and Greentwig just beginning their race.

She followed Clamshell as he left the hollow and turned past the triple stump, until Sundrop jumped out from behind the dead cypress and tagged him. But instead of running on up to them, Faun stopped short while she was still concealed by a tree trunk. Clamshell and Sundrop hadn't seen her, so she waited until they stood back to back, and then raced in and tagged them both before Sundrop could give the word.

"That's not fair," Sundrop shouted, stamping her foot.

"Yes it is," Clamshell said, while Faun danced laughing around them both, eager to be on with the game. Sundrop pouted for just for just a moment, then joined in their laughter. Then they put their backs together, Faun gave the word, and they raced off again.

Lonebriar, Sunset, and Suretrail were taking an easy time of it. They had counted taal several times in the short while they'd been a team, but each had been counted in turn more than once. Now they were on the far south side of the taal area, and seemed to have lost track of everybody. At least, they hadn't seen another elf for long enough that they felt safe in letting down their guard. It gave them a chance to catch their breaths, but if they'd really wanted rest, they'd have stayed back at the holt, or gone fishing with Bluesky and Starflower. It was action they wanted, and so they were heading back north toward the center of the taal area. Their casual movement meant that they were vulnerable, but at the moment that was all right with them.

When they first heard the commotion, off to one side, they all had the same thought and went immediately up into the low branches of the oak under which they were passing. Even as they hid themselves in the thick foliage they realized that it wasn't elves they had heard, not the sound of somebody count-ing taal, more like an animal hunting. But the sounds, half whistle, half bark were not like those of any animal with which they were familiar, so with only a few quick glances to each other by way of communication, they went back down to the ground to investigate.

As they neared the noise they heard a wood pig squeal in pain, but somehow more agonized than if it were just being killed by a predator. They gave up caution and hurried on until they came to a small clearing, where they found two swordfeet, like giant birds but with green scales instead of feathers, and grasping claws instead of wings, attacking a very small wood pig. It was the calling of the swordfeet they had heard while in the tree. No wonder they hadn't recognized the sound.

One swordfoot was a large adult, the other a nearly-grown juvenile. Swordfeet hardly ever came this far north and, in fact, only Suretrail had ever seen one before, when he and some others had gone ten days' journey to the south long ago during a bad, dry summer of no rain and no game.

He was just as fascinated as Lonebriar and Sunset as they watched the two creatures leaping at the small animal. The great claws on their hind feet, which gave them their name, slashed at the poor animal over and over again. The wood pig was bleeding from several deep wounds, but still too quick to let the swordfeet get a killing blow. As he watched, Lonebriar felt a strange sensation in his mind, like a sending, but different.

The larger of the two swordfeet was taller than an elf, but had been crippled at some time and was not as agile as it should have been. The smaller one, nearly as tall as Lonebriar, was quicker but clumsy. Together they kicked out at the frantic, dancing wood pig, sometimes leaping over it for a better blow, working together to keep it from getting away, chattering at each other in their strange voices.

Eventually the wood pig tired, and the younger swordfoot got lucky. It lashed out with a powerful kick and it's long talon caught the wood pig just under the shoulder. The blow tore through skin and ribs, ripping the animal open so that its insides fell out on the ground.

As if they were very hungry, the two intruders from the south immediately started tearing the wood pig apart, even before it was fully dead. The strange sensation Lonebriar was feeling became stronger. It was thin and sharp, almost a taste in the back of his throat. And while it was like a sending, it had no content, other than a feeling of great hunger at last being satisfied.

But in their fascination with the killing, and their excitement, the elves had gotten careless, and had let the wind get behind them. The swordfeet suddenly caught their scent and, jealous of their prey and chirping angrily, turned toward the elves and leaped to attack them.

The elves were taken by surprise, and discovered that they were a lot nearer the swordfeet than they had thought they were. The swordfeet made two great leaps toward them before the elves realized what was happening, and they had to scramble to get out of the way. Each elf jumped in a different direction, which fortunately confused the swordfeet for just a moment.

But it was only for just a moment. The swordfeet were incredibly fast and quick, and immediately turned their attention to Suretrail, who barely managed to get up into a tree before being ripped apart by the swordfeet's huge talons. Lonebriar and Sunset, while they had the chance, decided to follow suit, and each climbed the tree nearest them.

The swordfeet, frustrated, dashed from one tree to another and back again, but soon gave up since the elves no longer presented a challenge to their prey. As they returned to eat up the wood pig, too small really for a decent meal, Lonebriar felt the sending sensation again, like an acrid taste in his mind, not very strong but very clear.

Let's get out of here, Suretrail sent to his companions. The others agreed whole-heartedly.

They quickly worked their way higher up into the trees, and then away from the creatures at their meager meal. When they were far enough away to pose no further threat to the swordfeet, they returned to the ground and headed on toward the center of the taal area. Lonebriar felt the odd sending diminish, until at last it faded away altogether.

He started to tell the others about it, but Suretrail was talking very earnestly with Sunset about what to do about the swordfeet.

"We can't just let them run around up here," he was saying.

"But there are only two," Sunset said, "and the older one looks like it won't live very long."

"That's as may be," Suretrail said, "but they're both female, and the younger one looks like it's carrying young. If she has her litter up here, we'll have more trouble than we can handle."

"A few swordfeet won't be much competition," Lonebriar said.

"That's not the point," Suretrail answered him. "The trouble is, swordfeet attack anything — deer, big cats, wolves, elves. I've seen healthy adults kill a gray bear. They're fast, and strong."

"These two don't seem too impressive," Sunset said.

"They are not a good example. Another problem is that wolves can't smell them — or at least they don't pay any more attention to swordfeet than they do to lizards and small birds. And swordfeet are smart, very smart. But they are different from other hunters, they don't think the same way a wolf does, or a cat. No, we can't let them stay up here in our hunting grounds. And if more swordfeet came north, we'd have to find a new place to live."

"So should we go back," Lonebriar asked, "and destroy them now?"

"Tomorrow will be soon enough," Suretrail said, "but destroy them we must, and the sooner the better. But right now

I want to find somebody to count." He patted his taal-stick and grinned.

    Raindance inched her way through a tangle of thornbushes, moving so quietly that a robber bird just four arm-lengths away didn't notice her. She knew there was another elf nearby, maybe two, though she had seen or heard nothing so far. She was good at the game, had counted many times with her taal-stick, and had not been counted herself yet even once. Graywing had once said that she thought that maybe Raindance could sense other elves even when they weren't sending to her, but Raindance didn't agree with that. Maybe it was smell.

    She paused to listen, heard the robber bird, now behind her, preen its deep blue feathers, heard something that sounded like maybe a fox, some way off, digging up a mouse burrow, heard a slight rustling up in a tree ahead of her, just a scratching. She looked up toward the sound, like tiny claws on bark, and saw a squirrel running along a branch. There was something about its movement —

    She looked back along the way the squirrel had come, and heard a chattering there, where another squirrel was scolding at something concealed among the oak leaves. Nearby was the ball of leaves that was its nest, and further out on the limb were, yes, two elves — Freefoot and Shadowflash. Raindance let her breath out slowly and watched them for a moment, then backed away, just as quietly and carefully, until they were out of sight.

    She circled around their tree, far and fast, until she was well ahead of them and, she judged, on their line of movement. Then she climbed a tree of her own. She went high up, as high as she could, then out on a limb which overhung a lower branch which, she hoped, would be the one Freefoot and Shadowflash would take when they went by. There was a free drop between her limb and that one. Now all she could do was become a part of the tree and wait.

    After a few moments she heard the faintest of sounds approaching — bare elf feet on tree bark. She did her best to become even more invisible, and even more silent than she was. And her guess, if that was what it was, had been correct. First Freefoot, then Shadowflash stepped out onto the branch below her.

When they were directly underneath her she dropped down to their branch. She landed just behind them, and struck them both, one right after the other, with her taal, even as they were reacting to the impact of her landing. Freefoot, in fact, was so startled that he nearly fell out of the tree.

"Easy," Raindance said, laughing, as she helped him regain his balance.

"What did you do," Shadowflash asked, "fly?"

"Just watched the squirrels," Raindance said. "Who are you tracking?"

"Suretrail," Shadowflash said, "and Lonebriar and Sunset, if we can judge by the marks."

"At least," Freefoot said, "we know Suretrail has two others with him."

"I left them together a while ago," Raindance said, "I suppose they could still be teamed up. Can I join you?"

"Sure," the other two said together.

"There's Suretrail's mark, right there," Freefoot went on, pointing to a tiny disturbance in the bark of the limb a few paces further on.

They followed the trail, which went down from the tree at last. Shadowflash, as the longest sighted, took the lead, while Raindance kept on the alert for anybody who might have been following them. Ater a while the trail began to get rather vague, and they all had to work hard to follow it. So intent were they on this task that they almost stumbled across a bear cub before they were aware of it.

"Not good," Freefoot said. The mother bear had to be near by, and none of them wanted to deal with her if she thought they were a threat to her cub, so they backed away from the little animal, who was not at all afraid of them, and indeed seemed to want to play. But before they could get fully away, two strange green scaly creatures, as big as elves, jumped out, without warning, from behind a fallen tree behind them.

The larger of the two swordfeet misjudged its leap, and its huge talons missed Freefoot, but it hit him with its body and knocked him to the ground. Shadowflash was not so lucky. The smaller swordfoot caught him a glancing blow on his right side with one great claw, ripping through his jacket and the flesh beneath.

Raindance had little time to think, but she was nearer Freefoot. She leaped for a branch that nearly overhung her chieftain, then swung from it, aiming a two-footed kick at the swordfoot adult which was about to attack him again. She hit it on the shoulder and knocked it away even as it was jumping.

Shadowflash, meanwhile, had recovered enough to be able to jump on the juvenile, just above its kicking feet, and struck at it with his knife. But the swordfoot's scales were tough, and his blows hardly scratched it.

The adult swordfoot had turned toward Raindance, who was still swinging from her branch, and raised one foot high to kick at her. The momentum of her swing just barely took her out of its way. Freefoot got unsteadily to his feet, drawing his knife as he did so, and stabbed at the swordfoot, aiming just under its foreleg. The blade bit through the softer skin and scales there, but did not penetrate the ribs. The swordfoot leaped away and turned to face him again.

Shadowflash was having trouble hanging on to the juvenile. It jumped and twisted and threw itself about, and at last threw Shadowflash to the ground. With almost the same motion, the creature turned on him.

Raindance, at the same time, was taking advantage of the adult's momentary distraction to swing away to the ground, but she was so concerned for Shadowflash, who was stunned by his fall, that she fell clumsily herself, and that left the larger sword-foot free to pursue Freefoot, who now was trying frantically to get away from it. Raindance lurched upright, then froze — as did everyone else — at the roar of a large animal thrashing through the undergrowth nearby.

It was the mother bear, about which they had forgotten in the fight, which came crashing out of the brush toward them — and they were between her and her cub.

Freefoot was directly in the black bear's path as it charged, upright on its hind legs, forepaws outstretched, more than twice as tall as an elf. He tried to duck out of its way, but the bear swung one paw and knocked him backward, through the air and against the trunk of a tree. The adult swordfoot continued its attack by leaping at the bear, and slashed at it with both talons. The bear was saved from serious injury only by virtue of its dense fur and thick summer fat.

Raindance had to choose and Shadowflash, this time, was nearer, so she jumped to his aid even as the smaller swordfoot turned away from him. But before she got to Shadowflash she saw the bear grab the larger swordfoot in a mighty hug, and couldn't help but watch. It looked like the adult swordfoot would surely be killed, but the juvenile leaped high at the bear and struck her with both talons on the shoulder.

Shadowflash, without Raindance's aid, got unsteadily to his feet, and staggered off, away from the battle. With just a glance at him over her shoulder, Raindance turned her attention to Freefoot, who was lying very still at the base of the tree against which he had been thrown. She circled around the battling bear and swordfeet to him. Even as she did so, the bear swung a forepaw at the juvenile swordfoot and knocked it away, and the adult, which had not been unscathed by the bear's hug, attacked it again.

Raindance knelt beside Freefoot. He was unconscious. She grabbed him under the arms and dragged him away from the fight, in the same direction Shadowflash had gone. As she had to pull him backwards, she was able to see the two swordfeet suddenly run away from the bear. The bear followed only a pace or two, then stopped to search for her cub, which was running toward her and squealing with fright.

Freefoot began to mutter and toss his head as Raindance pulled him to his feet. She half carried him after Shadowflash, whom she found leaning against a small elm tree, as if unable to go any further. He straightened up when he saw her coming, and tried to help with Freefoot, but he was too badly injured himself and was barely able to follow her away from the bear. They did not go far, but stopped when they came to a big, sturdy tree with low branches. Raindance pulled Freefoot up first, then helped Shadowflash clamber up after. They got themselves to the next higher branch with some difficulty, where Raindance propped Freefoot up against the trunk.

After a moment to catch her breath and to make sure her two companions would not fall, Raindance looked to their wounds. Freefoot had several broken ribs, and was still dazed from hitting his head on the tree trunk. Shadowflash's wound was not deep, but it was very long and he was bleeding badly and in shock. Raindance bound his wound as best she could, and tried to reassure him that the loss of his taal-stick was really not very important under the circumstances. She had lost her taal-stick too, though Freefoot still had his in his belt.

"We'll have to find them," Shadowflash insisted. His words were slurred, his shock was worse than she had thought.

"We will," she reassured him, "but later."

There was no hope for it. Freefoot and Shadowflash were too injured to move, and they needed healing right away. The only thing Raindance could do was to make sure they were secure, then hurry back to the holt for help and proper weapons.

Lonebriar, Sunset, and Suretrail were moving quickly through the taal area. They had seen or heard no other elf in quite some time, and were eager to find someone to pursue or elude. They went along through a stand of pines, which had carpeted the forest floor with a thick layer of needles, so that nothing else grew between the trunks of the trees.

Lonebriar felt something tickling the back of his mind, like the memory of a dream that comes back unbidden. It was another strange sending like before, over almost before he could start to pay attention. It was — had been — sharper than before, and yet very faint, as if it had come from a great distance. He tried to puzzle it out, but the only sense he could make of it was anger and pain. He started to mention it to the others, but before he could speak they came to an open glade.

They stopped at the edge and looked out at the sunlit place. There was no cover higher than an elf's knee — all low ferns, flowers, thumb-bucket plants, and clumps of grass. It wasn't a very large glade, maybe only a hundred paces across, but the verge surrounding it was dense — a good place for an ambush.

"Shall we go around?" Sunset asked. "If there's anybody watching and we go across, we'll draw them out."

"That's just what I was thinking," Suretrail said, "and that's why I think we should go out in the open and take our chances. It's no fun tromping through the forest all by ourselves."

"That's true," Sunset said thoughtfully. "And come to think of it, if we lay a good trail, whoever is following us will go through here too, and we'll be safe on the other side in ambush."

"Is there somebody following us?" Lonebriar asked.

"Where have you been?" Suretrail said. "Didn't you hear that branch break back at the draw?"

"I'm sorry," Lonebriar said, and started to go on to explain his distraction, but Suretrail and Sunset were already in the glade. He followed after.

They went across it quickly, keeping all eyes open in all directions at once but, almost with disappointment, they got to the other side without anybody jumping out at them. Once back in the forest they became more careful about the trail which, as a part of the taal, they had to leave for others to follow, and circled around just inside the verge of the forest, so that they could keep a watch on the open glade in case their pursuer was closer than Sunset thought. When they had gone about half way back to where they had entered the glade, they paused to rest a moment and enjoy a little sit-down. Lonebriar was just about to mention the strange sending sensations when Stride appeared, at the side of the glade, right at the spot from which they had entered.

She looked out across the glade, even as they had done, and for a moment seemed to hesitate. Then her gaze went to the ground, and a moment later she started forward, with many glances from side to side, but obviously following their carefully laid trail.

The three elves in ambush did not speak nor send — sending would have been unfair — but a few quick glances from one to another, a few gestures, and their plan was set.

Suretrail, as quietly as he could, started to circle back through the woods toward the point where they had left the glade, going well in from the edge. Sunset, in the meantime, went on around the other way, and when Stride was nearly to the forest verge, came out of the forest behind her, boldly but silently, and nearly caught up with her, just as she was about to enter the forest. Suretrail must have made some slight noise just then, because Stride, who had been about to turn around, hesitated a moment, and stared intently into the forest ahead of her, and did not see Sunset, who was in plain view behind her, but now frozen absolutely still. That was Lonebriar's cue. He went in the direction Suretrail had taken, but just at the edge of the glade, and so was able to see all that happened.

Stride waited by the verge just a moment longer, but the sound she had heard was not repeated. She felt nervous being out in the open like this, and hurriedly made her way in past the thick growth to the forest proper. She felt immense relief at being back in cover, and was about to turn around to see if anyone were following, and surely would have seen Sunset had not Suretrail, just at that moment, jumped out from behind a tree and touched her lightly with his taal-stick.

"Rats and mice!" Stride exclaimed, jumping involuntarily into the air. "Were you there all along?"

"More or less," Suretrail said, grinning.

"But I heard you —"

"I threw a nut," he said. And just then Sunset raced up from behind, leaped through the verge, and struck Sunset with her taal.

"Puckernuts!" Stride exclaimed. She had seen Sunset at the last minute, but hadn't been able to drop into the face-off stance that would have invalidated the count. "Where did you come from?"

"Right out there in the open," Sunset said, laughing.

Stride was so perturbed she didn't even notice Lonebriar who, by this time, had come up behind her and was standing next to Suretrail. "That was a pretty clever move," she said to Sunset. And then Lonebriar touched her with his taal, and she jumped into the air again.

"Oh, come on!" Stride cried when she saw who it was. "Not you, too." But she couldn't help laughing herself now.

"Me, too," Lonebriar said, or tried to say through his own laughter. "What a blow! count three in a row."

It was the best taal count any of them had ever been involved in that day, and they all enjoyed it immensely, even Stride. But they were having such a good time that they didn't notice, until it was too late, Moonblossom dropping down out of the tree right over their heads. She hit both Lonebriar and Suretrail with her taal, but Sunset and Stride were a bit further away, and though very badly surprised, managed to face Moonblossom off. But just barely, they were laughing so hard.

"Were you in on this too?" Stride asked her.

"No," Moonblossom said, "I was up in that tree the whole time."

"Why didn't you get the three of us," Sunset asked, "when we came through just a few moments ago?"

"You were being too careful," Moonblossom said, "and I was afraid to take the chance."

"You couldn't have picked a better time," Lonebriar said. "Too bad you couldn't have gotten us all, I don't think anybody's done that before."

"Raindance has," Moonblossom said, "the last time we counted taal, four summers ago."

"Well," Suretrail said, "we found the action we were looking for, and a bit more besides. Let's change partners."

"I could use some help," Stride said. "Why don't you and I go together for a while?"

"That's fine with me," Suretrail agreed.

"Then let's us three make a team," Moonblossom suggested.

"I think I'd like to go alone for a while," Lonebriar said, "if that's all right with you two."

"It's okay with me," Sunset said. So they split up and went their separate ways.

Faun was getting tired of playing tag. She was, she felt, getting to old for that kind of thing. After all, she would be taking her adult name in not too many more summers, and elders didn't spend their time playing tag. She told Clamshell she was quitting, and went to find her mother.

Dreamsnake was busy in the treeless area between the stream the clay cliff which gave Halfhill its name, and in which the elves had dug their dens. She was making pants for Sprig, and having trouble with her needles. They kept on breaking. They were all old, but there was no antler left to make new ones, and there would not be more until the fall. That meant she had to be especially careful in boring holes in the pants leather, and would have to stitch each seam twice, since the only needles she had left were small ones.

Faun came up to where she was sitting cross-legged, and waited while she finished a thread of jumper gut. "I want to go out to the taal area," she said.

"Just a minute, cubling." Dreamsnake straightened out a new piece of jumper gut by running it several times between her fingers. It was fine enough for the needle she was using, but the needle had already begun to show a crack near the eye and she wanted to be careful with it, to make it last as long as she could.

Faun waited a moment as her mother threaded the needle. The sound of the other cubs' laughter, coming from across the stream, made her want more than ever to be grown up. "Can I go?" she asked. "I'll be careful."

"Go where?" Dreamsnake asked as she picked up the half-sewn pants.

"Out to count taal."

"Oh, goodness no." She smiled up at her daughter. "You're not nearly old enough for that. Now let me finish this so Sprig won't have to go around naked."

Faun wanted to argue the point further, but her mother was obviously so concerned for her sewing that she knew that to interrupt her further would only make her angry, so she wandered off, looking for Graywing or Glade, the only two other elders left at the holt, hoping that maybe one of them would give her permission to go.

She went upstream — which just happened to be in the direction of the taal area — but before she went very far she heard adult voices. There, just beyond the edge of the holt, were both Graywing and Glade, talking with Raindance. Grizzle, Raindance's wolf, was with her, and that made Faun wonder, because she knew Raindance was counting taal and that wolves weren't supposed to be a part of the game.

"Hello," she called as she ran up to them.

"What is it, Faun?" Graywing asked. Her face was troubled, and for a moment Faun thought she had done something wrong.

"I want to go out and count taal with Raindance," she said.

"Oh, no," Graywing said. "You're too young for that."

"I'm nearly full grown!"

"And besides," Graywing went on, "there's been some trouble, Freefoot and Shadowflash are hurt. You'll have to stay here."

"I can help," Faun tried to say, but Bentfang came bounding up to them just then, and Graywing turned away to nuzzle her wolf.

"Go tell Dreamsnake," Raindance said to Faun, "that Graywing and Glade are going with me."

Faun turned to Glade. He had often let her do things when the other elders wouldn't. "Please, Glade," she begged, "can I go with you?"

"Not this time," Glade said, and she knew by the sound of his voice that he meant it. He started to say something more, but Streak was loping easily toward them, and he turned his attention to his wolf.

Faun couldn't understand their preoccupation. Raindance was saying something about litters, though it was not the time of year for wolf cubs, and what they could possibly have to do with anything was beyond Faun's comprehension.

"Are we ready, then?" Graywing asked.

"We'd better get going," Glade said. He turned to Faun. "Let your mother know where we are," he said, "and we may want you, too, when we get back."

"At least now we know," Graywing said to Raindance, "why Lightpaws left so suddenly a little while ago." Lightpaws was Freefoot's wolf.

But Faun wasn't paying any more attention to what the elders were really saying than they were to her. She wanted so badly to go out and prove herself grown up that she could think of nothing else, not aware that her behavior was proving her to be the child she thought she wasn't.

So, being childishly selfish and feeling put off, she left the adults to their adult business and wandered back toward the bank. As soon as she could see Dreamsnake, bent over her work, she stopped, and looked back just in time to see Graywing, Glade, and Raindance, all fully armed, go into the forest with their wolves.

She looked back at her mother. Dreamsnake was very busy, and not watching her. She was supposed to give her mother a message, but the opportunity was too good to miss. She would surprise her elders, and show them how good a tracker she was. As quietly as she could, she ran after them.

She hadn't gone very far into the woods before Bouncer came bouncing up to her. Bouncer was her first wolf, and getting rather old. She stopped to greet him with a nuzzle and a wrestle.

"You can't go with me," she told him. "I'm going off to count taal, and wolves can't play."

He sat up and looked at her, his head cocked to one side, almost as if he understood.

"Now you stay here," she told him, "and I'll tell you all about it when I get back." Then she ran off after Graywing, Raindance, and Glade. She knew approximately where the taal area was, since the elves who had gone off to play had planned its boundaries that morning before they left, but she wanted to practice her tracking skills by following the three elders. She easily found their trail, and then proceeded with more caution since, she knew, if she were caught, they would send her back home in disgrace.

Lonebriar had a strategy. First, he was sure that most of the other elves were in the northern part of the taal area, and he wanted to get to them as quickly as possible, to try to catch somebody by surprise. Second, he was sure that the companions he had left behind would be coming after him, so, though he had to leave a careful if subtle trail, he wanted to get well ahead of them, circle around, and get behind them if he could.

When he had covered half the distance across the taal area, he climbed up into a beech tree and paused a moment in a crotch to catch his breath and listen in case anybody else were nearby. But he heard nothing but the sounds he expected to hear if he were alone in the forest, sounds with which he was most familiar. Maybe, he thought, his strategy wasn't so good after all, if it left him with nobody to compete with.

As he got down from the tree he remembered the strange sending he'd felt several times that day. It had seemed to have come from the swordfeet, but he didn't know how that could be. He opened up his mind and tried to see if he could catch that almost taste again, but nothing came to him but his own thoughts.

Oh, well, he'd have plenty of time to worry about it later. He tried to guess the best direction to go to find some elves to count taal on and went off, looking for a trail.

He hadn't gone more than a hundred paces when he found tracks — two elves. He examined the bent leaf, the torn bit of moss. That looked like Stringsong. A little further on there was a scratch in the bark of a tree trunk. Catcher maybe. The trail wasn't very old. He put all thoughts of swordfeet and strange sendings out of his mind and went in pursuit.

Sunset and Moonblossom followed a trail into the marsh. It had not been a wet summer, but there was always lots of standing water here, and the ground underneath was thick, sticky mud.

The going was especially tricky in the marsh, in several ways. Only occasionally was the ground firm enough to keep a footprint, and the rushes and reeds were always bent and torn anyway, so the marks left by the elves they were pursuing were hard to distinguish. Besides that, it was hard to move fast — the mud sucked at their feet, or the water was too deep, or the rushes too thick to push their way through. There were a few trees in the marsh, but they were either dead, or spindly water willows, and in neither case any good for climbing. And to top it off, the mud and the reeds made it almost impossible to be quiet.

Still, this was the way the trail led, and crossing difficult ground like this was part of the contest. But at last, when they came to a bit of firmer ground, they were able to stop for a moment and listen. Up ahead, barely audible over the rustling of rushes, the screaming of red-wings, and the gentle susurration of the marsh itself, they could hear what they were sure were other elves, their quarry perhaps, having as difficult a time of it as they.

There was a dead pine nearby. Moonblossom decided it was worth the chance, so she shinnied up the barkess trunk as high as she dared, both for fear of being seen and of bringing the rotten tree crashing down. Sunset stared up at her anxiously as she searched the marsh in the direction of the sounds. After a moment she froze in place, and then slowly slid back down to the ground.

"It's Quickthorn," she whispered to Sunset, "and Rillwalk-er. They're not that far ahead."

As quietly and as quickly as they could, they worked their way through the mud and rustling rushes toward the other two elves, and at last could see them, moving very slowly toward where the marsh merged with the little lake. But Quickthorn and Rillwalker were not taking any chances. Each was covering the other's back, so that they both were almost walking sideways. It would be impossible to come on them by surprise.

Sunset had an idea. She touched Moonblossom's arm, drew her back just out of sight of the others, and whispered in her ear a moment. Moonblossom liked the plan, so they circled around until they were parallel to the others' line of travel, and at a place where there was a relatively clear stretch of shallow water leading away from where Quickthorn and Rillwalker were, then stood up.

"Where did you come from," Sunset said, not very loudly, but trying her best to sound surprised.

"I was waiting right there," Moonblossom said, "in that clump of willows."

"Want to team?" Sunset asked as Moonblossom carefully stomped around in the willows, making it look as if she had actually been there.

"Sure," Moonblossom said, and they hurried away up the clear stretch, leaving a muddy trail in the water.

They rounded a very dense clump of rushes and reeds, went on further leaving a more than obvious trail, then doubled back to the clump. Moonblossom wormed her way in among the stalks of the tall plants, while Sunset went opposite, along a fallen log to hide behind the moss-covered stubs of its branches.

They didn't have long to wait. Sunset was barely in place, and painfully aware of a damp footprint she'd left on the log, when sure enough, Quickthorn and Rillwalker came up the trail.

Just as they passed her hiding place, Moonblossom jumped out of the rushes and tapped Quickthorn on the shoulder with her taal-stick. But Rillwalker, just a pace ahead, had time to turn and face off.

"I told you it was too good to be real," she said as Quick-thorn ruefully straightened up from the crouch he had automat-ically fallen into

"And you were right," he said, but where's the other —"
But before he could finish, Sunset leaped out from her hiding place and lunged at Rillwalker, who was turning even then, and poked the end of her taal into her chest.

"Owl droppings!" Rillwalker said. "Can't even follow my own advice." Then she laughed, and the others joined in with her.

"That was a good trick," Quickthorn said. "Are there any more of you hiding in the muck?"

"Not that we know of," Moonblossom said. "I've counted ten taal today, how about you?"

"I can count only five," Rillwalker said, "but I've been hit seven times."

"Poor luck," Moonblossom said, "but I've been counted nine times — twice by Raindance."

"She got me once," Sunset said, "Lonebriar got me once, and Grazer got me once, but I counted nine taal."

"I'm even up," Quickthorn said, "done and got six times each."

"Has anybody gotten Raindance?" Moonblossom asked. Nobody had.

"She'd make a good target," Quickthorn said, "don't you think?"

"Do you suppose," Rillwalker said, "if we worked together, at least one of us could count her?"

"It's worth a try," Sunset said. "Somebody should get her at least once before the day is over, and it might as well be one of us."

Lonebriar was sitting near the top of a high rock, sur-rounded by the down-hanging branches of a beech tree that grew from a cleft half way up behind him. He had been been waiting there for a little while now, sure that his quarry would pass this way. He'd followed Stringsong's and Catcher's trail until he had noticed that it overlapped yet another, older track. So he'd circled around, gotten ahead of them, crossed their line of travel, and found that other track, which had led him here to the rock. It was the track of a solitary elf, he didn't know who, and it curved around the base of the rock. But Lonebriar had followed it no further. Instead he had climbed up here to wait in ambush.

He had begun to wonder if he had made the right decision when a subtle movement back along the trail, in a stand of maple saplings, caught his attention. It was Stringsong and Catcher all right, intent on that other track he'd noticed. They came, cautiously, up to the base of the rock, but even as Lonebriar got ready to slide down its face and count them both, the two elves got suspicious, and he hesitated when they backed off a pace or two.

"There's been somebody else here ahead of us," Catcher whispered to Stringsong.

"They're going the same way," Stringsong said, "and this other trail is fresh."

"If we're lucky," Catcher said, "we can count them both. But isn't this first trail just a bit too obvious?"

They started to go around the rock the other way, hoping to meet their quarry face on. Lonebriar quietly changed his position so that he could watch, and then saw that their move had been anticipated — there was someone else waiting just a quarter of the way around, in a hollow in the rock. It was Smarthand, no other elf had that much girth. Lonebriar had not been all that careful when he'd climbed up, how had Smarthand missed hearing him?

It was a good trick, and Lonebriar grinned as he watched Stringsong and Catcher near the hollow. Smarthand could not see who it was that was approaching, but jumped out just as Stringsong came in view and jabbed him in the chest with his taal. Catcher, two paces behind, was able to face off in time.

"How long have you been waiting there?" Catcher asked Smarthand, laughing so hard she could hardly stand.

"I nearly fell asleep," the fat elf admitted with a chuckle. He wiggled his taal under Stringsong's nose. "How did you fall for such a trick?"

"It was Catcher's idea," Stringsong said, poking at her good-humoredly with his own taal.

"You could have gone the other way if you'd wanted to," Catcher said as she eluded his stick. "Then you could have gotten both of us maybe."

It was time, Lonebriar thought, to make his move. The three elves were getting a bit silly, joking at each other, and might not notice the slight sound he made as he started to slide down toward them. He had almost reached the ground when Smarthand looked up, but Stringsong and Catcher were caught unaware, and he counted them both.

"It's you," Smarthand said, "who woke me from my nap."

"You should have heard me coming," Lonebriar said with a grin. "This makes my count eight for the day."

The three rescuers and their wolves entered that part of the forest which the elves had designated as the taal area, and had to pass through a depression, filled with hand-leaf bushes. If Raindance did have a special skill in detecting animals or other elves, it did not serve her now, for without warning they almost stepped on the two reclining forms of the swordfeet. Even the wolves had not detected their scent.

The swordfeet were just as startled as the elves, and jumped up, hissing and waiving their long, clawed forelegs. Raindance staggered back into Graywing, but managed to throw her javelin at the larger swordfoot before it could attack, striking it in the chest. The swordfoot, already injured, fell sideways and knocked the smaller, younger one aside. That was when the wolves finally realized they had an enemy to deal with, and Grizzle and Streak leaped at the younger swordfoot, while Bentfang harried the older one.

Graywing recovered her balance, and she and Glade joined in the fight with their spears, while Raindance now had to use her ax. The swordfeet — old and injured, young and clumsy — fought like demons, leaping, slashing, kicking, even biting though that was not their way. Elves and wolves pressed them, stabbed and bit.

At last it was too much for the green, scaled monsters. Though the juvenile was only superficially wounded, it was inexpert at this kind of fight — one on one was more its style — and seemed reluctant to take chances. The adult was bleeding badly from several wounds, including a deep ax gash in its neck, and its previous wounds had already sapped much of its strength. As soon as there was a moment's pause, the swordfeet turned away from the elves and wolves and dashed off out of the bushy hollow and into the woods. The wolves did not try to pursue, nor did the elves, who were glad enough to fall exhausted to the ground and watch the swordfeet disappear through the distant undergrowth.

"You got her real good," Glade said to Raindance, who's ax-blow it was which had caused the older swordfoot so much damage. "See," he pointed at the leaves of the bushes through which the swordfeet had run. They were spotted, almost sprayed with blood.

"Let's get it over with," Graywing said. She pushed herself to her feet and started after the animals, but Raindance grabbed her arm and stopped her.

"We can take care of them later," she said. "Right now we have to find Freefoot and Shadowflash."

Lonebriar, Stringsong, Catcher, and Smarthand were on their way back to where Lonebriar had last seen Raindance, in order to pick up her trail. They went by a slanting tree, one that had been blown half way down in a storm, long ago, but which had continued to grow until it was almost full size, though its top rested against its neighbors which now, too, had grown crooked. There they came across another trail and paused a moment to try to figure out who had made it.

"It's not Raindance," Smarthand said as he examined the all but invisible footprints on the smooth bark of the slanting tree.

"That's Fire-Eyes," Catcher said, "and it looks like Fangslayer is with him."

"Let's get Raindance first," Stringsong said. "I've counted Fangslayer once already."

Lonebriar wasn't paying much attention, and missed what Catcher was asking him. "I'm sorry," he said. "What did you say?"

"I said, shall we still look for Raindance, then?"

"Yes, sure."

"What's the matter?" Smarthand asked. "Are you all right?"

"Yes, I'm fine, it's just —" He hesitated as he felt, once again, that strange almost-taste in his mind, which now he was sure meant that the swordfeet were not too far away.

"Well, let's go then," Stringsong said. "You have to show us the way."

"All right," Lonebriar said, but as they went he told them about the sensations.

"You ought to talk to Dreamsnake," Catcher told him, laughing gently as they went on.

It was a very dark and dense part of the forest where Sure-trail and Stride were following, not so much a track — the undergrowth was too thick — as the vague sounds of other elves. It was impossible to be quiet here.

But they weren't always sure whether they were trailing someone, or someone was trailing them, because sometimes the sounds seemed to come from behind them, or from one side or another, as often as from ahead.

Meanwhile Fire-Eyes and Fangslayer, not that far off in the same dark part of the forest, were nervously trying to get away from the sounds which they were sure were being made by pursuing elves. But sometimes the sounds were not so much behind them as ahead, or off to one side. The forest canopy was so thick here, and the forest floor so dark and tangled with shade-loving bushes and vine-stems, that it was easy for even an elf to get turned around. More than once Fangslayer had lost his sense of direction. It was not a part of the forest the elves usually visited, except in winter.

And so the two pair of elves stalked each other, all unknowingly. They got ever more confused, sometimes mistook the sounds of other animals for elf sounds, and eventually completely lost track of where they were, or where the more open forest was.

Fangslayer was getting more and more tense with every passing moment. Suretrail was decidedly jittery. Stride was beginning to think that this wasn't any fun any more, and Fire-Eyes was almost ready to call out and give up.

The two pair of elves continued to become ever more lost. They alternated between trying to be as cautious and quiet as possible, and being almost careless and quite noisy, for elves, in their movement through the undergrowth.

Once Suretrail and Stride tried to backtrack, but the forest became unfamiliar, and they had to admit that they'd lost their own trail. Once Fire-Eyes and Fangslayer thought they had found a clear trail for sure, only to realize after going twice past the same tree, with its distinctive shelves of fungus, that they had been following themselves.

The sounds of other elves, and maybe of other creatures too, continued to confuse them and at last they actually became frightened, wondering if maybe there was a real enemy out there. Each of them, privately, wanted to stop the hunt, but none of them cared to admit it to their partner.

At last, as it had to happen, they all came together unexpectedly, each pair meeting the other as they came around a huge tree from different directions. Their startlement was so great that they all leaped clumsily back from each other, Suretrail actually falling to the ground, shouting and waving their taal-sticks as if they were weapons.

"By the High Ones," Fire-Eyes said, gasping for breath. "I thought we were done for there."

Stride helped Suretrail to his feet. "Let's get out of this place," she said.

"Yes," Fangslayer said, "I agree. At once."

They were so relieved to end the hunt that they didn't care that none of them had been able to count taal. Without further hesitation they started off, not paying any attention to which direction they took, so long as it got them out of the darkness. But even as they went, they thought they could hear … something … behind them … stalking them ….

Lonebriar, Stringsong, Catcher, and Smarthand, having finally picked up Raindance's trail where Lonebriar had left her, followed it to the place where she had met Freefoot and Shadowflash.

"Now remember," Catcher said, "whatever we do, we count Raindance first."

"Maybe," Stringsong suggested, "if one of us makes a try for Freefoot or Shadowflash, that will distract her and give one of the rest of us a chance at her."

"Let's see where we find them first," Smarthand said.

They followed the triple trail until they came to a place where the ground was torn up, and the foliage beaten down. And there were bloodstains. Lonebriar knelt by a large, half-dried spot. "It's elf blood," he said.

As far as they were concerned, the game was over. They examined the ground all around the signs of struggle, looking for a clue as to what had happened.

"Bear tracks here," Smarthand said. His hands went to his waist, where he normally carried his two axes, one on either side, but of course, he'd left them at the holt.

"They're too smart to tangle with a bear," Catcher said. "Something else must have happened."

Lonebriar was looking at some other footprints in the ground, dug in with such force that their maker could not be identified. And yet … he touched the track with a finger, and felt, in the back of his head, a ghost of that strange sending taste he'd felt before. "The swordfeet were here," he told the others.

"Are you sure?" Stringsong asked.

"I can … feel them, sort of, in these tracks."

"You've been into the dreamberries again," Stringsong said.

"Maybe not," Catcher said. "Think about Dreamsnake."

"But she doesn't actually send to snakes and lizards," Smarthand said.

"No, but she knows them, maybe it's the same way with Lonebriar and swordfeet."

"Now is not the time to argue about that," Smarthand said impatiently. "Elves have been injured, we've got to find them, and find out what happened. Let's follow the blood, and hope they're still alive."

"They were able to get away," Stringsong said.

"Maybe," Lonebriar told him, "or maybe the swordfeet ate them."

"So let's stop arguing about it," Smarthand said, "and go!"

But before they could follow the trail of blood, Lightpaws, Freefoot's wolf, came bounding up to them, in obvious distress. The wolf didn't even pause to greet them, but sniffed around, smelled the blood, turned away from it — it wasn't Freefoot's blood, then — and dashed to another place where he started to howl, softly, in the back of his throat.

"Easy," Catcher said to the wolf. "We'll find him, show us the way."

Whether Lightpaws understood or not didn't matter. Another wolf answered his howl, and they all ran in that direction as quickly as they could.

Faun had been having a hard time keeping up with Raindance and Graywing and Glade, and at last she decided to throw caution to the winds and just run after them. After all, they had not been trying to disguise their trail. She didn't understand that, she thought that leaving an all but secret trail was a part of the taal.

The elders seemed to have gotten awfully far ahead of her, as if they, too, had been running. No, their footprints were not that far apart. But they had been hurrying.

The tracks led her to a hollow where a bunch of hand-leaf bushes had been trampled down. What in the world had they been doing there? Then she noticed blood splatters on some of the leaves, and suddenly she was very frightened. Had they been hurt? Had they been hunting? She didn't have a weapon, and besides, whatever they had been fighting, it had left horrible huge tracks in the ground. But there, their footprints went on beyond the place. She hurried after them.

It seemed to take forever, though actually it wasn't very far, but at last she heard movement up ahead and, now that she was away from the scene of the fight, she forgot her fear and re-membered that she had wanted to prove to the elders how good she was at tracking. She became more careful about making noise herself, but still hurried on, until she finally saw Raindance, Graywing, and Glade, with their wolves, up ahead beneath tall trees, where the ground was clear enough to see a long way. They were moving quickly, but now she had no trou-ble keeping them in sight. She continued to play her game, always keeping a nearby tree between her and them as she ran after them.

She was able to close the distance to the elders, until at last they were so near that to go any further would reveal her to them, so now was the time to try to tag them. She left the shelter of the last tree and ran toward them, trying to be as quiet as she could, but it wasn't quiet enough. All three elders turned toward her before she was half way there.

"What are you doing here?" Graywing demanded. She sounded angry.

"I came to count taal," Faun said. She was disappointed to have been discovered without even tagging one of them.

"We are not counting taal," Glade told her. He, too, was angry. "Freefoot and Shadowflash have been hurt, and there are swordfeet in the forest."

"She must have gone right by where we fought them," Raindance said. "Listen, cub, you are very lucky. If the sword-feet had come back while you were there, they would have had you for lunch."

"I didn't know," Faun said. She suddenly felt very young.

"You'll have to go back to the holt," Graywing told her. "Did you tell your mother where we were going?"

"No."

"Oh, dear. We can't just send her back alone, the swordfeet are between us and the holt."

"I'll take her back," Glade said, "and if any other elders have come in, I'll bring them back with me." Then he took Faun by the arm and led her away.

Lightpaws didn't have to lead the four elves very far. The wolf bounded up to a huge tree, with low, overhanging branches, where Shadowflash's wolf, Snapper, was pacing and leaping, as if he were trying to get up into it. Not too far up, on one of the low-hanging limbs, the elves could see two forms, huddled and still.

"Freefoot," Catcher called up. "Is that you?"

"He's here," came Shadowflash's weak voice. "He's unconscious."

"Hang on," Stringsong said, "we'll be right up." He grabbed the lowest branch, out where it was just above head height, and pulled himself up.

Catcher and Lonebriar were just behind him, but before they could follow, something huge and black came out of the bushes beside the tree, came so fast that Smarthand, who was nearest, didn't have a chance. It was the wounded bear, angry and looking for trouble. She caught Smarthand utterly by surprise, and sent him flying with one great swing of her mighty forepaw. Smarthand crashed up against the tree trunk, and slumped down unconscious.

Catcher reached over her shoulder, her hand fluttering in the air where her javelin should have been. Lonebriar fell backwards a pace, then ran to get between the bear and Smarthand, who was bleeding from his nose and mouth, as well as from the four long gashes across his chest. Stringsong crouched on the limb, drew his knife, then dropped down on the bear's back and started slashing at the animal's face, its nose and eyes.

Which might not have been too smart a thing to do, because the bear turned around in place and, thinking Catcher was the cause of her pain, struck at her and hit her a glancing blow, which nonetheless sent her spinning to the ground. Stringsong was just barely able to hang onto the bear's thick fur.

Lonebriar knelt by Smarthand, and touched him gingerly. The fat elf was still alive, though his breathing was ragged. Lonebriar left him, looking frantically around for something to use as a weapon, and heard a mewing from the bushes where the bear had been hiding. He looked and there was the cub, standing on its hind legs, excited and frightened by the battle.

Stringsong was still clinging to the bear, stabbing at it any way he could. Catcher was struggling to her feet, holding onto a dead branch, one end of which was reasonably sharp. Smarthand was choking. Lonebriar looked at the cub, at the bear, then back at the cub. He didn't like what he was going to do, but elf lives were at stake.

Crouching low, hoping the bear wouldn't notice him, he ran to the cub and grabbed it. It was surprised, and started to struggle. He threw it to the ground, pressed it down with his knees, then wrenched its ears until it cried out. Then, as the mother bear turned to see what was wrong, he stood and kicked it, not toward her but at an angle. It yelped with pain and crashed to the ground. The bear took two steps toward him, bellowing in utter rage, then the cub ran off and the bear, still wanting vengeance, decided instead to drop down on all fours and chase after it.

Stringsong leaped from its back at once, and ran toward Lonebriar who, having made sure that the bear was really leaving, had gone back to Smarthand. Catcher, staggering and holding her chest with one arm, got to Smarthand too, just as

Stringsong did. The three elves turned their attention to their unconscious companion.

"Something's broken inside," Lonebriar said as he wiped the blood away from Smarthand's mouth and nose.

"Do we dare move him?" Stringsong asked.

"If we don't," Catcher said, gasping with the pain of her own battered chest, "the bear will come back and finish the job."

"Are you all right?" they heard Shadowflash's weak voice call down from the tree.

"No," Lonebriar said.

"I'll take care of Smarthand," Catcher said to Stringsong. "You help Lonebriar bring those two down. We've got to get away from here."

They could hear the bear, chasing its cub and bellowing, getting further away, but they knew they would have precious little time before it returned. Stringsong and Lonebriar quickly went up into the tree, where they found Shadowflash, conscious but weak, holding onto Freefoot, who's eyes were open, but who's mind was elsewhere. They brought Freefoot down first, then Shadowflash.

"We need to get help," Lonebriar said. "We can't carry all three of them, and Catcher can hardly walk by herself."

"Let's find a place to hide first," Stringsong said.

So as best they could, they dragged their injured companions away from the tree.

It was getting late in the afternoon when Suretrail and Fire-Eyes decided to go one way while Stride and Fangslayer went another. As much fun as it was counting taal, it would soon be dark and time to quit and go home for a more than welcome supper. But they were reluctant to give up too early. After all, not every summer provided them with so much game that they could take the time to just go out and burn off some fat. This year had been especially rich, even better than the last time they'd counted taal, four turns of the seasons ago.

Perhaps it was the time of day, or their hunger, but Sure-trail and Fire-Eyes were not being as careful, or as perceptive, as they might have been. They were working their way around a juniper thicket when Moonblossom, who had been hiding there in ambush, jumped out and counted them both.

"That's twice you've gotten me," Suretrail complained to her. But even as he spoke, Stride, whom he'd thought he had left behind but who had in fact left Fangslayer almost at once and had been following him and Fire-Eyes, ran up from behind, her taal-stick waving, and counted Moonblossom.

Suretrail dropped into a face-off crouch, laughing as he did so, but Fire-Eyes dashed off around the juniper thicket.

"What do you suppose has gotten into her," Moonblossom said.

"Go after her and fine out," Suretrail suggested. "I want to go toward the stream."

But just then Fire-Eyes came back around the far side of the thicket, and with raucous laughter and wildly swinging taal, counted both Stride and Suretrail, then ran off into the woods again.

Stride and Moonblossom glanced at each other, then grinned and, caught up in Fire-Eyes' wild mood, ran after her before she could get completely out of sight. It was a chase, and Fire-Eyes led them laughing around a batch of brambles where they all three, literally, ran into Quickthorn and Sunset, who were coming the other way. Everybody fell in a confused pile, and were laughing so hard it was some moments before they could get to their feet again. There was no count of course.

But even as they were regaining their composure, Suretrail leaped out from a clear place in the briar patch and counted Fire-Eyes and Quickthorn, and Rillwalker dropped down from the branches overhead and struck Suretrail and Quickthorn with her taal.

Quickthorn had been counted twice in a row now, and was beginning to feel picked on, but Rillwalker was confused by their near histeria.

Fangslayer, too, must have been confused, since he just walked up to them from another part of the forest and asked, "What is going on here?"

He failed to notice Sunset — though the others did not — who was tiptoeing up behind him. She reached out her taal-stick with an elaborate gesture and tapped him on the head, then burst into laughter along with the others.

In spite of this, Fangslayer was hardly startled. He rubbed his head as he looked at Sunset over his shoulder, a wry smile on his face. "I see," he said to Rillwalker, "that things are beginning to get a bit silly around here."

But even as he was speaking, Stride, Fire-Eyes, and Sunset dashed off, and then Suretrail and Moonblossom ran away, and then Fire-Eyes came swooping back from another direction and got Fangslayer fair and square, and Quickthorn too, though he might have argued the point, but missed Rillwalker altogether.

And so it went. In no time the taal degenerated into a hysterical parody of the game that Faun had wanted so much to be too old for. For a little while, everybody was a cub again.

Lonebriar sat just inside the edge of a briar patch, his favorite place for solitude. Deeper within, made as comfortable as they could be, were the four wounded elves and the two wolves. Even Catcher, the least injured of the four, was sleeping now. For which Lonebriar was grateful. Ever since Stringsong had gone back to the holt for help, Catcher had complained that either she should have gone instead, or should have remained on guard while both Stringsong and Lonebriar went, or should have gone with Stringsong. Lonebriar knew that this just showed that though she had been able to walk, she was in shock. But her constant muttering had made him uncomfortable. Now, at last, he had some peace.

They had chosen a briar patch not just because of Lonebriar's preferences. A tree would have been far safer, but Smarthand was so badly hurt that they had feared that the exertion of getting him up into a suitable branch would have hurt him more, if not killed him. He and Freefoot and Catcher all had broken ribs and more, and flat ground was better for them to lie on. And the two wolves, Lightpaws and Snapper, couldn't climb trees. They were now lying near their companions, half asleep but with their ears pricked for any sound.

The briar patch, Lonebriar hoped, would keep the bear from being too casual about intruding, but he still felt vulnerable. He had sent a mental call for Blackbrush, his own wolf, and was waiting for him to arrive.

Catcher had sent for her wolf too, but she had been weak and in pain, and wasn't sure she had gotten to her. Smarthand, of course, had been unable to do anything. His breathing was still ragged and shallow, and he had bled a lot from mouth and nose when Stringsong and Lonebriar had dragged him into the dubious shelter of the briar patch. If Stringsong didn't get back with help soon, he would die.

But it wasn't really the bear Lonebriar was worried about, it was the swordfeet. He could feel them in his mind, the sharp, almost-taste of their peculiar and involuntary sending. He felt hunger there, and fear, and pain, and anger. At least, that was how he interpreted the images that were not images. The sensation flickered, and it was getting stronger.

He saw the swordfeet before he heard them. They were an eight times eight of paces off, upslope from the briar patch, where the forest floor was relatively clear. Even from this distance Lonebriar could see that the adult was in a bad way. The two green-scaled hunters moved uncertainly, raising their heads now and then to sniff the air, but the larger swordfoot would pause every eight paces or so to sink into a crouch, as if she were very weak. Considering the wounds she had taken, Lonebriar was surprised she was still alive at all.

As quietly as he could, he crept back under the briar canes to where Catcher and Shadowflash were resting, and gently nudged them awake.

We're going to have company, he sent to them. He didn't know whether the swordfeet could hear a whisper or not, and he didn't want to find out just now.

Catcher came awake quickly, but Shadowflash moaned, and Lonebriar, who had not taken his eyes off the approaching swordfeet, saw the juvenile turn her head toward them. Catcher looked out of the briars and saw the creatures, then turned with a stifled moan of her own to quiet Shadowflash. But the damage had been done. And injured elves would be perfect prey for injured swordfeet. There wouldn't be much of a fight.

It was Smarthand's blood that finally made the difference. The swordfeet came closer to the briar patch, though apparently they could not see the elves concealed under the leafy, spiny canes. But even though there was no breeze, there was enough of a scent of blood in the air that the two swordfeet were able to catch it. Lonebriar could tell by their sudden tension and total attention. They did not run, but now they came toward the briar patch with eager determination.

Lonebriar felt sick. Aside from his knife he was unarmed, and though both Catcher and Shadowflash were alert to the danger now, they could not help him. The thoughts of the Swordfeet, tickling in the back of his mind, were a combination of desperate hunger and raging recognition — they knew it was elves who had been the cause of their pain. And help ... help was so far away.

Lonebriar crept to the edge of the briar patch and slowly stood up. He would fight them alone, and maybe he could hold them off long enough for Stringsong to come back. Behind him he heard the wolves stirring, but neither of them had fought a swordfoot before, and they did not recognize the enemy. The swordfeet kept coming nearer, but when the adult moved as if to attack from one side, the juvenile stayed with her, instead of taking the other side.

That, Lonebriar thought, might be his only chance to save his four companions. If he attacked the adult, the juvenile might just stay near by to protect her instead of going into the briar patch alone. If he could keep them out here, he might be able to live long enough for help to come. Maybe.

Then the swordfeet's thoughts, tasting like sour berries around the edges of his consciousness, suddenly became

stronger, as if they were sending directly at him. ~Hatred!~
~Anger!~ ~Hunger!~ ~Pain!~ ~Revenge!~

Lonebriar grabbed at the thoughts, held onto them, felt
them with his mind. He tried to send his thoughts back at them
in the same way. ~Stop!~ he sent. ~Go away!~ And to his
surprise, the swordfeet stopped.

~Lunch!~ the adult swordfoot sent or at least, that was
what her thought clearly meant. ~Swordfoot-killer!~ the
younger one sent.

~Yes!~ Lonebriar sent back. ~Kill swordfeet. Powerful elf.
I defend my family as you defend your mother!~ Or at least,
that was the intent of the image he formed in his mind and sent
at the creature.

Both swordfeet stood up a little taller, their heads twitching
from side to side as they looked at Lonebriar. He could feel the
more muted flavor of their private communication. They were
surprised, uncertain. No other animal had ever spoken to them
in their own language before. The younger swordfoot chirped,
the older answered. That was their talking, they didn't know
they were sending to each other.

Behind him, Catcher and Shadowflash watched in fascination and utter surprise. They did not know what was happening,
only that the swordfeet had hesitated only eight and two paces
away, and that Lonebriar seemed to be communicating with
them somehow.

Which he was. He could not imitate their chirps, but he
could put his thoughts into their strange minds. ~Leave us
alone,~ he sent. ~Eights of eights of elves coming. Defend to
the death. Go away.~

And the swordfeet went away.

Stringsong raced back toward the holt, sending a mental
call for Ranger, his wolf, as he ran. He pulled up short when he
saw, off at an angle through the trees, two elves with their
wolves, hurrying back in roughly the direction he had come. He

called out to them, and shortly stood talking with Raindance and Graywing.

He quickly explained what had happened, and they followed him back toward the briar patch. Ranger joined them just as they caught sight of Lonebriar, at the edge of the patch, suddenly sitting down and dropping his head into his hands. As they hurried up to him, Shadowflash and Catcher came creeping out from the briars.

"What happened?" Stringsong gasped.

"It was the swordfeet," Catcher said. She sat down beside Lonebriar. Shadowflash just lay where he was, half out of the briar patch.

"Are you all right?" Raindance asked Lonebriar. She knelt beside him.

"My head hurts a bit," he said. "I think Smarthand is bleeding to death."

Stringsong, Graywing, and Raindance pushed their way in through the briars and found Freefoot, awake but very groggy, and Smarthand, who was lying in a pool of his own blood. Gently they dragged him out, then went back for Freefoot. He was very weak, had difficulty breathing, and was still quite dazed, but with any luck he would be all right in time. It was Smarthand they were worried about. The wounds across his chest had closed over. It was his internal injuries he was dying of.

"We should have brought Faun with us," Graywing said, and told them about how the cub had followed them to count taal. Though still very young, Faun was already showing signs of becoming a healer.

"We'll have to make drag litters," Raindance said. "So what's this about the swordfeet?" She started to cut down long, straight branches.

"They came looking for us," Lonebriar said as he got to his feet to help. "They left just before you got here."

"You fought them off by yourself?" Stringsong asked as he peeled oak bark to tie the branches Raindance and Graywing brought him.

"It wasn't exactly a fight," Lonebriar said. He was still tired from his exertions and the strangeness of the swordfeet's thoughts.

"He sent to them," Catcher said, and told them what she had seen.

"They would chirp at him," Shadowflash added, "and he just stared at them, and then they went away."

"I wish I'd seen that," Freefoot murmured.

"I don't see how that's possible," Raindance said. She helped Lonebriar fashion another drag litter.

"I don't either," Lonebriar said, "but that's what happened."

"So Lonebriar is a swordfoot-talker," Graywing said. "Dreamsnake has a way with snakes and lizards. And Treewing can talk to birds. I've known a few other elves who had a special talent with animals. It's not very common, but it does happen now and then."

They continued to talk about it as they finished the three drag litters — Catcher was able to walk, and would have to — in part to keep their minds off what they could not help, Smarthand's pale gray face and shallow, labored breathing. They then made harnesses from more oak bark so that Snapper and Grizzle could drag Shadowflash, and Lightpaws and Bentfang could pull Freefoot. Because Smarthand was so badly injured, Graywing would drag him herself, to be sure that his trip was as smooth as possible.

But Stringsong, with Ranger, and Raindance and Lonebriar, had other business to attend to.

"The swordfeet have to be dealt with now," Raindance told the others. "You'll have to lead us to them, swordfoot-talker," she said to Lonebriar. "Can you do that?"

"I think so," Lonebriar said. "I wish we didn't have to kill them. I mean, I've talked with them."

"We'll do what we have to do," Stringsong said as Blackbrush finally came in answer to Lonebriar's mental summons.

"I know," Lonebriar said.

Stringsong could sympathise with him. He had had to destroy a wolf of his own once, when it had gotten the frothing fever. The memory still hurt, though he had had no choice. Rage had bitten his father, Hickory, and the elf had died of the fever too.

Then, when the injured elves were securely fastened to their litters and harnessed to the wolves, the three hunters went off in search of their prey.

Faun was very subdued and contrite by the time Glade brought her back to the holt. He had explained to her about Freefoot and Shadowflash, and about swordfeet, and how important it had been for Dreamsnake to have known about it so that she could have sent more help if any of the elders who had not joined in the taal had come back, and how Faun herself might have to use her fledgeling healing powers when the wounded were finally brought in.

Dreamsnake was cutting meat for the other cubs when they came to the bank. "Where have you been?" she asked. She put down the haunch of antelope and her knife and went to meet her daughter. "I've been so worried about you." She looked at Glade for an explanation.

"I've got to get back," Glade told her, then turned to Faun. "I'm depending on you now," he said. Then he hurried back into the woods.

Sprig and Clamshell came up to listen as Faun told her mother about Freefoot and Shadowflash, and how she had gone to count taal, and where to send any elders. Dreamsnake let her remorseful cub tell the story to the end.

"I'm very disappointed in you, cubling," Dreamsnake said when Faun had finished. "Fairheart and Fernhare were here while you were gone, I could have sent them out to help."

"I'm sorry, mother," Faun said. She was nearly in tears, and was little comforted when Bouncer came over to greet her.

"I know you are, cubling," Dreamsnake said. "But you must promise me that you won't run off like that again. You're just not old enough yet."

"When will I be old enough?"

"When you remember to do what you're supposed to do before you do what you want to do. Now don't go too far away. We're going to need your help when the injured come home. And you," she said to Sprig and Clamshell, who were giggling behind her, "it's time for your supper, and stop making Faun feel worse than she already does."

Faun felt very sad indeed. She had been bad, she hadn't been as grown up as she wanted to be, as she had thought she was, and Sprig and Clamshell had witnessed her disgrace. Fighting back the tears, she ran off to where a low tree branch made a bridge across the stream, with Bouncer bouncing happily along beside her. On the other side she went upstream to a large, flat rock where she sometimes went to sit and think, and there found Sundrop and Greentwig, talking quietly and trying to grab the little fishes that swam by in the water just below the edge of the stone.

"Where have you been?" Sundrop asked as Faun climbed up on the rock beside them and sat down to dangle her feet in the water.

"I went out to count taal," she said, and told them all about it.

Lonebriar, Raindance, and Stringsong followed the bloody track of the swordfeet. Raindance felt strange, not having Grizzle with her. Lonebriar and Stringsong had made Blackbrush and Ranger sniff the blood, hoping that they would recognize the smell, but the two wolves had showed little interest, and paid little attention to the blood on the trail.

The trail did not run straight, but did go through more open woodland for the most part. There had been quite a bit of blood at first, though later it diminished, and from it Lonebriar could get a distinctive feeling of the swordfeet, not a smell exactly, though in his mind that was the way the image formed.

"I don't want to kill them," he told the others as they hurried along the trail.

"I know," Raindance said. "But what else can we do?"

"They're not evil," Lonebriar went on. "They're just being themselves, like any hunter."

"If we were south," Stringsong said, "in their part of the forest, then we'd have to let them be. We would be the intruders then. But they don't belong here, O Speaker to Swordfeet. We can't let them stay."

"I know that," Lonebriar said. "And the younger one is carrying pups. I could feel it in her when we 'talked.'"

"If she has her pups up here," Raindance said, "we'll never be rid of them. I'm sorry, Lonebriar."

"Just lead us to them," Stringsong said, "and we'll do what we have to do."

"I remember Rage," Lonebriar told him. "You couldn't let anybody else destroy him. It's the same now, I have to do this."

The trail descended into a lowland part of the forest, where the ground was wet and did not keep footprints. There had been no blood for the last few hundred paces, and they lost the trail. Blackbrush and Ranger were no help. Though they had smelled swordfoot blood, they could not follow the scent. It was almost as if swordfeet did not exist for them.

They tried to pick up the trail again on the far side of the lowlands, but found no signs. They then coursed back along both sides of the wet area, but without any luck. The swordfeet couldn't still be in that part of the forest, the elves could see across the whole of the lowland area, even though it was not small. The undergrowth was mostly mosses and a few low ferns.

"There was some hard ground over there," Raindance said, pointing. "They might have gone out that way."

"I think you're right," Lonebriar said. He could feel a tickling 'smell' in the back of his mind.

"Are they sending?" Stringsong asked.

"Not the way we think of it, their thoughts just — leak out. But yes, I'm feeling them. The adult is in great pain."

"Let's go, then," Stringsong said gently, and Lonebriar led the way.

The tickle in his mind, the acid 'taste' of the swordfoot thoughts, led Lonebriar across the hard ground and upslope to where the trees were very large, but very close together. There was no undergrowth here. The tickle became stronger, but he remembered that, unless the swordfeet were 'talking' directly to him, they would seem further away than they really were, so he was cautious. Every tree trunk was a possible hiding place, the gently sloping ground had many shallow hollows and depressions. But he was concentrating so hard on the swordfoot sensations that it was Raindance who saw them first.

There they are, she sent to her companions, and pointed. An eight of eights of paces upslope, in a grotto formed by the trunks of two huge trees which grew almost out of each other's roots, were the two swordfeet. The adult was lying down, her head up-slope, the juvenile crouched beside her, her back to the elves.

She's dying, Lonebriar sent. His emotions were tangled like wine-berry vines. The swordfoot's thoughts were so alien, so strange, and yet it was a sorrow to him that she should be dying here, in a strange land she didn't understand, so far from her home. Swordfeet were terrible killers, so great a threat that elves could not share the same forest with them, and yet, because he could 'read' their thoughts, he felt a kinship with them. The adult would not live long, but could he actually kill the younger one? And if he did, what kind of scar would he bear? Stringsong knew about that, he could help him afterward.

We only have to deal with the juvenile, then. Raindance's sending intruded on his thoughts. Lonebriar looked up. Stringsong was nocking an arrow in his bow.

I can't be sure of a kill at this range, Stringsong sent. **We'll have to get closer.**

They went as quietly as they could. Lonebriar's feet felt like they were caught in tangle-vines. When they were half way up the slope, still too far for even Stringsong to make a sure shot, the juvenile jumped up and turned to face them. Its thoughts were like sharp smoke in Lonebriar's mind, ~Rage: Despair: Threat.~

Raindance hefted her ax. The swordfoot kicked out at the empty air in defiance. Stringsong held his bow at ready. The swordfoot barked harshly. Raindance glanced at Lonebriar, saw that he had no weapon, and offered him her ax. The dying swordfoot raised her head and looked back at them.

"I'll cover you," Stringsong told Lonebriar.

But Lonebriar refused the ax.

"It's all right," Raindance said, "we'll do it for you."

"No," Lonebriar said, "I want to try something first." He stepped between his companions and started up the last of the slope toward the swordfeet.

"What are you doing?" Stringsong cried, alarmed.

"Just give me a minute," Lonebriar said. The young swordfoot kicked at the air with both feet as he neared, but did not leave her mother's side. He was able to come within six paces of her before he stopped.

The older swordfoot hissed, but could not rise. The younger one lashed out again and again with one foot, but stood her ground. Lonebriar stood before her, feeling her hatred, her anger, her grief. Then he closed his eyes and sent to her, in her own special way.

~I won't hurt you,~ he sent, or simpler thoughts that amounted to the same thing. ~You are in no danger from me.~

~Enemy,~ the swordfoot sent back. ~Destroyer. Food.~

She was such a powerful animal. Her green scales, though dirty now, scarred, and spotted with blood, were large and brilliant and glossy. Her huge hind-foot talons were perfect weapons, her grasping forelegs strong and agile, her needle-teeth perfect for grabbing and tearing flesh, sharper than a wolf's. Lonebriar let his admiration for the swordfoot form his thoughts. She had been so brave, so smart, so caring of her mother. In essence, what he sent was, ~I like you.~

The swordfoot stopped kicking, and stretched her head toward him, as if to see him better. ~Pain,~ she sent. ~Anger. Grief for Mother.~

Lonebriar thought of himself as a terrible hunter, of the swordfoot as a terrible hunter, both hunting the same ground, both defending their own lives, their right to take whatever food came their way. The swordfoot echoed his thoughts, as if it acknowledged the truth of that.

Lonebriar formed an image of two great hunters in competition, but, ~I win,~ he finished. ~It is the way.~ The juvenile's sending was simple acceptance.

Lonebriar looked into the large, yellow eyes of the young swordfoot, eyes like those of a snake. He almost heard Raindance and Stringsong, behind him, cry out as he went up to the creature and put out a hand to touch her, gently, beside her deadly mouth. The swordfoot reached up and touched him in the same way.

For a moment, the elf and the swordfoot just shared their minds with each other. Then Lonebriar sent, ~Go home now. But when you bring forth your pups, come back to me.~

The swordfoot seemed to understand. She dropped her wickedly clawed forepaw from Lonebriar's face and looked back at her mother.

The adult was lying stretched out on the ground. Lonebriar could feel her mind, flickering, fading. The young swordfoot stepped up to her, sniffed at her, licked her wounds one more time. Then the adult died.

The juvenile straightened, looked once at Lonebriar, looked past him at the other two elves with a thought that they, at least, were fair game, then went away up the slope to the crest of the rise and out of sight.

"What happened?" Stringsong and Raindance asked together as they hurried up to Lonebriar. "You let it get away!" Raindance accused.

"I sent her away," Lonebriar said. He drew a deep breath and turned to smile at his two companions. "She's going home."

"How do you know that?" Stringsong asked. He was looking past Lonebriar at the dead swordfoot.

"I told her to."

"But it'll be back," Raindance said.

"Yes, after her pups are born, when they're old enough to travel."

"Listen, Talker to Swordfeet," Stringsong said, "I think you fail to understand the seriousness of the situation. One sword-foot loose in our hunting grounds is bad enough, but if this one comes back fully grown with a half-grown offspring —"

"Four," Lonebriar said. "She's carrying four."

"You're crazy," Raindance said. She knelt beside the dead swordfoot, touched its great talons, fingered its fore-claws, rolled its head to one side to look at the terrible teeth in its half open mouth.

"She knows me now," Lonebriar said. "She will come to me first." He stooped beside Raindance, then drew his knife and cut the two great talons from the dead swordfoot's back feet.

"How can you be sure?" Stringsong said. He kicked at the carcass. "We've got to hunt it down."

"No," Lonebriar said, "we don't." He stood up, the bloody trophies in his hands. "We shared minds, Stringsong. They are alien, yes, but they have no concept of deception. They didn't try to fool us when they left the wet place, they were just looking for higher ground. They never hide except when they sleep. She — said — she was going back home. Really."

Raindance stood up beside him. She looked at the deadly, sharp, sword-like claws in his hands, each as long as an elf's forearm. "It's your responsibility, Talon," she said. "When the swordfeet come back, you have to protect us from them, even as you now protect them from us."

"I accept that," the elf who had been Lonebriar said.

"It's a big responsibility, Talon," Stringsong added.

"I know," Talon said. "That's fine with me."

"I wonder if this thing is any good to eat," Raindance muttered.

Talon, as Lonebriar would be known from now on, sat by the fire in front of the bank of the holt, surrounded by cubs. Only Faun was not there, as she was with Raindance and Glade, who were tending to the wounded elves.

She was more than glad to have a chance to make up for her childish behavior that day, even though she was not yet very good at healing, and healing sometimes hurt. Especially with someone as badly injured as Smarthand. He was so broken up inside that she was afraid, at first, to even try. Glade suggested that she start with Catcher, and then do what she could with Freefoot and Shadowflash. Her success, little as it was for one so young, gave her confidence, and at last she put her hands on Smarthand again, and felt inside him. She lacked experience, but Raindance and Glade guided her, talked to her, suggested things for her to do. It took great effort, and a lot of courage on her part, but she succeeded in stopping his internal bleeding. By then she was exhausted, and could do no more. At least Smarthand would live until morning, when she would try again.

Though it was full dark, Dreamsnake and Stringsong were the only other elders at the holt. None of the rest had yet returned from the taal, or the few who had not joined in from their other expeditions. They sat with the cubs, as fascinated as they by Talon's story, of how he had first felt a swordfoot sending, had fought with them, and at last had made friends with the young one and sent it back home.

"Is it like that with you and snakes?" Stringsong whispered to Dreamsnake.

"Sort of," she whispered back, "except snakes don't have much of a mind to talk to."

Talon had to tell the story several times, and answer all the questions Greentwig, Sprig, Sundrop, and Clamshell had to ask. The cubs delighted in using his new name whenever they could. For his part, Talon wasn't sure he deserved so much attention. After all, he had gotten his old name because he liked to be alone a lot. But there didn't seem to be any help for it.

He was relieved, then, when Sunset, Suretrail, and Fire-Eyes finally returned, tired and hungry, but laughing and obviously pleased with the day's events. Though, of course, he would have to tell the story all over again to all the elders, too.

"It was a great taal," Suretrail said as the three came over to the fire. "Everybody else will be here soon."

"Did you come back early?" Sunset asked when she saw Talon and Stringsong. "You should have stayed out with us. You missed all the excitement."

The Deer Hunters

It was a warm summer day at Halfhill. Four elves sat in the afternoon sun in the treeless space between the wide, nearly vertical cliff that gave Freefoot's holt its name, and the broad, gurgling, gravel-bottomed stream.

Suretrail, his back to the clay cliff — more than twice as high as an elf — was carefully weaving a plait of fibers and feathers with which to decorate his spear. The two javelines beside him had already been painted with red ochre and blue berry-juice. Rainbow, on Suretrail's left, showed him some tricks with the white, green, and black feathers. Her own spear was stained and carved with elaborate patterns.

On Suretrail's right was Graywing. She took off the rawhide thongs that bound the flint point to her spear-shaft. It had become dull with use, and needed to be replaced. Fangslayer, across from Suretrail, was carving a new handle for his white quartz ax. From somewhere across the stream behind him came the occasional sounds of the four children laughing.

In the face of the cliff behind Suretrail were the dens of the elves, dug back into the hard clay among the supporting roots of the large, overhanging trees that grew above it, and down its gently sloping back side. In the deep shadows at the top of the cliff sat five other elves in a line. Four of them were no longer children, but not yet adults in the eyes of their elders. Shadowflash, the fifth, as old as Suretrail, sat at the end.

Brightmist, beside him, was not thinking about Shadowflash at the moment, though for several seasons now they had been a little more than playmates, a little less than lovemates. Rather, she was trying to figure out how to make Suretrail give in to their wishes.

Deerstorm, on Brightmist's other side, plucked a frond of fern and set it in her brown hair. Beyond her, Greentwig sat with crossed legs, staring down into his hands folded in his lap. At the far end of the line was Crystalmoss. She was quite a bit younger than the other three, but already showed tremendous promise.

Somewhere off to the north a wolf howled. Shadowflash left off his thoughts and turned toward the forest behind him. The cublings across the stream became silent. The four elders on the bank below him put down their work and looked up toward the sound. The howl came again.

"Freefoot's back," Shadowflash said. He started to rise but his companions did not move. After a moment's hesitation, he sat down again.

There were more wolf-howls. Fangslayer and Rainbow answered back. The hunting party had been gone for three days. A few moments later, Freefoot and Starflower, Fairheart and Moonblossom came through the trees from the upstream western end of the cliff.

They and their wolves looked tired, and well they mind be, for on the back of each of the wolves was an antelope, each nearly as big as an elf, caught out on the prairie to the north of the forest. The waiting elders greeted the hunters and helped take the carcasses down from the tired back of the wolves. There would be feasting tonight.

"The antelope are doing well this year," Fairheart said. "Can you believe it, these are the weaklings."

Suretrail and Graywing began to butcher one of the antelopes while Fangslayer and Rainbow started on another. then there was a crashing in the brush on the other side of the stream, and four very young elves came racing across the stones set in the water. Dreamsnake, who had been tending them, came a moment later.

The cublings — Dayshine, Warble, Starbrigtht, and Feather — hurried up to where the elders were carefully skinning the antelopes, and begged for treats. suretrail and Fangslayer handed out bits of rich liver. It was all they could to to keep the from offering more "assistance" than was good for them, for for the antelopes.

Freefoot spread out one of the skins, on which Fangslayer and Rainbow placed the meat as they cut it from the bones. Fairheart hacked off the horns and hooves and put them aside. Graywing carefully split the leg bones, not only to remove the marrow but also to save the bones themselves for javelin points, awls, find scrapers, and other tools.

Catcher was the first of the other elves to arrive. She greeted the hunters cheerfully and displayed a brace of ravvits, which she had taken from the traps that only she knew how to make.

A moment later Glade and Fernhare came from downstream. Glade glanced up to the top of the cliff, where his son Greentwig and his friends were still sitting with Shadowflash. They should have come down to help with the butchery. Instead they just sat, rather sullen and grumpy about something. Not Shadowflash; he was his usual cheerful self.

Starflower and Moonblossom carefully separated the edible organs from the intestines. These Freefoot and Catcher took down to the stream to wash. Later they would be stretched and dried for cord, bowstrings, and thread.

Two-Wolves and Grazer joined the group. Two-Wolves took the job of prying the teeth from the antelopes' skulls. Grazer, who was a full head taller than any other elf, helped keep the children busy while the butchery was finished. Bluesky came last.

At last Shadowflash and the four young elves came down from the top of the cliff. Antelope was not that common a meal, and just enough different from deer to make it special. Graywing, Bluesky, and Catcher passed around chunks of meat, choice pieces of liver, kidney, lungs, and brain.

Four antelopes proved to be just barely enough. It was fortunate that so many of the other members of the tribe had gone off on hunting expeditions of their own. All those present were able to eat their fill, and by the time Fairheart found it necessary to bring out fire for lights, there was nothing left of the antelope but belches, smiles, and some greasy faces.

By then the children were getting sleepy. Fairheart and Moonblossom collected their daughter Starbright and went off to their den at the downstream end of the cliff. Warble's father was one of those out hunting, so Dreamsnake took her to her place. Dayshine's parents, too, were away, so she went to sleep with her grandmother Bluesky. That left only Feather.

Freefoot reached down to pick up his cubling son and hold him for a moment, then handed him to Starflower.

"Aren't you coming?" his mate asked.

"In a bit." He pointed to where Brightmist, Crystalmoss, Deerstorm, and Greentwig were sitting by the stream dangling their feet into the water. "There's something wrong and I want to find out what it is."

"They've been awfully quiet this evening," Starflower said.

"And they've been avoiding Suretrail," he told her. He nuzzled his son again, then Starflower took Feather away.

Freefoot waited until all the others had gone off for the night before he went over to join the four young elves. "Why don't we take a little walk," he suggested.

They seemed pleased to see him, almost as if they had been hoping he would come to their rescue. They got to their feet and walked with him downstream, away from the cliff.

It was almost full dark, and the sounds of night had begun. Beside them the stream gurgled pleasantly. Somewhere an owl hooted, in preparation for its night's hunt. Chirpers and other insects were calling stridently.

They walked without talking until they could no longer see the lights left out at the holt, then found a place where a rock shelved over the edge of the stream, mossy and soft and big enough for them all to sit on. They rested for a while, silent in the deepening night.

At last Brightmist spoke up. "We want to go on a hunt," she said.

"By ourselves," Deerstorm added.

"Well," Freefoot said, "I don't see why you couldn't do that."

"Suretrail said we couldn't," Greentwig said. "Fangslayer said it would be all right, but when we asked Suretrail, he said no."

"I see. Well, he must have had a reason."

"But now that you're back," Brightmist said, "maybe you can tell him it's all right."

"It's about time," Greentwig said. "We're not children any more."

"We can take care of ourselves," Deerstorm insisted. "We've been on lots of hunts with the elders."

"But we always have to hunt what they want to hunt," Crystalmoss said, "and let them attack first, and sometimes we don't even get in on the kill until it's all over."

"Except for ravvits," Greentwig said, "and chuckers."

"Will you let us go?" Crystalmoss asked.

"I can't if Suretrail told you you couldn't," Freefoot said, "but maybe we can work something out. We saw tapirs at the clearing when we came by this afternoon."

"They're no fun," Brightmist said. "You can walk right up to them."

"How about the otters at the pool?"

"Yeah," Greentwig said with innocent enthusiasm. "They put of a good fight."

"No," Deerstorm insisted, "two of the bitches died this spring."

"Besides," Crystalmoss said, "Suretrail told us we couldn't."

"Hunt otters?" Freefoot asked.

The four were silent. They hadn't asked to hunt otters.

It was an old story. Children had to be protected while they learned to live and survive in the forest. But sooner or later they wanted a real challenge. The transition between childhood and adulthood was never easy. "All right," Freefoot said. "I'll see what I can do."

Suretrail and Bluesky were sitting in front of Bluesky's den when Freefoot got back to the cliff. In spite of the late hour they were both making arrowheads. Suretrail, who was putting thong-notches on the delicate flint points, seemed to know what Freefoot had come for. He put down the piece he had been working on and looked up at his chief. "Are you going to let them go?" he asked.

"I told them I'd talk with you about it," Freefoot said. "They want your permission."

"They're good cubs," Suretrail started to say as Fangslayer, then Catcher joined them.

"They're not cubs anymore," Fangslayer said.

"But did they tell you what kind of hunt they have in mind?" Suretrail went on. "They want to go to Tall-Trees for black-neck deer."

"Oh," Freefoot said. "I see."

"I think they ought to do it," Fangslayer said.

"They have to learn sometime," Catcher said.

"Of course they do," Suretrail said. "But you need at least four to hunt black-neck. If they wanted to go out with a couple of more experienced hunters, okay. I'm not worried about Brightmist or Deerstorm. It's Crystalmoss."

"She's the best thrower in the tribe," Fangslayer said.

"With stones and darts and javelins," Fangslayer said. "That's not heavy enough for black-neck. And she's not even fully grown yet."

"It's Greentwig who's the real problem," Bluesky said. "He's just not ready.

"He's old enough," Fangslayer said.

"They don't have enough experience," Suretrail insisted. "None of them are ready for this kind of hunt yet. Black-necks are too tough, especially at this time of year."

"And Tall-Trees is too far away," Bluesky said. "It would take them half a day at least just to get there."

And besides," Suretrail said, "I've already told them they couldn't."

"I still think they ought to have their chance," Fangslayer said.

"They'll never learn," Catcher said, "if they don't find out for themselves."

Glade, Grazer, and Dreamsnake came to join them. They already seemed to know what the discussion was about. Bluesky added wood to her fire so that they could be included in its light. The others made room for them.

"Talon and I," Glade said, "took Greentwig and Crystalmoss out hunting yesterday. Beaver, up by the marsh. Crystalmoss did all right. But Greentwig, I don't know. I don't predict a long life for him."

Bluesky brought out a pouch of dreamberries and passed it around.

An elf his age should have an adult name," Fernhare said. "Crystalmoss has hers."

"I think Deerstorm has what it takes," Grazer said, "and not just because her father. Brightmist, too."

"They want to do this for themselves," Fangslayer said.

"Of course they do," Glade said. "They want to prove themselves. But Greentwig is … just … the combination just won't work."

"He is something of a disappointment," Dreamsnake said gently. "But Glade, you and Fernhare can't take care of Greentwig all his life. He must learn — somehow — or die trying."

"I know," Glade said sadly.

"If Longreach were here," Bluesky said, "maybe they'd let him be a part of their hunt. He's not that much older than Greentwig. With five, that would be fine."

"If they could bring in a black-neck," Grazer said, "They would certainly prove themselves."

"They would indeed," Freefoot said. He chewed another dreamberry, then sat back to think.

"We can all remember," he said at last, "when we were first give the chance to hung, not with our elders but on our own — not just for ravvits but for serious game." The others listened without comment. "We can all remember when we were first given full responsibility for our own hunt, whatever game and whatever place we chose. For some of us that's been a long time."

Suretrail looked away. His decision was being challenged. Fangslayer just stared into the fire.

"Suretrail," Freefoot said, "you did the right thing when you told them not to go."

Suretrail muttered an acknowledgment.

"But it's my responsibility now," Freefoot went on, "not yours. And Fangslayer," he turned to his elder son, "you are right too. Those four are nearly of an age, and they must become adults. We cannot deny them their chance, as we all have had, even though they die. Even though."

For a moment, all were silent. "And it's not fair to Brightmist or Deerstorm," Freefoot went on, "who will be full adults soon enough. Now is the time. Let us hope they all come back alive."

The next morning Shadowflash went with Brightmist and the other young hunters when they left Halfhill. The weather was cool, and there was a slight mist in the forest. Shadowflash liked it when the forest was that way. Of course he liked the forest any way when he was with Brightmist. He wanted to go with her today, but he knew he would not be welcome this time. He was only going to see them off.

They went upstream a way and then the four young hunters paused to call their wolves. Answering howls came back from different parts of the forest.

The four youths were excited about the hunt, and now that they had finally gotten permission, a bit apprehensive as well. That was good.

After a moment Fog, Brightmist's gray bitch, came walking toward them. She was a big old wolf and seemed to know that something special was about to happen. Then Scarface and Mask appeared, bounding lightly through the brush. Scarface was Deerstorm's wolf, who bore the marks of a less than successful encounter with a forest pig. Mask was Greentwig's companion, black across the eyes and tawny brown elsewhere. Behind them came Dancer, long-legged and swift, bounding up to Crystalmoss's side. The elves greeted their animals, in the way of elves and wolves.

Then Brightmist turned to Shadowflash and put her hands on his chest. **We'll be all right,** she sent to him.

I know. Keep an eye on Greentwig. He did not look at the youth, tall for his age, handsome sturdy, and somehow younger than Crystalmoss.

This could make a difference for him, Brightmist sent.

It will, if he survives.

"Let's go," Deerstorm said. "You two can cuddle when we get back."

The wolves were impatient too. They could sense their companions' excitement and wanted to get on with it. Shadowflash touched Brightmist's pale ruddy hair, then turned and went back to Halfhill.

The hunting party went upstream to the west. The mist dissipated before they got to the big south loop, which they cut across instead of following, and by the time they got to the marsh the day was warming. They had been too excited to have breakfast so they caught a few of the marshrats that lived there. The animals were so plentiful and slow that it was hardly hunting.

The stream went on beyond the marsh, but they crossed the water there and head southwest. The ground rose. Bald Hill was directly to the south, though its rocky top was not visible from this far away. They passed its sloping shoulder, moving quickly, ignoring the plentiful small game. It was an easy walk, though the forest was dense with undergrowth.

Still, it was nearly noon by the time they got to the edge of Tall-Trees. Brightmist had not been there before. She couldn't help but pause as they left the denser forest and entered the parklike area.

The trees were huge deciduous junipers, each one twenty or thirty paces or more from its nearest neighbors. The ground was covered with a ruddy-gray carpet of fallen foliage, scalelike and ankle-deep. The branches overhead completely covered the sky, so high that they got dizzy looking up at them. The tree trunks were so big around that the four of them together holding hands could not encircle one. The bark was shaggy and loose, and gave no purchase when they tried to climb.

The forest floor was not completely bare. Here and there were a few small plants and shrubs that preferred deep shade, but they hardly obstructed the view. They could see for hundreds, maybe thousands of paces in every direction.

Some ways off was what, had it been in a clearing, they would have called a copse. It was a dense, rounded mass of brush and vines that grew where the trees were farther apart, and where the sun was able to come down from the canopy of branches overhead. It was maybe thirty paces across, it's verge abrupt, and the taller trees within it were about four times as tall as an elf. Still, the lowest branches of Tall-Trees were many times higher than that. There were other similar copses farther off, some smaller, some larger.

They were all in awe of Tall-Trees. Even the wolves seemed to know that this was a special place, the last of an ancient forest left over from some previous age.

"Look," Greentwig said. He pointed. There, so far away they could not tell what kind it was, was a buck deer. It was walking alone, and they watched it as it went from one great tree to another, then disappeared into a copse.

"That's where we'll find the black-necks," Deerstorm said, "in the copses."

"Then let's go hunting," Brightmist said.

They went to the nearest place of brush, shrubs, and vines, several hundred paces from the edge of the forest. Except for the one deer, they had seen or heard no other life in the park. But there was plenty in the copse — birds, squirrels, insects, bats hanging asleep from the head-high branches. The copse was small, and there were no deer there, but they did startle a forest antelope, its head barely chest-high on an elf. They did not chase it as it went bounding off in search of a safer refuge.

They left the copse and went toward a larger one more likely to shelter their chosen prey. It felt strange, walking in an openness that was still roofed by branches. They could see so far in all directions that for the first time the realized they were truly alone, truly on their own here. They felt rather small and young. They great clear spaces between the trees was not like a clearing, or the meadow, or the prairie; it was different.

As they went deeper into Tall-Trees, the copses became larger and farther apart. They quickly learned that while they could see great distances here, so could the other animals. They had to move carefully from one copse to another, to avoid being heard or seen before they got to the shelter of the brush. More than once they heard some unseen animal bounding away from the far side of a copse as they approached uncautiously.

Sometimes they saw white-tail deer, occasionally red deer, in the copses or crossing the park between them. The wolves wanted to hunt, and it was not easy to explain that that was the wrong game. They took an occasional ravvit or pouchrat, to fortify themselves, but avoided the prickle-spines and the badger they surprised out of its burrow. They found no traces of black-neck deer.

Black-neck were uncommon in the elves' hunting range. Most of the year thy lived in the upland forests to the south and came here only during the month or so just before the mating season. They were far bigger than the white-tail or even smaller red deer, which lived here year round.

And at this time of year they were dangerous. The bucks, which would not eat much until the mating was over, were antsy with the upcoming rut, nervous, cautious, and prepared to fight with anything. The does, though not territorial, could also be deadly. Besides anticipating the mating, they would be protecting fawns and yearlings. White-tail or red deer would be far easier game.

But it was black-neck they wanted, and at last, in the seventh and largest copse they had visited, they came upon traces of their quarry. The smell of the black-neck droppings was distinctive, and now that the wolves had the scent they could follow it.

The deer were not in that copse, but the trail was fresh and led them bast several smaller copses toward another large overgrown area, some distance away. They hurried toward it, but cautiously.

The hunt was serious now. They entered the copse as quietly as they could, one step at a time, penetrating the dense growth of vines, bushes, tall grasses, and leafy herbs with as little noise as possible. The scent of the deer was strong, and fresh. They paused frequently to listen. There were squirrel sounds, bird calls, a ravvit dashed off through the brambles. But there was also the sound of a branch moving, and there was no wind, not even a breeze. They moved closer and could hear the sound of bark tearing. That was the deer grazing.

They kept in touch by sending as they closed in. They were excited when they saw the deer — two big bucks, five does, as many yearlings, and maybe four fawns. The wolves were naturally cautious.

The bucks were huge, over twice as high at the shoulder as an elf, their black manes thick, their antlers at full growth, broader than an elf could reach, with spear-sharp points. One of them could provide more meat than the four antelopes Freefoot and his hunting party had brought in. The more they watched, the more fascinated the elves became, and the more frightened.

Which one should we take? Greentwig asked. **There's a yearling.**

If we wanted that spindly thing, Deerstorm sent back, **we might as well have gone after red or white-tail.**

We don't dare try for a buck, Brightmist sent. Unless they dropped it on the first strike, they would be in danger of their lives. Later these two bucks would become deadly enemies; right now they would help defend each other and the rest of the herd.

How about that doe, Crystalmoss suggested, **the one on the far side.** It was the largest of the does, but also somewhat slower.

She won't have many more breeding seasons left, Deerstorm agreed. **The younger does could easily replace her.**

They circled into position, then Greentwig, who was farthest around, sent, **Wait!**

What is it? Brightmist asked, then she heard it too.

There was another animal nearby, in a thicker part of the copse, not that far from the doe. The wolves one by one caught the scent, and they, too, were distracted. The animal sounded large, and its scent was unfamiliar. Carefully, they moved to where they could see the creature.

At first they thought it was just a forest pig, but it was nearly half the height of the buck deer — taller at the shoulder than Crystalmoss — and fully as heavy. No forest pigs got that large. Its body was angular, it's shoulders high and sharp, its face was knobby and very long, its head huge, with a crest of dark reddish hair. And it had two tusks growing up from each side of its lower jaw instead of just one, each tusk longer than an elf's hand.

It rooted around the bases of certain bushes, digging up tubers and occasionally pulling plump fruits off the branches. And even as they watched they all got the same idea. What if they brought back this animal instead? The black-necks would be around for several eights-of-days yet, but this might be their only chance at a strange pig like this.

Pigs were, pound for pound, more dangerous than anything except badgers and wolverines. Even wolves and long-teeth were cautious about taking one. They would have to be especially careful, not only because it was a pig, and so large, but also because it was unfamiliar and they didn't know its ways.

Quickly they planned their attack, then struck. Deerstorm's arrow bounced off the pig's boney face, Greentwig's lodged high in the shoulder, Brightmist's struck a rib, and Crystalmoss's javelin struck a flank.

The pig jerked up and squealed with surprise and pain as they readied for a second attack. The wolves closed in to keep the pig confused. The deer moved quickly away.

The three archers shot, but the pig's skin was tough. It squealed again and spun around. The wolves danced out of reach of its tusks. Crystalmoss threw her second javeline and hit the pig at the base of the neck, but the light weapon could not penetrate the bone and muscle. The pig crashed off, knocking Dancer aside.

They dashed through the brush in pursuit.

The wolves raced ahead to try to turn it. Brightmist got her spear ready for a charge, but the pig zigged and zagged out of her way. Deerstorm and Greentwig couldn't get a clear shot with their bows through the dense undergrowth.

Crystalmoss threw a dart, which did little more than scratch along the pig's back. Then the pig turned abruptly south and burst out of the copse. The elves and wolves raced in pursuit. Crystalmoss recovered one of her javelins as it fell from the pig's neck.

The pig was running away fast. It seemed so very strong and touch. But there was blood on the ground, and as the pig ran it shook itself as if to dislodge the arrows still sticking into it.

They had committed themselves now. The pig was wounded, and they could not just let it go and eventually bleed to death. They had to kill it if they could.

Elves and wolves ran, just keeping up with the pig. They hoped it would wear itself out or come to a place where they could attack it more effectively. It led them southwest, in almost a straight line, and stayed away from the copses.

Once in a while one of the wolves closed in and snapped at it. Once in a while one of the archers drew up and tried a running shot. The pig almost ignored them.

One time Deerstorm and Crystalmoss raced up, one on either side, and both threw javelins. they hit the pig under its shoulders, but it just kept on running. Greentwig came up once and tried to hamstring the pig with his ax, but his blow went wrong and only cut the skin.

At least the pig was bleeding a lot and would eventually lose its strength. But when they finally killed it, how would they ever get such a heavy animal back to the holt?

They came to a part of Tall-Trees where there were many copses closer together, some of them only a dozen paces apart, and the pig had to swerve and turn frequently to stay on the clear ground. At one point the pig suddenly found itself confronted by a newly fallen tree, too gib to jump over and too low to run under, and it was almost trapped. For a moment the pig was at bay, the wolves closed in and snapped at it. The pug swung its huge heavy head to one side, Mask tried to bite at its throat, the pug swung back and caught the wolf and tossed him into the brush.

Mask yelped, the other wolves hesitated, the pig charged through the elves and around the stump end of the fallen tree, and all but Greentwig turned in pursuit. He went to help Mask get to is feet. The wolf's side was badly cut, his ribs bruised, but he wanted to go on, so they did.

After that the wolves didn't try to get too close. Instead they ranged ahead, as if looking for another place to corner the pig. The pig, though bleeding even more, was running harder now, and the elves and wolves had to work just to keep up.

They came to the far side of Tall-Trees by the middle of the afternoon. On their left was the verge of the river, which formed the southern border of the park. The pig headed toward it, then veered more to the west again, toward the denser forest. While they could they got off a few more arrows into the pig's blanks. The elves hoped that the thicker brush of the forest would slow it down.

But the pig charged into the brush unhindered, and the elves and wolves, lighter in weight, and to work to get through the tangles of vines and creepers. The pig ran along the bank of the river, where the brush was thicker, and began to pull ahead of them.

As the chase continued through the thickest growth they lost sight of the pig now and then. It continued to gain until they could no longer hear the noise of its passage, and had to follow the trail the wounded animal had left. It was not difficult. The brush was broken, there were hoofprints in the ground, blood spots and smears on the foliage. The scent of the pig was strong: fear and blood and sweat.

It seemed as though the pig was never going to tire, though the elves had. Even the wolves, especially Mask, were beginning to show strain. Most game, when chased through the forest, were as encumbered by the brush as the hunters.

The chase went on, into a broad valley. There was a subtle change of vegetation here, the undergrowth was more luxuriant, the trees were broadleaf red-twigs more often than not. The pig's trail still led along the bank of the river, too wide even here to cross.

They wanted to rest, but they dared not. Only the splattering of blood here and there assured them that the pig, though now far ahead, was worse off than they. At last the ground began to rise, the river beside them ran more swiftly. The water was broken by occasional rocks, and the forest on either side became somewhat clearer. Then they could hear noisy splashing up ahead. They knew they must be getting to the top of the valley, and, indeed, they soon came to a long expanse of rapids, between rocky banks. And there was the pig, still a good way ahead, running and stumbling along the bank, as if looking for a place to cross.

The river splashed through a thousand paces of jumbled rocks, a treacherous ford across the river. The pig was choosing its path carefully, but jumping strongly from one rock to another. The hunters fanned out and started to cross, in hopes of meeting the pig on the other bank, where they could attack it again.

But Mask was tired and whimpering. Greentwig paused to talk with his wolf and told him to rest there a moment and then go back to the holt. Mask was sorry to miss out on the kill, but knew his own strength. The wolf sat, and Greentwig hurried after the others, who were now partway across the river.

What a hunt! Greentwig nearly fell into the water as he hurried to rejoin the others. The pig had almost reached the other side, angling upstream, and the hunters were gaining on it.

They all reached the other side at the same time, though spread out up and down the rapids. The pig, instead of following the river upstream, where Brightleaf and Crystalmoss were waiting, charged up the bank, leaving the river altogether. The elves pulled together to follow it into the forest.

This was more like the classical hunt. The forest was more open this high up, but the uphill work was strenuous. The pig chose a straight path, avoided gullies and brush, and the elves and wolves ran along beside and behind.

At last the land began to level. They had come to the uplands, and the pig was now running southeast. It was tiring, and
they were able to keep up with it easily. The forest was different
here, an older forest.

The pig occasionally stumbled as it ran. It was going to
have to turn at bay sooner or later. And then it came to a break
in the forest, a broad, semiopen glade. There were occasional
trees spotted through the mostly waist-high brush and grasses.
The ground was both soft and rocky, mud and moss between the
broken stones.

The pig was tiring rapidly now in the late afternoon. It
struggled across the glade, thousands of paces across. The pig
looked as though it was trying to get to the other side, so the
elves and wolves put on speed and circled around. If they were
going to finish it, it had to be here.

Luck was with them. Before the pig could get more than
three-quarters of the way across the glade they were able to
turn it into a shallow, rocky draw. Steep rocks formed the sides,
and three huge oak trees grew out at the far end, their roots a
tangle that the pig couldn't pass. It turned and charged back,
saw the elves and wolves, backed a step, then stood at bay.

The pig snorted angrily, kicked rocks and mud, smashed its
face from side to side against roots and brush. The wolves
ranged along the sides of the draw and snapped at the pig when
it tried to climb out. Once the pig nearly made it but Scarface
bit its nose, just out of reach of its tusks, and the pig squealed
and dropped back.

They used their few remaining arrows carefully, aiming for
the throat between the neck muscled and the shoulder bone.
The pig thrashed around heavily with each hit. Crystalmoss and
Deerstorm used the last of their javelins and hit the pig in the
belly in front of the flanks. The pig snorted in rage.

It was bleeding copiously now, its movements were erratic,
and it occasionally stumbled. Now was the time to go in for the kill.
But Deerstorm had no more weapons, and Crystalmoss had only a
few darts and a small ax. It would be up to Brightmist with her
spear, and Greentwig with his heavy ax, to finish the matter.

Deerstorm went behind the pit and half way down the rocky side to hit it with a rock. The pig turned toward her with a snort. Now Brightmist and Greentwig could enter the draw. Crystalmoss then distracted the pig from the other side. Greentwig and Brightmist got into position.

Brightmist planted the butt of her spear against the ground while Greentwig threw rocks until the pig charged. But Brightmist slipped on the muddy rocks and the pig, instead of impaling itself in its mouth or under its chin, ran into the spear at its shoulder, all the way through the muscle to the bone.

Brightmist lurched to the side, out of the stopped pig's way. Greentwig stepped up and swung his ax at the back of the pig's skull, but the animal half turned and his blow, though strong and deep, only struck it in the shoulder.

The pig screamed. The spear was lodged in its shoulder, and it was crippled, but now Brightmist had no weapon. She backed off. The pig screamed again. Greentwig trembled. Then, when the pig turned toward him, he struck again. He hit it across the forehead, barely avoiding its tusks. There was a lot of blood, but it was not a killing blow. The pig screamed again.

From all sides they heard the sudden response: heavy, deep grunts and bellows, squeals and snorts and moaning calls. The pig staggered back, panting and crying.

The elves stood paralyzed. There was a crashing in the brush not far away, heavy hooves clattered on rocks, sucked at the mud, getting closer. Brightmist, Crystalmoss, and Greentwig clambered half up out of the draw. Deerstorm was already out, crouching on the edge.

From all sides more pigs were coming, from the forest, from other parts of the glade where they must have been concealed by brush or wallows. They came at a full run, responding the way all pigs do to the distress of one of their fellows, to the rescue.

The four young elves had just a moment to realize that the pig they had been hunting, as big as it was, was only a juvenile. These four boars, and eight or ten sows, were fully grown. Each was as tall as a black-neck deer, each weighed maybe three or four times as much. Their faces, long and bristly, were covered with callused knobs, their tusks were longer than an elf's arm.

The wounded pig screamed. The rest of the herd, with a dozen or so juveniles as big as the wounded pig in the draw, and even a number of piglets, came on from all sides, at full charge. The forest was a long way off. There was no place to run.

It was dusk at Halfhill. A few lamps were lit. Over by her den Bluesky was making arrowheads. Beside her for company, Catcher was making a trap from a springy stick, a piece of bone, and some fine cord woven from hair. Nearby, Dreamsnake was telling the cublings the story of how Freefoot had gotten his name.

Closer to the stream, Fairheart, his shirt off, was making a bow, shaping the wood with sharp flint. Beside him, Rainbow was repairing his shirt and trimming it with fancy feathers. Suretrail, Glade, and Two-Wolves looked on.

Downstream from them, Freefoot, Grazer, and Fernhare were working on the antelope skins under Starflower's direction. Graywing, Shadowflash, Moonblossom, and Fangslayer sat between them and the others, talking, digesting, calming down for the night.

"The cubs ought to be back by now," Suretrail said.

"If they got a deer," Catcher said, "they'll have a hard time bringing it back."

"One of them could have come on ahead and asked for help," Rainbow muttered.

"No," Fangslayer said, "they've got to do that themselves."

"After all," Moonblossom added, "Tall-Trees is a long way off; they might have to stay the night."

"I don't think we should have let them go," Suretrail insisted.

Freefoot ignored the implied challenge. "It has to happen some time," he said softly. "They're of that age. If we hadn't given them our blessing, they'd have gone off anyway."

Suretrail knew that was true, but it didn't make him any happier. He tried to put his thoughts and worries out of his mind by watching Rainbow stitching on Fairheart's shirt.

One by one, as night fell, the elves finished their tasks and retired to their dens. At last only Suretrail, Rainbow, and Bluesky were left. The three just could not go to sleep. To keep busy they set about making arrows. Shafts, fletches, heads. They could always use more arrows.

Overhead the two moons were shining. They had been approaching each other during the last few nights. Would they kiss when they passed?

Just before dawn Freefoot, who was more concerned than he cared to admit, came out of his den with Starflower and little feather. He saw Rainbow and Bluesky asleep, saw Suretrail coming back from the stream, and waited for him as Starflower, with a reassuring word, took Feather off for his morning bath.

"How much longer should we wait?" Suretrail asked him softly. Rainbow muttered in her sleep.

"Give them a chance," Freefoot said. "If they got a big buck, they'll have a hard time bringing it back."

Bluesky woke and looked up at them. "We made a lot of arrows last night," she said.

Now Rainbow roused too. "Are they back yet?" she asked.

"Not yet," Bluesky said, and went with her to wash up.

"And besides," Freefoot went on, if it was a long hunt, they'll have to sleep. Other hunts have turned out that way before."

"I know that," Suretrail said, "but not hunts half of who's members were too young or incompetent." And then he saw Glade and Fernhare, just coming out of their den. "I'm sorry," he said, "but it's true."

"I know," Fernhare sighed.

Glade didn't say anything. On the one hand he agreed with Suretrail. On the other, he was the keeper of the Way, and knew better than anybody that Freefoot was right. He just went upstream, and after a moment Fernhare followed.

The conversation was rousing the other elves now, and one by one they came out of their dens. Freefoot went off to wash. Suretrail started to pick up all the arrows he and Bluesky had made. He was exhausted.

Shadowflash and Catcher came up from the stream. "Were you up all night?" Catcher asked.

"Made a lot of arrows," Suretrail said, showing them to her.

"They'll be all right," Shadowflash said as Bluesky and Rainbow came back with Fangslayer. "Deerstorm has been there before, she's got good sense."

"So has Brightmist," Fangslayer said. "We had to give them the chance. We wouldn't worry about any other party of four."

"That's just the problem," Rainbow said.

"I guess we can wait a while longer," Bluesky said.

The daily hunt was a minor affair, as the elves went after smaller game closer to the holt. By noon, most had returned for a light meal. But Suretrail, Two-Wolves, and Rainbow couldn't stand it anymore. They went to sit with Freefoot, Starflower, Fangslayer, and Feather.

"I think we should go looking for them," Suretrail said.

"I have to agree," Starflower said.

"If they were all right," Two-Wolves said, "they'd not have kept Crystalmoss out this long."

"Then I guess somebody had better go after them," Freefoot said to Suretrail.

"I'm going too," Two-Wolves said.

"How about Shadowflash?" Starflower suggested.

"That's good," Freefoot said. "Grazer and Fernhare too. But it's getting on toward afternoon, you won't make it to Tall-Trees before dark."

"I know," Suretrail said, "but I think we should start out anyway. Tomorrow might be too late."

Mounted on their wolves, the five elders traveled as quickly as they could, following much the same route the four younger elves had taken two days before. It was indeed dusk by the time they came to Tall-Trees.

The area was too large to search, so they tracked first one way along the verge, then the other. At last Snaggletooth, Shadowflash's wolf, caught a trace where Brightmist had put her hand on a branch to move it aside.

They followed the faint trail from copse to copse, circling rather than going through. Always they found the trail on the other side. As they went they occasionally saw distant shadowy forms of deer — white-tail, red, even black-neck. But there was no smell of deer blood anywhere.

"I think it's time to shed some," Two-Wolves said. "It's late, I'm hungry, and Loper and Springer don't want to track elves with so much game nearby."

The others agreed, so when they saw a white-tail yearling they brought it down quickly and ate. By the time they finished it was full night. The dark did not slow them as they went on, but fatigue and full bellies did.

Some time later, in a large copse, they smelled pig blood. They entered the brush, smelled the spoor of black-neck, and saw the place where the pig had been struck.

"It wasn't a forest pig," Shadowflash said.

They followed the blood smell out of the copse and through the dark parkland. At one point the trail crossed bare ground, and they knelt to check for prints. It was a big pig, and had been running hard.

"If they just wanted supper," Grazer said, "why did they choose a pig that size?"

"Why a pig at all?" Suretrail wondered. "There were black-neck right there."

"More of a challenge," Fernhare suggested.

"It looks like it must have led them quite a chase," Two-Wolves said.

"Foolish thing to do," Suretrail said.

"At least," Shadowflash said, "they decided to finish the job after wounding it."

Later they came to a place where they smelled wolf-blood and stopped, alarmed. Their wolves howled in distress. The elves howled too, and sent. There was no reply to their sending, but there was an answering howl.

They hurried toward the sound and found Mask. Green-twig's wolf was tired and sore and stiff, and the skin along one side was badly cut and it seemed that some ribs were cracked.

"He can't be the only survivor," Suretrail said.

Two-Wolves put his hands on Mask's head and stared into the wolf's eyes. But Mask was not his wolf, and the animal was tired, hungry, and thirsty, and not interested in wolf-talking. About the only thing Two-Wolves could learn was that Green-twig had sent Mask back from some place. After a bit Two-Wolves instructed Springer, the smaller of his two animals, to accompany Mask back to the holt where he could be tended.

The trail continued in almost a straight line through the park to the river, where they could see the trampled brush where the pig had gone. They followed, into the denser forest.

It was dawn by the time they came to the rapids high in the back of the valley. The sun, though still hidden by the forest across the river, was just coming up. The trail led to the rocks of the rapids, and was lost. Two-Wolves looked around. "Here's where mask turned back," he said.

They were very tired now and had to rest a bit while they decided what to do next. They slaked their thirst, and Shad-owflash and Grazer went to catch a few fish for breakfast. They came back with several large salmon.

When they had eaten and caught their breath they searched along the river, then forded the rapids where it was easiest and cast up and down the other side. At last they found wolf-prints in the mud, and followed the trail away from the river, upslope into the forest, and eventually to the uplands.

They pushed as hard as they could until, by midmorning, they came to the semiopen glade. Here they could finally see the pig tracks clearly, of the wounded animal and many others. The smell of pig was strong.

"Look," Fernhare said, pointing to the tracks. "The pig our deer hunters were after was just a juvenile."

"Are you sure?" Two-Wolves asked.

"See for yourself," she said. She pointed out other, much larger hoofprints. "Mountain-swine. I've seen their tracks before, way to the south."

They scouted cautiously. There could be other swine nearby. The pig smell was everywhere, bushes had been rooted up and small saplings knocked down.

"At least twenty animals," Suretrail said, "maybe more."

"Look at the size of those tracks," Grazer said. "Bigger than a deer, heavier than a bear."

They didn't see any swine at the moment, but the ground was uneven, there were hollows, rocks, bushes, and the occasional tree where they could be concealed. The rescue party moved deeper into the glade. Some of the pig marks had been made recently. One pile of droppings was still warm. The wolves were quiet, slinking along. They didn't like this place at all.

Then they heard sounds to one side, distant snorting and grunting. They approached cautiously, well spread out and ready to run. And there they were, dozens of swine, of all sizes, the biggest truly huge, loosely gathered and moving around a place where three tall oaks stood, still some way off.

Two-Wolves looked up at the trees. Maybe … **Crystal-moss!** he sent.

Father! came the answer they could all hear.

Then the four young hunters yelled, and the swine thrashed around in the rocky-bottomed draw.

"They're up in the trees," Shadowflash said with obvious relief.

Are you all right? Suretrail sent.

The four young elves all answered at once, a jumble of thoughts and images. They were fine, but they were tired, cramped, and hungry. The pigs had stayed under their trees since the middle of the afternoon the day before yesterday, even during the night. Their prey had died last night, and they had hoped that, with its death, the other swine would leave, but they hadn't. The nearest other trees were too far away to jump to, and the forest was too far away to run to even if they could have gotten past the herd below them.

Even worse, Deerstorm's wolf had been killed shortly after they had gotten into the trees. Fog and Dancer had escaped, but Scarface had gotten cornered, tossed, gored, trampled, and later half eaten. Deerstorm was more distraught about that than her own predicament.

Hang on, Grazer sent. **We'll get you down.**

The elders tried to get closer, but the juvenile pigs and most of the piglets were out at the edge of the herd and could easily alert the adults. As they tried to decide what to do next, Dancer and Fog came slinking up from the forest. The other wolves whimpered softly, the elders hushed them up.

The forest, on the side of the draw from which the wolves had come, was not too far away, and the elders circled around to it.

"Let's see if we can make them chase us," Grazer suggested to Shadowflash. Shadowflash just grinned.

They left the others and walked toward the herd of swine. Then they started yelling and shouting and waving their spears. The piglets set up a commotion, some of the juveniles started to chase them, and they ran back to the forest. But most of the swine stayed at the draw, and those in chase gave up quickly.

The rest of the swine were not more upset than ever. Suretrail and Two-Wolves went around to the side and again taunted them by throwing stones at them. They, too, were chased back, by a sow and three juveniles.

But the other swine just got more upset. The elders could see the branches of the three oak trees shaking as the boars and sows shouldered against the trunks, as if they would knock the trees down.

"They're digging around the roots," Greentwig called to them.

"We've got to do something," Fernhare said.

Suretrail thought about it, then went toward one of the narest juveniles and threw a javelin, which struck the pig square in the side. The pig screamed, the nearer adults turned and lunged, Suretrail ran.

Several swine gathered around the wounded pig, but Suretrail's shot had been too good. Even as other adults came to the rescue, the pig died. The swine jostled it, Rolled it over, but didn't pay any attention to the elves. Instead they snorted and went back to the three trees.

"It was a good idea," Fernhare said.

"But not quite good enough," Shadowflash said. "Make some cord, as much as you can."

He took one of Suretrail's javelins, took off the bone head, whittled the end of the shaft to a point, then refastened the head backward, as a long barb. The others cut strips from their clothes and plaited a long and thin but strong cord which he tied to the butt of the javelin.

"I guess throwing it is my job," Grazer said. He was the strongest of the elves. He coiled the cord loosely over one arm and then went boldly out to pick a target.

The other elves followed at a short distance, to give him help if he needed it. Grazer moved carefully toward the herd of swine and picked out the piglet that was nearest the forest. Holding the end of the cord tightly with one hand, he took careful aim and launched the javelin in a high arc. It struck the piglet through the thick of the thigh, at nearly the full stretch of the cord.

He didn't pause but turned and ran back as hard as he could. The barb on the javelin held and the weight of the now screaming piglet nearly jerked the cord from his hand. The boars and sows bellowed in rage at the piglet's screams as he dragged it along behind him, and before he was halfway back to the trees the whole herd came running after him.

Two-Wolves and Shadowflash were waiting by a tree, and as Grazer came up they gave him a boost into the branches. As soon as he had a good hold he pulled in the cord and dragged the screaming piglet up after him. He was barely in time. A boar crashed hard into the trunk of his none-too-large tree, and it was all he could do to hold the tree and the piglet at the same time.

The swine trampled the undergrowth, snorting and grunting and shouldering the trees. Fernhare, Suretrail, and Shadowflash fanned out through the branches, making as much noise as they could to distract them. Though most of the swine trampled around under Grazer, others dashed back and forth following the three elders who squealed in imitation of the hurt piglet as they moved slowly away. It was enough to keep the swine from knocking down Grazer's none-too-large tree. Meanwhile he was holding the piglet, wishing he could put it out of its misery.

But Two-Wolves moved quietly off through the branches, away from the swine, and went back to the ground. He called all the wolves and hurried with them to where the youths were even now coming down from their refuge. The four young elves, tired and cramped, mounted the borrowed wolves and raced with him back to the forest. Some of the swine came to investigate and started in pursuit, but the elves went up into the trees as soon as they could and the wolves scattered.

As soon as they were all safe, Grazer slit the piglet's throat. Now the other elders became quiet and slowly, one by one, moved off through the high branches. Grazer kept the piglet as he left the place. No sense letting good meat go to waste.

When they were a safe distance away they came down to the forest floor. The wolves rejoined them as they went back toward the river. When they could no longer hear the swine they paused to rest.

Shadowflash held Brightmist as they sank down to the ground. The other three young elves all sat, very subdued. The elders, too, were quiet. Even the wolves seemed relieved. Suretrail butchered the piglet, and let the kids eat it all.

"I thought you were going after black-neck," he said.

"We could have had one, too," Greentwig answered.

"At least that was something you could have handled," Suretrail told him.

"Would we have done any better," Fernhare asked, "if we had hunted that pig?"

"I guess not," Suretrail said reluctantly.

"Under the circumstances," Fangslayer said, "I think our deer hunters are probably wise enough now to take care of themselves."

"Sure," Grazer said, "they didn't bring back a black-neck, but anybody can get in trouble."

"It's not the kind of trouble we're likely to have in the future," Brightmist said from Shadowflash's arms. "And besides, it was a good hunt before we got trapped."

"I guess it was at that," Suretrail said. "You did all the right things up until then."

"And then, too," Crystalmoss said. "We could have tried to run away."

Then Suretrail reached out and hugged her. "I'm so glad you're safe," he said.

Fernhare looked fondly at Greentwig, who still felt unappreciated. "Nobody can argue about your hunting alone now," she said. "You four seem to make a good team."

"And as long as we have to go back through Tall-Trees anyway," Greentwig said, "let's get us a black-neck."

"That's a good idea," Suretrail said.

———————————

Howling Time

Freefoot woke at first light, from a dream that made him feel strange. There was going to be a Howl.

It was late summer, when the days were still hot but the nights were decidedly cool, when all the leaves were very dark green, and a few of the understory plants had begun to get edges of gold and red and brown. It was a rich time of year, just before the harvesting of the fruits and nuts, when the deer and bear and smaller animals were getting fat for the winter. There had been light rains a few days ago, but by now the ground was dry.

He had been sleeping at the south edge of a small grove of trees, separated from the forest proper by only a few minutes walk through a narrow strip of the prairie, a vast sea of grass which extended north, east, and west as far and farther than any wolfrider had ever gone, even he. He had been away from the holt for three eights of days, a rather long time, even for him, and was less than half a day from Halfhill.

He should be at the holt. He could easily get there by midday if he set off at once. The elves had not planned the Howl, it was just going to happen, as it sometimes did. All the elves would be at the holt. That seldom happened, and it was reason enough for them to celebrate.

He sat up, watched the sun come up and brighten the narrow stretch of prairie between the grove and the forest, and thought about the feeling, trying to figure out what it meant. The Howl was a part of it, but there was something more, something which eluded him, something which made him sad.

Dawn passed into midmorning. Even at this distance, he could feel the other elves as they went about their business. Streak, his wolf, became restless and hungry. His thoughts remained a jumble, but after a while they began to take shape, and they did not comfort him. He thought about maybe not going back to the holt after all, but just missing the Howl that night.

That made him stop thinking altogether. It also made his stomach hurt, and the back of his throat ache. Not go back at all? He had had, he realized now, that thought many times before, though until this morning it had never come clear, just a remote longing which he had easily put aside. It frightened him, now that he knew what it was, and in more ways than one.

The most important thing was that his absence would be obvious to everyone. The gesture would not be misunderstood. It would be an abdication, and Suretrail would take over as chieftain of the tribe.

The thought persisted, in spite of the dismay he felt. He had never liked being a leader. He preferred to wander. That was why they called him Freefoot. It was just an accident of birth that he had inherited the chieftainship from Huntress Skyfire. That was long ago, he wasn't sure just how many eights of eights of eights of the turns of the seasons. Since Skyfire's time, when they had crossed from the west, fleeing the humans, and had found this place of peace and plenty, the elves had been free of conflicts, and could concentrate on just living. Almost nothing important ever happened, and that was the way everybody liked it. Freefoot's life had not been at all difficult. But still…

If he didn't go back, it would mean giving up Starflower, his lifemate. Though they had never Recognized, they loved each other, and she was more dear to him than anybody since his mother … and that one time in the tall grass so far away, so many years ago.

If Freefoot did not go back tonight, he would not be welcome later. He would never see Fangslayer, his eldest child again, or Fangslayer's lifemate, Deerstorm, and their cubling Ebony. Nor would he see his own younger child, Feather. The thought was an ache in his head and his throat and his chest.

He had always wanted to go to the places from which the elves had come when he had been a cub, or to those from which his people had come before that, or go on to other strange places, further east and south and away. To wander and see places and just survive, that had always been his desire. He did as much of it as he could, and it was never enough, and he always felt guilty that it took him away from his people as much as it did.

The temptation was strong, even with the thought of what he would miss if he went. Someday, someday, he would have to decide, one way or another. But he didn't have to make up his mind just yet. He patted Streak and told the wolf to go ahead and find something to eat.

Brightmist, Shadowflash, and Bluesky, with their wolves, young Starjumper, old Snaggletooth, and Blinky, arrived at the far side of Round Hill, over by Little Hill, at first light, to collect the best fruit they could find. They had panniers and baskets with them, and would have to cover a large area to get enough of the late summer fruit to make the expedition worth their time. There were crab apples, blackberries, grapes, and sugar cones, which were especially sweet this year. They worked until midmorning when they stopped to catch some squirrels for breakfast.

Though fruit and vegetables made up only a small portion of the elves' diet, it was important for pleasure and nutrition. They sampled freely of what they had collected, and thought that maybe they had enough for several days, until Shadowflash suddenly thought, "What if we have a feast tonight?"

"Why would we do that?" Brightmist asked.

"No special reason," Shadowflash said.

"Unless we Howl," Bluesky said. She sucked on a sugar cone and looked at her two companions.

"Why should we?" Brightmist asked.

"Just because," Shadowflash said.

———

The sun was barely up, and what little of the sky which could be seen through the trees was a deep blue. The surrounding forest, dense and deep, was still quite dark. It was quiet.

A very young elf-child, with streaming long black hair, came out of his den on legs that were still not too steady, and sneakily and gleefully scampered along the base of the cliff to another den and went in. After a moment or two, he and another elf-child came out, her hair so white it was almost transparent. She was just slightly older and almost ready to talk. They giggled at each other, though they tried to be quiet, and went to yet another den a little further along the cliff and went in.

After a few minutes, Dreamsnake came out with the the two cublings in tow, and a third one tagging along behind. The one with black hair was Ebony. The white-haired child, Silvercub, was feeling very grown up compared to him. The third was Dewdrop, small, pretty, with pale gold hair, Dreamsnake's own girlchild, a bit more shy than the other two. Almost immediately a huge gray and brown wolf came out, a gentle creature who's name was Bearcub.

The cublings skipped clumsily as they went down to the stream. They were excited but they were quieter now, with Dreamsnake to mind them. When they came to the water the cublings, who weren't wearing very much anyway, took off their few clothes and went in. The water was cold, and now that they were away from the dens they could no longer restrain themselves, laughing, and calling out, and making up noises and imaginary words. Dreamsnake sat on the grassy bank and more sedately washed herself while the cublings played. All cublings were excited first thing in the morning, but today there was something else in their play and laughter, something which they all shared. Bearcub drank, then went off looking for breakfast.

Dreamsnake didn't know why the cublings were so excited, but their pleasure was infectious, and she really didn't care. After all, cubs will be cubs. They splashed from one side of the stream to the other, threw water on each other, and at odd moments actually spent some time getting clean.

The sky got brighter, the light began to shine on the common yard and, in spite of the noise of the children, the forest became alive with its own sounds. Dreamsnake, who often felt guilty about spending so much time with the young ones, instead of going out hunting, watched them play with a strangely intense contentment. Something about today was surely going to be different.

Fire-Eyes lay wrapped in furs in the sleeping-chamber of her den. She heard cublings splashing and playing down at the stream. She had known since long before dawn that the day would be strange. Her night had been filled with more dreams than was usual, even for her, and she felt very muzzy. She had had this kind of feeling before, a little bit different maybe, not so intense. She had no idea why, and hoped it would not take too long before it all became clear to her. All she knew now was that today was going to be weird.

She got up quietly, so as not to disturb Ironwood, her lifemate, who was still asleep beside her. Brown-haired Spinner, her very young boychild, woke when she did, and looked up at her as she dressed. She looked back at him, and tried to see him through the colors in her eyes. He smiled up at her. He knew his mother was weird again, which meant that something exciting was surely going to happen. He got dressed too, and went out with her.

She hesitated at the entrance to her den. Spinner, beside her, saw Ebony, Silvercub, and Dewdrop playing down at the stream with Dreamsnake. He forgot about his mother and ran off to join them.

A moment later Dayshine, with his father Puckernut, came out of their den. Then Starbright came from her den. Her parents, Fairheart and Moonblossom, had come out earlier to wash up, and were a few eights of paces upstream from the children. Deerstorm and Fangslayer came and found their own place in the water. Then Rainbow and Two-Wolves, then Starflower and her young son Feather, then Stringsong and his girl Warble, then Talon and the boy Whistle, and even Suretrail, who dared the stream in spite of the cubs, who now were making a veritable party of the moment.

Fire-Eyes watched for a while, but she was still struggling with her dreams, even though she was awake, and she didn't really see what was going on. She tried to remember her dreams, to make some sense of them, but they kept eluding her, like trying to pick up a slippery mellon seed. When dreams escaped like that, it usually meant that one was waking up, but that wasn't true this morning.

She tried to shake off the weird feeling but it got stronger. She began to have visions of those elves long dead, that everybody thought of as ancestors whether they actually were or not. At first these visions were just flickering images, but after a while they became more consistent, more insistent, and more intrusive.

In one vision she saw an elf, standing by a structure of shaped stones that would not come apart. It was set on a hot flat land with no trees anywhere. There were elf skulls all around it.

In another she saw an image of an elf who was more wolf than elf, with a hairy body and luminous eyes, heel-sitting with a — a High One beside him, who kneaded his hairy neck gently. He arched with pleasure, then rolled over on his back to expose his belly, as if asking for more.

She saw a she-elf, seeking with her mind, with her sending power, for a lost child. She saw the child, though the cubling was far away, looking at a flower. It was a poisonous green and veined with black, with heavy down-curved petals, unnatural among the other flowers. The child touched the flower, and the she-elf got no more sending, no answer to her call, just an emptiness.

There was the chaser, in a time of sickness, his head filled with dreams of sky-mountains coming down to the land. He found his wolf eating the snow. The wolf did not know him, and none of the other wolves knew their riders either.

Most frightening of all was a vision of a long-legged wolf-elf and another, more elf-like. It was a mother and her son, struggling mind to mind, to try to prove which one had the Way. The she-wolf lived and the child died.

Fire-Eyes was not aware of time passing. These visions frightened her, but at last, by midmorning, the worst of them was over, and she found that she had wandered to the top of Halfhill. She stood on the edge of the clay cliff, looking down at what was happening below on the common yard in front of the dens. At last one part of it came clear. "There's going to be a Howl tonight!" she called out.

Those who heard her called back, laughing, "Of course, we thought you knew."

Fire-Eyes laughed too.

Stringsong sat in front of his den, watching the morning activities but paying little attention. He was tuning his harp while Warble watched. He plucked one of the six strings. It was nearly right. He tightened it just a bit, then he tightened another string. Now that one was okay, but the first string was now too loose. It took him a long time to tune his harp, and then it wouldn't stay the way he wanted for more than a couple days.

"Why are you doing that?" Warble asked him.

"We're going to sing tonight," Stringsong said, without really being aware of his words.

"You mean Howl?" Warble asked.

"Yes," Stringsong said, surprised, "that's what I mean." He started on another string.

Two-Wolves came to them and said, "We should get some meat for tonight."

"You're right," Stringsong said. He gave his harp to Warble, went into his den for his spear and bow, and went off with Two-Wolves, while Warble plucked the harp strings pretending to make music.

By mid morning all the elves who were awake were out doing things. They were aware of a sense of excitement, and would have shared it even if they had not had the children as an example, but each had gone about their daily business until the truth began to come to them, by ones and twos and threes.

Catcher, Puckernut, and Suretrail had started mending weapons after their wash-up, and it was while Suretrail was putting a new edge on a flint knife that he felt something in the back of his throat, as if he were howling. "A Howl," he said.

Catcher and Puckernut looked at him. "Sure," Catcher said. "That's what it is."

Deerstorm, Fangslayer, and Starflower were sharing a late breakfast when the realization came to them, all three at the same time. Deerstorm nearly choked, Fangslayer stopped with a bit of meat halfway to his mouth, and Starflower sat with her mouth full. They looked at each other with sudden understanding. Deerstorm's choke turned into a chuckle.

Dreamsnake was still at the stream, with Dayshine, Dewdrop, Ebony, Spinner, Silvercub, and Starbright. Rainbow and Two-Wolves had come down to help for a while. The cublings were standing around in a circle, passing some intangible thing from one to the other, and every now and then one of them would howl. Two-Wolves watched them with a strange concentration.

"They're howling," Rainbow said.

"Of course," Dreamsnake said, "that's what it's all about."

Fairheart and Moonblossom were eating a leg of two-day-old venison for breakfast. It was a bit on the gamey side, but Fairheart liked flavor in his meat. They were a very close couple, and shared their thoughts by sending more than other people did. The idea of the Howl came to them simultaneously.

Graywing, with Feather, had gone down stream a little way to gather water leaves. These were used sometimes for seasoning bland meat, or for making a strong tea or, when dried, to put with other greens for flavor. Feather was fairly bouncing as he reached under the water for the broad, smooth leaves, which he plucked and handed to his elder. Graywing, who was related to him three generations back, watched him, and her throat tensed with emotion. The only way to relieve it would be to howl, and she almost did so. But no, not now, tonight, with everybody else.

Greentwig and Hornbird met each other outside their dens. They had let themselves sleep late. They sat down in front of Hornbird's den. They didn't speak much, Hornbird was not talkative, and Greentwig had little to say. Hornbird offered to share a ravvit, fresh last night, and Greentwig accepted. They heard a sudden shout from the cubs by the stream.

"We're going to Howl tonight," Greentwig said.

"Not tonight," Hornbird said. Her correction of the slow one was habitual. Then she realized that she was wrong. "I'm sorry," she said. "Of course we are."

Every four of eights of turns of the seasons or so, the elves would feel the need to re-establish their identity, to remember their past, to bring themselves all together and become one with each other. Sometimes they did this when there was a death, but not always. Sometimes when there was a birth. Sometimes events changed the course of their lives, or they escaped such change, and they would Howl. And sometimes they did it just because they hadn't done it in a while.

But this was none of those occasions. There was no because, it was just going to happen, and nobody had any idea why. Since there seemed to be no reason for this Howl, it would in itself be cause for a celebration.

The last time there had been a Howl, the elves had been away from the holt, out on the prairie, and that had been to celebrate a kill of several huge humpbacks after a long and starving autumn. Before that, the Howl had been in the deep woods south of the holt, when Sunset had died defending the tribe's cublings from an angry gray bear. Before that — well, it hardly mattered now. The elves had not had a Howl at their holt in far too long a time.

Ironwood rose late and found that his lifemate and cubling had already left the den. He went out and looked for them in the common yard. Spinner was with Dreamsnake, but he couldn't see Fire-Eyes. He thought about having a piece of chucker for breakfast, then going out to get fresh meat, then thought about getting a lot of meat and sharing it, then wondered why, then realized that there would be a Howl that night.

Fernhare and Glade saw Fire-Eyes on the edge of the cliff overlooking Halfhill, heard her shout though they did not understand the words, and went around by the upstream end to see her, but by the time they got there she had wandered away somewhere. They were concerned for her, though they had seen her caught up in her visions many times. Today it was more intense somehow. They sat down on the edge of the cliff, with their legs dangling over, to talk and think.

"I think we're going to have a Howl," Glade said at last.

"I think so too," Fernhare said. "And that, I'll bet, is what's got Fire-Eyes going today."

"Well of course it is," Glade said.

Fernhare sat there a few minutes longer, then stood up from the cliff edge, went down to the common yard, and found Ironwood, Talon, and Starflower. They all felt the need to be something, perhaps they could make a Howling Place for that night. Fire-Eyes wandered by, distracted and distant. They gazed after her as she went past them to the river bank and then downstream.

The Howling Place had to be big enough for all the elves and their wolves to gather together, where they could build a huge bonfire, where they could feast far into the night and eat dreamberries and, most importantly, where they could share their thoughts and feelings for each other and their past.

It wouldn't do to build the bonfire right on the common yard. The scar would be there until the next spring. The ground across the stream was open enough and the fire-scar wouldn't hurt it, but it was too wet this year, and soggy.

There was a huge blackwood tree, a kind of broadleaf evergreen, at the downstream end of the holt, on the left hand as the elves come out of their dens, and just beyond it was a ring of small trees that had grown up in a kind of circle, where older cublings sometimes went just to get away. But the clearing within the circle, though sheltered, was only a few paces across, eight and four or so, not big enough for everybody.

Just upstream a way was a grove of smaller maples and beeches, a strange mixture of trees, none of them bigger around than an elf's arm. It wasn't much good for anything, they couldn't hunt there, and after a few eights of eights of turns of the seasons it would be too dense to be good for anything. Still....

They went to look it over. It would take a lot of work, but it would do quite well. Quite a few trees would have to be cut. The stumps, though small, would not be easy to get out of the ground, but they could do that. They went back to get axes and digging-sticks.

Treewing had been out for an eight of days with her wolf, Whisper. She had wakened early in her camp on Flat Hill, gathered up the feathers for arrows, bones for needles, and other things she had collected so far, and went down into the valley between Flat Hill and Bald Hill, where she hunted more birds until late morning. As she got to the top of Bald Hill, looking around for her next target, she got the clear thought that there would be a Howl. She would need to get special feathers for the celebration, so she went to the marsh, on the stream which ran through the holt, to hunt the more exotic birds which lived there.

She didn't have names for them, but one kind of bird had bright red tail feathers almost as long as her hand, and another had iridescent blue feathers along its throat. She collected a few of these, ate what meat she could, and gave the rest to Whisper. She left the swamp and kept on the lookout for other birds, those with yellow wing feathers, others with black crests, and the kind with long, brown, spotted tails, to add to the collection. She would prefer to spend several days doing this, and going further afield, but time was getting on. She found most of her wants by the time she got back to the holt at midday.

———————

Fire-Eyes saw Treewing come in, but she didn't say anything. She had been feeling very much like a child for the last while, so she had gone to play with Dreamsnake and the cublings, who were near the stream as usual. While they were on the bank, the cublings got all muddy and grassy, and had to go back into the water to rinse off, but that was part of the game. Catcher and Glade brought food for them all and stayed to share it. Fire-Eyes ate too but, now that she was no longer distracted with play, her visions came on her again, and she participated very little in the meal or the conversation.

Bluesky, Brightmist, and Shadowflash finally decided that they had enough fruit and started back to the holt. On the way they came to a bush of dreamberries, all ripe.

"This is good," Shadowflash said. "We can use these tonight."

"What a good idea," Bluesky said. She and Shadowflash started to collect them. Brightmist found another bush nearby, and when they had finished with the first bush, they cleaned that one too.

They now had almost more berries than they could carry, and Brightmist wanted to sample them, but Shadowflash said it might be more appropriate to wait the Howl that night. They got back to the holt by early afternoon. They saw Fire-Eyes sitting with Dreamsnake, her back to the stream where the cublings were playing. She was staring into unseeable distance, at something which no one else could see. She wouldn't need dreamberries today.

Graywing and Feather came back from gathering water leaves, and joined Puckernut and Hornbird for some lunch, and to talk about the preparations for the Howl. Greentwig wanted something fresh to eat, so he went off to hunt with his wolf, Longtoes.

After eating, Graywing took Feather, and Warble who had wandered by, to where Fernhare, Ironwood, Talon, and Starflower were making the clearing for the howl. Graywing told the cublings that it was going to be their job to take charge of the food. They would feast tonight after the Howl, and they needed some place to put the food that would be coming in. Bluesky, Brightmist, and Shadowflash had already brought the fruit, and Treewing brought her bird-meat. It all had to be put out of the reach of pests, and hungry cublings, and wolves that didn't know any better.

They took the slenderer trunks and straighter branches to build high platforms, tying them to the trees still standing around the circle of the clearing, using strips of bark from the trees which had been cut down. The platforms would be as high as an elder could reach and would completely encircle the cleared ground. This would mark out the Howling Place and make it special. As food came in they put it up onto the platforms which they had built. There would be a lot to eat tonight. Their work would take them until dusk, and it was hard work, but it was worth it. The cublings were learning, and that was important. The three elder elves did most of the work, but Feather and Warble took their helping seriously.

Stride, with her wolf Spot, had been gone for two eights of days, mostly in and around the marsh at the north of the forest, living off fish and whatever else she could catch. Early in the morning she had made herself a little reed punt, from which she hunted turtles for shell and bonefish for their bones. She became aware of the Howling at midday, and decided that though she preferred her solitude, it was time to head back.

She paddled her punt out of the marsh and across the lake, calm but deep, into which the waters of all the streams and rivers that went through the elves' hunting ground and beyond emptied, and which, in turn, went north across the prairie into the unknown. She went past Southern Island, and by early afternoon she got to the mouth of Small River. On the east shore was the forest swamp, where elves seldom went. The water was too deep for walking, the trees and marsh plants too close together for punting, and the snakes and long-jaws too hungry to mess with.

She could use her pole now, which she preferred, especially against a current. She stayed close to the shore, and soon came to the mouth of the stream which ran past the holt. Half way there she paused at Tiny Lake to catch several trout. It was mid-afternoon, and she hadn't eaten since breakfast.

Rillwalker had been on the uplands for three eights of days, exploring the upwaters. She had left them the day before, taking her time, following Small River to Tall Trees. She had camped that night in the rocky hollow near the three threes where, three turns of the seasons ago, Greentwig, Deerstorm, Brightmist, and Crystalmoss, all barely adults, on their first hunt alone, had been trapped when they had roused the ire of a whole herd of Mountain Swine. She left her camp in the early morning, and a little later she spotted a small red deer. It was easy for her and her wolf, Smoke, to take it. Ordinarily she would eat her fill, and let Smoke have his, and then have brought back just the best of the meat, but she had felt the call for the Howl, and for that she wanted a whole deer.

Going through Tall Trees was easy, even while carrying the carcass. The huge evergreens were widely spaced, and there was almost no undergrowth, except in the domed clumps, peculiar to Tall Trees, which she could just go around. The ground was firm and cushioned with a thick layer of dead needles.

It got more difficult when she left Tall Trees and entered more typical forest. She was strong, and used to hard work, but the deer was getting heavy, and now even small branches, clumps of fern, and shallow irregularities in the ground were a nuisance and slowed her down.

At midday she got to the source of the stream which ran past the holt. and paused there a while to catch crayfish for lunch. Smoke didn't like these so much, but she wouldn't let him have any of the deer.

After her brief rest she followed the water downstream, as it changed from a brook to a creek to a stream, to the marsh. After that it was slow going the rest of the way to the holt.

Glade and Catcher decided that they needed Ancestors. This was something the elves could not make if they were out in the wild somewhere. They were symbolic images representing the spirits, memories, and histories of the five chiefs before Freefoot — Timmorn Yellow-Eyes, Rahnee the She-Wolf, Prey-Pacer, Two-Spear, and Huntress Skyfire. Freefoot would represent himself.

They began working on it in the early afternoon. They assembled the things they wanted to use — fur, leather, feather, wood, paint, stones, and whatever felt right to them — and started putting the Ancestors together, getting more stuff as they needed it and thought of it. When finished, these emblems would each be mounted on a smooth straight stick stuck into the ground. Some small thing from every member of the tribe, present or not, adult or child, was added to each of the Ancestors. Fire-Eyes came and sat with them, but did not help. They let her be.

They paused when the elves making the Howling Place finished cutting a narrow path to the common yard. "Come see what we've done," Talon said. So they went with them to the freshly cut clearing. Fire-Eyes tagged along, hardly aware that she was going with them. All the smaller trees had been cut down in a circle, to knee-height, leaving something for them to hold on to while digging the stumps out. Glade and Catcher looked around to see where they would put the Ancestors, to make sure they would fit in. Fire-Eyes just stared into some other place. When they knew where they would be placed, they went back to the common yard to work on the images.

Fire-Eyes left the Ancestor makers shortly after that, and went downstream to the flat rock. Her visions and waking dreams were beginning to get tedious, and oppressive, and she wanted some time to think by herself. Visions were her talent, and her curse was that she couldn't always see the meaning of the visions she got. Sometimes she never did understand.

She lay face down on the rock and looked at the rippling water, just a few hand-spans from her face. There was going to be a Howl, okay, she knew that, and so did everybody else, they had understood that even before she had. So why this persistence? There were no recent events to make it special. So that meant that something was going to happen tonight to make it so, or might happen.

She thought about the visions she had had so far, and the only ones that seemed meaningful were the ones about the ancestors, the five chiefs who had gone before. Whatever it was, it had to do with Freefoot. He was the sixth chief, the blood of the five chiefs preceding him. But more than that would not come clear.

After their brief, late lunch, the elves making the Howling Place began digging out the stumps. The ground would have to be leveled and packed hard, the tree-poles and branches and brush trash would have to be hauled off, and suitable wood would have to be stacked to one side to be used to make platforms for the food, and some as poles on which to hang the Ancestor figures. As the afternoon wore on, other elves came to see how the work was coming, saw how much there was yet to do, and took over much of it so the first four could rest and "supervise" them in finishing the job.

Stringsong and Two-Wolves had gone due south until they came to Tiny Glade at midday. There they found traces of several deer, and followed the trail of the one which was largest, judging by its hoof prints. It went through the forest to the river, where it crossed to River Island, which they reached at mid afternoon. The hunt, from there on, was fairly straightforward.

The two elves directed their wolves to go around beyond the deer and, by sending instructions to them, had them drive it back toward them, where they caught and killed it easily. They butchered it and brought it back north, and returned to the holt. Except that the meat would be eaten at the Howl, instead of while it was fresh, it was a perfectly normal hunt, with nothing remarkable about it at all.

Grazer and Quickthorn, with their wolves, were in the narrow valley that climbed to the highlands south of Tall Trees, tracking a bear which had come down from the uplands. Its scent was strong, though the dashing river filled the air with the smell of water, and they heard an occasional stone move under its feet, though the noise of the river was loud. At last they came around a boulder and saw it, rooting among the mud and rushes at the water's edge, nearly as tall at the shoulder as Quickthorn's chin.

The elves readied their spears and got closer. The bear looked up at them. They thought of the meat, saw the bear move, and for a moment were distracted by images themselves and the rest of the clan howling around a bonfire that night. That was enough to eliminate the benefit of surprise. The bear charged. Their wolves had not shared their confusion, and so did not lose track of their immediate purpose, and kept the bear busy so that Grazer and Quickthorn, after being knocked aside by the bear's first rush, were able to recover themselves quickly.

Both elves and wolves took wounds during the fight. Quickthorn suffered a deep cut down his right side when the bear swiped at him with a forepaw, and Grazer got slammed against a tree-trunk, which cracked two of his ribs. Grazer's wolf, White-Eyes, got stepped on, which wrenched her shoulder and back, while Quickthorn's wolf, Briartooth, was bitten clear through the skin of the neck, though the bear missed the muscle and bone. They killed the bear at last, when Grazer and Quickthorn ran it through with their spears simultaneously from either side. It was not a clean kill

Everybody needed to sit for a while, to rest and bind their wounds. Quickthorn wanted to take the bear back entire, but there was no way they could carry that much meat that far, so they skinned it, feasted off the best parts, cut the rest of the meat from the bones, and wrapped it back up in the skin along with the claws and teeth. Then they built a drag litter, loaded it, and hauled it through the forest. They crossed Small River at the lower rocks, came past the west end of Stoney Ridge, and crossed their home stream when they came to the fern brake opposite the holt.

Suretrail and Rainbow, who had been with her wolf Foxbane birthing a set of six cubs, joined Catcher and Glade to help them make Ancestors. They kept at it on through early evening to first dusk, when they at last set the five images in their places around the perimeter of the Howling Place, just inside the ring of food platforms. They went back to the common yard for a brief pause, for a light meal and a wash-up before going back to the Howling Place.

Crystalmoss, with Whistle, and Spinner in tow, set off to the glade just north of the holt, a small clearing in the otherwise dense forest. Sometimes deer browsed there in the early morning or late afternoon, but Crystalmoss and the cublings wanted was honey flowers, which were far sweeter than sugar cones, though each flower held only a drop of nectar. They bloomed only at this time of year, and then only in the late afternoon and early evening. Picked too soon, they would not be fully sweetened. Picked too late, and they would go sour. Picked at the right time, which was just about now, they were well worth the effort, though they would not last the night. As they collected the flowers, Crystalmoss told the cublings as much as she could about the Howls, and elf-lore and traditions.

It was late afternoon by the time Stride got back to the holt. She met Glade, who took the deer and fish from her, then went down to the flat rock. Dreamsnake and some cublings were near it, and Fire-Eyes way lying face down on it, staring into the water. She got up from the rock when she came and distractedly went away.

She had a quick wash, then took the fish to the Howling Place, which was nearly finished. The stumps had been removed, the ground packed, and the rubbish cleared away, and everybody was now sitting and watching while as Graywing, Puckernut, Hornbird, Feather, and Warble continued working on the platforms for the food. As each was finished, Suretrail and Rainbow put Ancestors in their places. Stride gave the fish to Graywing, who cleaned them before putting them on one of the finished platforms, well out of reach, and carrying off the offal.

Fairheart, with his cubling Starbright, the cubling Dayshine, and strong, childlike Greentwig were taking it on themselves to provide fuel for a bonfire. Fairheart was the fire keeper, so it was natural that he would lead the expedition to gather the right wood for burning.

They stayed close to the holt and gathered as much as they could, cutting the larger fallen branches into smaller pieces, and taking down one or two small dead standing trees for their unrotted logs. Fairheart and Greentwig did most of the heavy work, while Dayshine and Starbright carried the wood back to the Howling Place, where they stacked it to one side on Fern-hare's instructions.

Fire-Eyes decided she needed some real privacy, so she went to her den. She heard the sounds from the common yard of the other elves coming and going, working and talking, getting more and more excited, even though they were tired by now. The sounds faded to a distant, almost musical murmur. And in a different kind of transparent rush, she saw elves past and future, places near and far, symbols and images that had no meaning for her, and over all there was Freefoot, and an empty place, slowly moving together. The closer they got, the more frightened and unhappy she became.

The sun, as seen from the grove just north of the forest, was sinking below the treetops. The sky overhead was turning a darker blue. Soon there being a few clouds in the west, there would be lots of color in the sky, something the elves seldom saw in the forest. Freefoot would see it, if he stayed there. The prospect didn't cheer him up any.

If he stayed away tonight he might as well stay away forever. He felt like he was teetering on a branch that was too slender to balance on or to bear his weight. He had to jump, right or left, or he would fall. Neither prospect pleased him.

At last he decided to go back, if only to take a last look, unseen, at the holt and his people. He stood, and beside him Streak stretched and licked his hand. The wolf had been patient all day, and wanted to hunt, but knew that his master was anxious and unhappy. Together they crossed the short strip of prairie and entered the forest. They walked quickly, and arrived within earshot of the holt by early evening.

He went up through the trees on the back side of the hill that ended at the cliff of clay, the half hill that gave the holt its name. He did not want to be seen, as that would make his escape impossible. But the prospect of leaving his people urged him on. He had to take one last look.

He stood at the edge of the cliff at last. The holt below him was so alive and full of activity and anticipation that it broke his heart to think of leaving it, but he hardened his resolve and turned away. After all, he was not really a leader, and never had been. He was not strong. He was away from the holt too much. And he never met his own needs and didn't really understand them. He went back down the hill, paused when he overheard people coming, and hid.

It was Crystalmoss, with Whistle and Spinner. He smelled the fresh honey flowers they carried, lots of them. Crystalmoss was too involved with the cubs, who were too excited about the Howl, to notice Freefoot, a few paces back through the trees. So perhaps it was only coincidence that Crystalmoss, as they passed by, happened to say, "I'm beginning to worry about Freefoot. He hasn't come back yet."

"He won't be late," Whistle said. "He *always* does what he's supposed to do."

"Of course he does," Spinner said. She was showing off what Crystalmoss had been teaching them all day. "Of all the chiefs we've ever had, Freefoot is the... "

He did not hear the rest, they had gone too far.

Those few words made him stop and think. If he had felt uncertain before, now he was completely torn. Because he really did want to go, he really did want to see the world. He could hear it, calling to him out of the night.

Crystalmoss and the cubs took the flowers to the Howling Place, and tied them in clusters of three and four as evenly around the perimeter as they could. Later, when the feast was over, the elves would be free to indulge in a few sweet sips, but for now they just perfumed the air. Then they went to the flat rock downstream from the holt, where Dreamsnake, who had spent the whole day, was watching over Ebony, Feather, Silvercub, and Warble. Ironwood joined them a little later and helped as Dreamsnake got all her charges out of the water and dried.

"Why are we Howling tonight?" Feather asked.

"I don't know," Dreamsnake said, "just because, I guess."

"We Howl for a bunch of reasons," Whistle answered. "But tonight I guess it's just because we're elves."

"We're more than just elves," Ironwood said. "There are other elves in the world, but they are not like us. There are elves on the prairie north of the holt, who ride animals like goats. And there are elves, I've been told, who live way back west where the humans live, and other elves in the mountains, and some think that there are still High Ones alive, who are the ancestors of us all. These other elves don't howl, only we do, and that's because we're wolf-riders."

"And because," Spinner said, "we are part wolves ourselves."

"That's very true," Ironwood said.

Dreamsnake got all the cublings back to the common yard. There they met other cublings, and she supervised them as they all began to get ready. When each of them was properly dressed and quieted, she led them to the Howling Place.

Freefoot liked to wander, but he liked it best when he had a few of his people with him. He wanted freedom, rather than solitude, he wanted to travel and explore, rather than to lead. He was uncomfortable with too many people, even such a small crowd as the population of the holt, a total of thirty nine including himself and the cublings. He preferred a few close friends, and his family, and what he enjoyed most was going on a long expedition with his lifemate Starflower, and maybe one or two others. But they didn't like being away for moons at a time, or going more than four or five days travel away from the holt. If he wanted to go exploring, he usually had to go by himself.

If he wanted to leave now, it would have be by himself. It would be easier for him to go if he could bring Starflower and Feather away with him. Maybe if Rillwalker and Puckernut and Dayshine were to come too, he could leave the holt to Suretrail and not be too regretful. But none of them would ever leave the holt, not if it meant forever. And even if they would, if he went back to get them, he would be there, and everybody else would expect him to be chief, and he would never get away. If he was going to go, he had to just go, by himself.

The thought made him ache. He loved his people. But this yearning, he knew now, had been with him forever, and whenever he indulged in it, even for only a few eights of days, he felt guilty for having been away while his people needed him. It would be better to just make the break, and let Suretrail take over. Then the elves would have a true leader, the kind they needed and deserved, and he could just go away. Everybody would be better off.

He felt empty. To distract himself he counted his resources. He could go a long way before the Howl started, and if he traveled all night and all the next day he could be beyond their reach by the time they started to search for him. If they did.

And yet, somehow, he couldn't quite make the decision.

Starflower was not at ease. She was, after all, Freefoot's lifemate, and she more than anyone missed him, had missed him for the three eights of days he had been gone. It was a quiet time now, before full dark, and though most of the elves remained near the Howling Place, there was some coming and going. She went to the top of Halfhill, and opened up her mind in the hopes of catching some stray thought if he were near, or some sending if he were far.

And she did sense him, not that far away after all, but still and solitary. Something was wrong. Her heart broke for him, but she did not call or send or go to him. She suppressed her anxiety and went back down to the common yard, where a few of the latecomers were tiredly and excitedly getting ready for the Howl.

Deerstorm, Fangslayer, and Moonblossom had gone out late in the morning with their wolves Stretch, Blackboots, and Fluff, to hunt for small game such as ravvits, chuckers, beaver, squirrel, and the like. They had gone west, and at midday they went past Round Hill, where they caught a small forest pig.

They ate the liver and brains, which wouldn't keep, and went on. By early afternoon they were in deep forest and were able to catch lots of small game, including a tapir and a prickleback. They kept moving as they hunted and, by mid afternoon, they reached the meadow at the foot of Long Mountain, where they caught lots of ground squirrels, quail, pouchrats, and more ravvits.

In late afternoon they headed back toward Bald Hill, collecting as they went, and in early evening went along the south side of the stream, still catching animals, this time some slow marshrats and otters. They got back to the holt at first dusk, loaded down with their quarry. There was nobody around on the common lawn, but they heard people talking upstream a way, so they took their burdens there, to the Howling Place, where they met Graywing and most of the other elders. They relinquished their game gratefully.

It was not often that everybody was at the holt. Usually only half or so of the elders and cublings were there at any one time, the rest being out hunting, exploring, or otherwise occupied. The Howl was bringing them all together, and for no reason that they could tell, which made the Howl special in itself. By this time, almost all the preparations were done, people were cleaned and dressed, and now were resting, eating a light supper, standing around or sitting and talking and taking it easy.

Fire-Eyes left her den. There was almost nobody in the common yard. Her thoughts would still not come clear, and she was getting more and more restless. She knew, she was certain, that there was some message, some reason for her visions, but no matter how hard she tried, the meaning would not come. She started to wander upstream as Stringsong and Two-Wolves came back with their deer. Talon saw her go and went with her. She didn't speak, and neither did he, he just kept her company. He had seen her caught up in ghost-talking before, but never for as long as this, or as deeply as this. After a bit, without actually arriving anywhere, Fire-Eyes turned around and started back. She looked once at Talon with silent pleading, but all he could do was put his arm around her as they walked.

Her day-long distraction still had a hold on her, and she was heartily tired of it. Nothing would come clear, it wouldn't go away, and the only thing she knew was that something was wrong. It wasn't just that there was going to be a Howl. It wasn't just that the spirits of the ancestors, and more than just the past chiefs, would be with them tonight. It wasn't just that all the elves were all together for once. It wasn't just this, or just that, or just anything. There was something wrong.

This was progress in a way. Now she had something a little bit more tangible to work with. She was not aware of talking to herself so quietly, and that Talon, who was staying so close to her, could not hear the words.

There was danger. The holt was in danger, or the Howl was in danger somehow, or the elves themselves, or something. She still couldn't figure out what it was. All day she had stumbled around, being a nuisance, and it wasn't for no reason. The feeling was there and, instead of looking for words, she closed her eyes and felt. There was a hole, broken threads, absence — yes, absence, someone was not there, it was someone who was not there. And at last she knew — there was great power, and great danger. In her vision she saw again the image of Freefoot and the empty place, so close together now that they almost touched. Her fear and her grief almost overwhelmed her, and she wanted to tell Talon about it, but she could not speak.

Freefoot watched Starflower from the shadows, not twenty paces from where he stood, and watched her go back down. He was angry. Crystalmoss and the cubs' words had reminded him of his responsibilities, and he didn't like it that these people put such a burden on him, such an obligation. He argued with himself that they deserved to be left to take care of themselves for a while, more than just a few eights of days, and see how they liked it.

"They won't like it at all," he heard someone say and, startled, he turned and saw his mother, standing a few paces from him. It was pitch dark under the trees, but he could see her as clearly as if it were day. Not by any light in the sky, or from her, or from nearby, but with some other kind of sight. She had been dead for nearly an eight of eights of eight turns of the seasons now, so it was her spirit only that he was seeing. One doesn't need light to see a spirit.

"Most blest of chiefs," she said, "you live with no enemies
and no hardships. Who will come after?"

He thought about an elf named Two Shadows whom he
had met and loved out on the prairie so long ago, and about
Feather, his youngest child here at the holt, and he knew that the
next chief was neither there nor here, but not yet born. It gave
him a pang sharper than any he had yet felt, and he looked up,
but his mother was gone.

Fairheart, Starbright, Greentwig, and Dayshine built the
bonfire in the middle of the Howling Place, with help from
Shadowflash and Brightmist. They took great care with it, while
the others watched, and finished at first dusk. Talon, coming
back from the stream with Fire-Eyes, brought them water and a
snack, and they stayed at the unlit bonfire the rest of the
evening until it was time for the Howl to begin.

It was a very exciting time for Greentwig. He remembered
previous Howls, and he was looking forward to this one, especially since it seemed to be just for the sake of Howling. He
really didn't understand why sometimes the elves Howled for an
important occasion, and at other times didn't, or why they
sometimes Howled for no reason at all. It didn't really matter to
him, as long as it happened every now and then. He enjoyed the
excitement, the emotion, the celebration, the food and dreamberries, and the feeling, strongest then, that he really belonged.
He liked having everybody around, and he especially liked it
when he had a part to play. Most of the time he had no more
responsibility than the cublings, even though he was big and
strong. But sometimes the elders would give him something to
do, and he hoped that would happen tonight.

It was just nightfall and everything was ready at last. Graywing was the loremaster, and at her word, Fairheart the fire
keeper struck new fire and from it kindled a torch. He looked
around at the gathered elves, saw that one elf was missing.

Freefoot should light the fire, but he was not there. Then he saw Greentwig, so innocent, so excited, but feeling a bit left out. He handed the torch to the child-elder. Greentwig's eyes lit up almost as bright as the flame. He straightened up, stepped forward with clumsy confidence, and thrust the torch into the hollow at the base of the bonfire. The flames caught, the elves stood, formed a circle, and got ready. All their wolves were with them. When the fire was burning fully, they began to chant. All the other wolves from the forest came in too.

Fire-Eyes stood outside the ring and felt the past, felt the ancestors, and asked them for help. The spirit of Huntress Skyfire seemed to come to her, and to answer her, to reassure her and calm her, so that at last she could take her place. As she did so, she sensed Freefoot's approach, before anybody else did.

He had been standing at the crest of Halfhill when he smelled smoke. He knew that meant that the fire had been struck. He felt within himself the communal sending, uncoordinated and uncertain at first, as the elves gathered their minds. He was not aware of himself down the slope and toward the Howling Place. It seemed as though he stood rooted to the spot, feeling the community come together, come into tune, and in his mind's eye he could see the fire. He heard the chanting before the Howl itself began, and opened his eyes just as he stepped into the circle, amazed at his own presence there.

Fire-Eyes watched Freefoot enter the circle, and now the pattern was whole. The empty place was empty no more. The danger was over. Her visions vanished, her thoughts came crystal clear at last as the ceremony began in earnest. The tone of the chanting changed with Freefoot's arrival, and became joyful as Freefoot pulled his knife.

He couldn't leave these people, he *was* these people, and they were him.

With the sharp tip of the knife he cut his arm, and with his fist clenched, he let the drops of blood fall to the ground, to mingle with the ground, the soil and the soul of his people.

"I am the blood of the five chiefs," he began, and now the elves could Howl.

———————————————————

The Naming of Stonefist

The day that Greentwig was finally given his adult name started out just like any other day at Halfhill, though it didn't stay that way long. The youngest elves, the cublings, came out of their dens at first light, where they'd slept the night away with their parents and older siblings, and went down to the stream to wash and play. Some of the older children came down to join them a little later. And some of the wolves, who had slept in the forest above the hill or across the stream, came around to find out if anything was up. It was a cool morning, but clear, and would get hotter as the day went on.

Many of the elves were away that day on hunting trips, or in pursuit of materials for clothes and weapons, or just wandering around, the way Freefoot often did, though he was at Halfhill that day. He wasn't up yet, but he was enjoying a quiet hour with Starflower, his lifemate, while Feather, his younger son, nearly an adult, was out with the cubs and cublings. His older son, Fangslayer, had moved into his own den long ago.

The noise of the children became louder, and the elders began to stir themselves. It was a good season, there was no need to hunt every day, no need to be constantly out and about. Every day since late spring had been about the same, and everybody assumed the days would continue to be the same until the first frost. And that was good, and the way it should be, since that was the way it usually was, year after year.

If Greentwig's coming of age were the only unusual event that day, it would be exceptional enough, and would have been remembered for many turns of the seasons following. After all, Greentwig was more than twice as old as any other elf had been when they became adults and assumed the responsibilities of being an elder. It seemed that he just never quite grew up. He was tall, and well built, and quite good looking, but he had never developed any skills, he showed no special talents, and seemed content, much of the time, to play with the younger elves, the juveniles.

Like the wolves who shared their lives, the elves did not bear the burden of an incompetent, did not support those who could not carry their own weight, and in the course of the years there were many occasions when Greentwig's parents, Fernhare and Glade, feared that this time he would die of his own ineptitude. His peers — Brightmist, who had been Sundrop as a child, and was now lifemate of Shadowflash; and Deerstorm, known as Faun when a youth, and mother of Ebony, a cub halfway to maturity, and lifemated with Fangslayer — despaired of him ever growing up at all.

And yet he somehow managed to survive, somehow managed to avoid catastrophe, was able to hunt well enough to feed himself and share with others. No one expected that he would ever stop being an overgrown child, certainly not today. And though they could not coddle him, they accepted him, as best they could, and did not drive him away. But he was a sadness for them, and they all knew that someday he would find himself in a situation which any other adult elf could easily survive, a situation which would kill him. It was some comfort to them that he did not seem to be aware of that.

In fact, Greentwig was very much looking forward to the day. He was going on a special hunting expedition, with Fernhare, his mother, and Fangslayer, and Brightmist, and Two-Wolves, and young Starbright, who was almost an adult, though she was less than half Greentwig's age, and for whom this expedition had been planned.

Coming of age was a difficult time for a young elf, when one had to prove one's competence, and maturity, and ability, and responsibility. Starbright had been dancing around the edges of it for half a turn of the seasons, ever since Silverknife had somehow crossed that imperceptible threshold. Starbright wanted to be an adult too, but she didn't know just exactly how to go about it. And so Fangslayer, the best hunter at the holt, had planned this trip, to the forested mesa, just north of the edge of the forest, and separated from it by meadow. It would not be a long trip, and the mesa was not a dangerous place to be, but the hunt he had planned would be a test of strength, cunning, courage, and endurance, and if Starbright did well, she would be that much closer to gaining her adult name.

As it was, things were not to turn out the way anybody had planned. Maybe if Freefoot hadn't been so busy that morning things might have happened differently. If he had not been so preoccupied with other problems he might have calmed Starbright when things began to go wrong, have encouraged her to follow through so that the hunters, when they got to the mesa, would have been better able to deal with what happend. On the other hand, if he had, Greentwig might not have been given his one and only opportunity to prove himself.

Starbright was still young, and whether she took her name this hot season, or during the snows, or with the next coming of the green, it wouldn't have mattered much, except perhaps to her pride. For Greentwig, though nobody could know it, there would be no other chance.

The first thing that happened to upset everybody's plans began when Two-Wolves was aroused from a languid late slumber by his sudden awareness of his wolf. Rainbow, his lifemate, had been awake for some time but had not awakened him. She was thinking of the hunt on which her mate would be going today, thinking of a place where she hdd found bright red clay for painting, thinking of a way to paste thin sheets of bark together to make a large, white surface for painting, just quietly waiting while her mate slept so lightly, uncovered in the cool morning. His eyes came open all at once, without warning and, though he did not move, he became as tense as a hunter at the moment of a kill.

"What's the matter," she asked him softly.

"Whitecollar is afraid," he answered, just as softly.

He had a special knack with wolves. It was his only exceptional quality. Every elf had a wolf companion, but Two-Wolves had two, most of the time, this time a mated pair. He was the only elf who could communicate comfortably with another elf's wolf, and besides his two he was on friendly terms with three other wolves who were unattached and lived alone in the forest. And so he was able to feel Whitecollar's fear, though the wolf was not in the den with him.

"But what could possibly frighten Whitecollar?" Rainbow asked.

"I don't know," he said, but he got up quickly and dressed.

"Where's Brushtail?" she asked, naming Whitecollar's mate.

"There's something wrong," was all he would say, and he left even while he was pulling on his vest.

He stood for a moment in front of the high clay cliff which gave Halfhill its name, and into which all the elves had dug their dens. The stream, beyond a stretch of grassy lawn which served as the common yard, ran from the right, as he stood facing it, and it was toward the down-stream end of the cliff, toward the left, that he felt the presence of his wolves. Whitecollar was definitely fearful, though he could not tell of what, but Brushtail's wolfish mind was somehow murky, skittery, angry, and confused, and very hard to read. He strode in that direction, ignoring the other elves he passed, not running, but taking long steps to get there as quickly as possible.

He came to the eastern end of the clay cliff, where the upper bluff came down to the river lowland. There was a cluster of small trees, which had grown up together, forming a kind of ring, just four paces across. The two wolves were inside this ring. Whitecollar, a brownish gray wolf with a circle of white fur around his neck, was crouched down, tail low, hackles up, head down, half curved around himself, against the far wall of the ring, through which he could have escaped if he had wanted, staring with frightened eyes at Brushtail. She, in turn, was standing in the middle of the dark of the branch-covered space, snapping at the air, turning around and around, her heavy tail with its black tip twitching, her jaws dripping white foam.

There was nothing he could do by himself, what he needed was a healer's help. Carefully, so as to not frighten the animals, Two-Wolves backed out of the clearing and went back to the hold and to Deerstorm's den. "May I come in," he called from the entranceway.

"Yes, of course," he heard Fangslayer answer.

He went through the narrow passage, with its corner to keep out stray drafts, to the main chamber, where he found Deerstorm helping Fangslayer get ready for the hunt. Fangslayer was tightening the bindings on his spearhead while Deerstorm was wrapping some ravvit meat in berryvine leaves.

Two-Wolves clapped Fangslayer on the shoulder, but turned his attention at once to Deerstorm. She was very large with the child that would be born very soon now. "Brushtail is sick," he said. "She's acting strangely, and she's foaming a the mouth."

"Oh, dear," Deerstorm said. She put down the bundles of meat and leaves, and Fangslayer put down his spear. "I suppose she could have gotten into some soaproot."

"Whitecollar is afraid of her. She keeps circling around and around her."

"Owl pellets," Deerstorm said. "I suppose I'd better go see." She had to work to get to her feet, her belly was so huge.

"I'm sorry," Two-Wolves said, "do you think it's the fever?"

"I'll know for sure when I see her." She turned to Fangslayer. He stood up to kiss her. "Have a good hunt," she told him. "Keep him out of trouble." Meaning, as they all knew, Greentwig.

"I will," Fangslayer said. "If Brushtail has the fever, you stay clear of her."

"I will," she said, and followed Two-Wolves out of the den.

They came out onto the lawn between the cliff and the stream and saw Silvercub come out of Two-Wolves' den. He ran up to them. "What's the matter, Father?"

"Brushtail is sick," Two-Wolves told him. "I think she has the frothing fever."

Silvercub's eyes got quite large. He was in the middle of his childhood, and took things quite seriously. "I'm coming along, Father," he insisted. "Maybe I can help."

Two-Wolves reached out and tousled his son's silver-white hair. "Maybe you can," he said. "But we hsd better hurry, Whitecollar is with her." Without further discussion the three went downstream toward the circle of trees.

They heard strange growling as they neared the place, not like the sound wolves usually made, and Two-Wolves leaped ahead. When the other two pushed their way into the little clearing behind him they saw Brushtail, foaming at the mouth, stalking Whitecollar, who backed away from her with his head down almost to the ground and his tail between his legs.

"She's bitten him," Silvercub exclaimed, and sure enough, there was blood on Whitecollar's shoulder. "So now he's infected too."

"I'm afraid you're right," Deerstorm said. "Now quiet a minute." She stood watching the two wolves, who paid no attention to her at all, and concentrated on her skill. To affect a healing, she had to lay her hands on the afflicted, but even from this distance she could make a diagnosis, especially with an illness as terrible as this. "It's the frothing fever," she said after a moment. "I'm sorry, it couldn't be anything else. And it looks like Brushtail has been ill for several days."

"What can we do?" Silvercub asked, while his father stood grimly, silently beside him.

"We might be able to save Whitecollar," Deerstorm said, "but I'm afraid there's nothing we can do about Brushtail."

"Will she die?" He clutched his father's hand.

"Yes she will," Two-Wolves said, "but it's worse than that. We can't let her just die of the disease. You can see how wild she's getting, it will get worse. She'll become like Rage, Stringsong's wolf, was so many years ago, biting at everything and everybody. She will have to be destroyed before then."

"Oh, Father, no."

"It has to be," Two-Wolves said softly. His voice was choked, and Silvercub looked up at his face, which was strained and pale. "I was there when Rage got the frothing fever," he said with an effort. "Stringsong didn't want to put him down, though Graywing told him he had to. We thought we could keep Rage confined, maybe he would get over it. But he got worse, and worse, and it seemed like he got stronger and stronger, and at last he broke free from his tether one evening when Hickory, Stringsong's father was walking by, and bit him severely. Stringsong had to destroy Rage then. We had no healer at that time, and Hickory got the fever, and began frothing and going wild and attacking people, so we bound him, rather than killing him, to let the fever run its course. We know now that that was wrong, a swift death would have been better than the madness and the pain which Hickory suffered until he died at last, screaming and biting himself."

Silvercub was very subdued. Deerstorm heaved a great sigh, and held her belly with both hands. The two wolves, across the small clearing, jockeyed back and forth. The three elves had to move around inside the ring of trees, to keep the two wolves as far from them as possible.

"I'm going to need some help," Deerstorm said.

"Get back to the holt," Two-Wolves said to Silvercub, "get whoever you can." Silvercub gave his father's hand another squeeze, and left.

Whitecollar's fear of Brushtail was apparently overcoming his fidelity to his mate, since now he seemed to be trying to leave the circle of trees. At the same time Brushtail seemed to be losing interest in the other wolf, and looked like she might try to leave the small clearing at any moment. Two-Wolves tried to keep the two animals together within the circle while Deerstorm kept out of the way.

It wasn't long before Silvercub came back with Treewing, followed a moment later by Freefoot. It took only moments for them to comprehend the situation, and the two elder elves worked with Two-Wolves to herd the animals into the one corner of the clearing where they couldn't escape between the trees. Whitecollar was confused and hurt, and did what he was directed with little resistance, but Brushtail was getting violent, lunging at the elves, backing, snapping at the air.

"Her disease is very far advanced," Deerstorm said.

Treewing paused to look at her. "Should you be here at all?"

"I think I can save Whitecollar," Deerstorm said, "if I can get to him."

Two-Wolves called Whitecollar, and the wolf came, frightened and uncertain. "See if you can calm him," he told Silvercub, "but be careful not to let him nip you or lick at you."

Silvercub worked to overcome his anxiety, and knelt before his father's wolf. This was not what Whitecollar was expecting, and this let Deerstorm come up on the animal's other side. She put her hands on the wolf's shoulders, a healer's hands, so that the animal did not flinch, but let himself be touched. Whitecollar was very nervous and in some pain, but the two elves attending to him meant that Two-Wolves was free to do what he had to do.

Two-Wolves, Freefoot, and Treewing consulted quietly for a moment, then they all *sent* to Brushtail, the same thoughts from all three, to calm her, to make her lie down and be quiet. The sick wolf had little resistance. She did, after a moment's confusion, what she was bid.

"Are we sure there's nothing we can do?" Treewing said when Brushtail lay as quietly as she could, twitching and growling softly and making a squeaking noise like a weak howl.

"Remember Hickory," Two-Wolves said. "Nothing we did for him helped at all, and he was not as far gone as this."

"We didn't have a healer then" Treewing said.

"— that's true," Two-Wolves said uncertainly.

Then Freefoot said, "I have seen the frothing fever several times before. Once the wolf, or elf, or other animal begins to spit white foam, it's too late. Even a healer can't repair the damage inside. Whitecollar has a chance, but Brushtail is beyond our hope. I don't know how to describe it in a healer's words, but Rellah, once very long ago, told me it was like trying to catch a school of shiners in the river with your bare hands. There are always more than you can hold at once, and the school as a whole always gets away, and when you grab at them they slip through your fingers. She was a strong healer, and I believe her."

Two-Wolves stood uncertainly for a long moment.

"I'll do it for you," Treewing offered.

But Two-Wolves knew that if it had to be done, he must do it himself. He drew his knife. He looked at Freefoot, who returned his glance, and once again the three elders shared a sending. And while Freefoot and Treewing kept Brushtail distracted, Two-Wolves moved around beside and behind the animal, and with one stroke to her heart, killed her.

Whitecollar had been watching nervously, in spite of what Silvercub and Deerstorm could do to keep the wolf calm and distracted, and when Two-Wolves struck, Brushtail yelped in surprise and pain. Whitecollar's reaction was instantaneous and violent. The wolf lunged across the tiny clearing toward Two-Wolves, who was half crouched over Brushtail, holding her dead body. Treewing was between them, and Whitecollar leaped upon her in his desperation, snapping and snarling. She drew her own knife as the wolf bore her to the ground, and though she didn't want to strike, she had to kill Whitecollar in self defense.

She pulled herself from under the dead wolf. Deerstorm rushed up, as clumsy as she was, and knelt beside her.

"Have you been bitten?"

"No," Treewing said, and turned to Two-Wolves, who was standing in shock. "I'm sorry," she said, "I..."

Two-Wolves stared past her at Whitecollar, trying to catch his breath.

"Let Deerstorm make sure you are unscratched," Freefoot said to Treewing, then he went to Two-Wolves and put his hands on the stricken elf's shoulders.

Two-Wolves came back to himself and looked into his chief's eyes, but could say nothing. He was a strong elf, but tears were streaming down his face.

"It is my fault more than Treewing's," Freefoot said, "that Whitecollar is dead. I should have taken him from here."

Two-Wolves shook his head. "It's not her fault. He would have torn her apart, and me as well, and I couldn't have defended myself. But what do I do now?"

"You will need healing too, of a different kind," Freefoot told him gently.

Ebony came crashing into the clearing, calling for his mother, and stopped short when he saw the dead wolves and the grief-struck elves.

Deerstorm stood, with difficulty, from where she had been examining Treewing. "What is it, my cubling," she asked. There were tears in her eyes.

"Fangslayer is about ready to get the hunting party together," Ebony said. His voice was almost inaudible, as if he could not completely comprehend what had happened here, as indeed he could not.

"I'll be with you in a moment," Deerstorm said. She helped Treewing to her feet. "You have not been infected," she told the older elf. "But it is important that all of us wash carefully after this." Then she knelt to look to Whitecollar. "He died instantly," she said to Two-Wolves. "Treewing's blow was right to the heart." She went to Brushtail and knelt close to the wolf without touching her. When she stood up she said, "Keep her here until she begins to swell. That will make sure that the fever will be burned by decay, and will not contaminate those who eat her flesh."

Ebony was very upset, and wanted to know what had happened, so Deerstorm told him briefly. Then she turned to Silvercub, who was in a state of shock where she had left him, and asked Ebony to come help her. Ebony went to Silvercub and they consoled each other for a while.

Then Deerstorm said, "I think I need your help to get back to my den." So with the two children supporting her, perhaps more than she really needed, she let them take her back home.

Two-Wolves sat in the center of the small clearing, his elbows on his knees, his face in his hands. When an elf and a wolf become partners, they form a bond almost as strong as that between lovemates. An elf's life is long, very long indeed, while a wolf's life is short, a few handfulls of years, so all elves know that they will lose their wolf friends, and while this does not make the pain any less, it makes it bearable. Another wolf will come along. But to lose a wolf suddenly, through disease or accident, is a terrible thing. Two-Wolves was special in this regard, more in touch with wolves in general, and his in particular. And he had lost both, in a single day.

Treewing and Freefoot came and sat beside him, put their arms around him, and helped him feel his grief.

"You should go back to your den," Freefoot said after a while.

Two-Wolves did not say anything, but Freefoot could feel his acceptance of that simple bit of wisdom.

Treewing and Freefoot helped Two-Wolves to his feet, and stood beside him to steady him. He looked at the two bodies.

"I'll come back to them later," Treewing said. "They'll be all right here for now."

Then, one on either side, Treewing and Freefoot helped Two-Wolves out of the little ring of trees, and walked with him back along the clay cliff toward his den. Other elves, having seen Deerstorm pass with the two children, were watching now, and their sympathy was evident in their expressions and postures.

The three passed the den where Greentwig was still living with his parents. He came out and asked them what was wrong.

"Both Brushtail and Whitecollar died this morning," Two-Wolves said simply. Treewing and Freefoot quickly told the rest of the story.

"I'm sorry," Greentwig said. "Is there anything I can do."

"Thank you," Two-Wolves said. "What I need right now is to be with Rainbow."

"Does that mean," Greentwig said, "that you won't be able to go hunting today?"

Two-Wolves could only stare at him incredulously.

"Yes," Freefoot said, "it means that."

The disappointment on Greentwig's face was obvious. Treewing, Freefoot, and Two-Wolves went on.

"He just doesn't understand," Treewing said softly.

Greentwig watched them leave, then went back into his den. His parents looked up, and saw his disappointed face.

"What's the matter?" Glade asked him

"Two-Wolves can't go hunting today," he said, and told them what had happened. Glade and Fernhare were shocked and saddened at the news. Greentwig was more than sympathetic for Two-Wolves' plight, but he was also disappointed that Two-Wolves wouldn't be going on the hunt, so he left the den again, looked around to see who was about, and saw Brightmist working, just in front of her den.

She was knapping some flints for arrowheads, in preparation for the hunt, and she looked up when she noticed Greentwig coming toward her. She had been sort of aware that something bad had happened regarding Two-Wolves, and was concerned, but this hunt was important, not only for Starbright, but for Greentwig as well. He was her age, though she had become an adult when she had been something more than half as old as they were now. She could see that Greentwig was upset, and guessed it might have something to do with Two-Wolves.

But as he drew near she began to feel strange, as if she were somehow larger than herself. Her arms felt long and seemed to float beside her. Her mind was shrunken inside her expanding self. Greentwig sat down beside her and spoke to her, but she was so preoccupied with these strange sensations that she didn't really hear what he was saying. He spoke again, but the strange feelings got stronger and she lost track of him altogether.

Greentwig looked at her face, saw the faraway expression in her eyes, the subtle jerkiness to her movements. Even to his slow mind it was obvious that there was something wrong here. "Brightmist," he said again, quietly, but more insistently, "what's the matter, can you tell me?" He reached out and touched her shoulder gently.

She tried to tell him what was going on, but found it hard to verbalize. She didn't really have the words to describe what she was feeling, both in her body and now, more and more, in her mind. And what she did say, Greentwig wasn't able, or didn't want to understand, she didn't know which, and at the moment didn't care. She was feeling very strange by now, as if she were floating in a place in between the lawn and a dream, and the whole world around her was somehow separated from her by more than physical distance. But Greentwig seemed insistant about something, so she forced herself to pay attention, looking at his mouth as well as listening.

"Will you be able to go hunting today?" he was saying.

"No," she said. "I'm sorry, I don't think so."

Greentwig looked at her silently for a long moment. Her eyes were unfocused, her face worked, and her hands were twitching as if there were something in them. He had never seen her behaving like this before, and it frightened him. He touched her shoulder again, and waited until she looked at him.

"Brightmist," he said, "are you all right?"

"I'll be okay," she said, but her voice was very odd. "We'll hunt together another time."

He rocked back on his heels. He knew that she was trying to be kind to him, in spite of her distress, knew that whatever was troubling her was not her fault. But he was disappointed again. Now his hunting party was down to four, and he knew that would make it more difficult, more dangerous, less likely to succeed. He tried not to feel sorry for himself, Brightmist looked so uncomfortable, so unhappy.

"Are you sick?" he asked her. "Should I call Deerstorm?"

"No," was all she said.

He watched her a moment longer, then he bid her goodbye, though he doubted she heard him, and went away.

He couldn't stop worrying about her though, so when he came to the den where Fangslayer and Deerstorm lived, he called out to her. After a moment Deerstorm, now looking a little wan, came to the entrance. Greentwig immediately regretted calling her, but she assured him that she was okay. Greentwig told her that Brightmist seemed to be ill, that she didn't want help, but that he was still worried.

"If she doesn't want help," Deerstorm said, "then let's leave it at that."

Fangslayer, dressed in unusually plain, greenish clothes, came out to see what was happening, and Greentwig told him about Brightmist. "And her hands were moving like this," he finished, moving his own hands as if he were breaking invisible reeds into small pieces. "So she won't be coming with us."

"That doesn't sound good," Deerstorm said. "I'll try to look in on her a little later, but right now I'm not feeling so well myself."

"Maybe I shouldn't go," Fangslayer said.

"No, I'll be all right. Besides, Starbright is counting on you."

Fangslayer met her eyes, and for a moment they shared a private sending.

"Okay," Fangslayer said at last to Greentwig, "We'll go hunting anyway." He ducked back inside the den for a moment and came back with his weapons, the bundle of meat wrapped in leaves, and something that looked like a lot of knotted rope. "Stringsong's best net," he said, showing it to Greentwig. He turned to Deerstorm and put his arm gently around her shoulder. "Let somebody else do the work for a while," he said. "We'll be back tomorrow."

"Good luck," Deerstorm said, then went back in to lie down while Fangslayer went with Greentwig back to his den.

There Fernhare, with Glade's help, was finishing the preparations for Greentwig. They had some meat in a bag of clean intestine, had his ax and bow and arrows ready, and had coils of light rope, Stringsong's best, which would be needed for this special hunt.

Fangslayer's news about Two-Wolves was distressing, and Greentwig's news about Brightmist was disturbing, but Fernhare was determined to go on with the hunt as planned. "Even with only four of us," she said, "we have a chance, and besides, it's not whether we get anything, it's how well we hunt that counts."

"I think you're right," Fangslayer said, "though I wouldn't give up our chances just yet. Two-Wolves is in good hands, and as for Brightmist, she's strong, and I think she can take care of herself."

But at that moment, Brightmist wasn't so sure about that. She felt power in her, not her own minor talent as a stone shaper, but something from outside that touched her talent and was working through it. She was the holt's flint-knapper, not so much because of her skill, but because of that bit of talent, just enough so that when she worked a flint, or whitecrystal, or other stone, it came out right. Now she picked up a piece of granite that she had been using as an anvil, against which she laid the flints to hold them steady as she worked them with a piece of antler, and started to work with it. She did not strike it with other stones, nor make it flow like she sometimes could, in an uncontrolled fluid sort of way, but molded it in her hands, as if it were pottery clay, shaping it with her fingers.

As she worked, aimlessly at first, Shadowflash, her mate, came out of their den behind her. He spoke her name, but she didn't hear him. She was sometimes like that, when she was engrossed in her work, and he came up quietly behind her, to see what she was doing, and stopped dead still, his breath caught in his throat. The speckled gray-black stone in her hands was slowly taking on the shape of an elvin face.

Shadowflash knew that something was wrong. Brightmist had done nothing like this before. He touched her shoulder. She didn't respond, but he felt an odd tremor running through his own body at the contact. It frightened him, and he went off for help.

Puckernut was just coming out of his den, with his life-made Rillwalker and their cub Dayshine, a youth of Starbright's age. With most other elves, Puckernut was as bitter and grouchy as his name, but he knew things, knew where things came from, where they had been, what was inside them, and Brightmist's behavior was something that Puckernut might just be able to make sense of. So Shadowflash stopped him and told him about what he had seen Brightmist doing with the granite.

"That doesn't sound right," Puckernut agreed. He saw Brightmist, not that far off from where they were standing, and what he saw didn't look natural to him.

"Can we be of any help?" Rillwalker asked.

"I don't think so," Puckernut said, so Rillwalker and Dayshine went on to the stream to wash up. Puckernut wanted a bath too, but he didn't like the way Brightmist seemed so entranced with her work, so he went over to her with Shadowflash and watched her for a while.

"Is she just coming into her talent?" Shadowflash asked. Brightmist was now holding a chunk of flint, slowly pushing it into a bowl shape.

"It doesn't feel like it," Puckernut said. "If it were, she shouldn't be so oblivious to us. This is magic, and it's from outside her somehow. I can feel it."

"But where has it come from?"

"I don't know. Brightmist?" he said. She didn't respond. "Brightmist," he said again, louder this time. Her attention did not waver. She was making the bowl larger, thinner, working the white rind of the flint up to the lip, leaving the main part of the bowl transparent black. Puckernut reached out and touched her shoulder. She was completely unaware of him. Then he took her hand, and felt a sudden thrill run through him, as if lightning had struck somewhere nearby. He jerked his hand away and sat back on his heels.

"What is it?" Shadowflash asked, his voice a hoarse whisper.

Puckernut wiped his hands on his thighs, as if to remove the contamination. "It's very strong," he said. "We'd better stay with her, at least for a little while."

Even as they settled down to watch Brightmist working the stone, Rainbow, Freefoot, and Treewing were getting Two-Wolves settled. He had held his grief for his dead animals in check, but now was the time to feel the pain, the loss. His mate and two good friends were with him, and he needn't be ashamed. It would be many days before he could begin to think about finding another wolf friend, and before then the grief of his loss had to be worked out.

Rainbow stroked her mate's forehead, cooed at him wordlessly, just letting him know she was there and that she cared. But as she did so she began to feel weird, as if she were somehow expanding, and shrinking inside herself at the same time.

She kept up her comforting reassurances, but as the moments went by her arms began to feel long and buoyant, and she held them up to look at them. They didn't look any different. The other people in the den seemed somehow far away and unimportant. She turned away from Two-Wolves and took out her art materials — pigments and white bark. It was as if she were watching herself from the outside — or from the inside, rather. She started to work, oblivious to Freefoot and Treewing, who were looking at her oddly, mixing red and yellow clays with a pine resin, which would make them water proof when they dried. She didn't hear when Treewing spoke to her. She just mixed up some blue berry-juice with the resin, and turned the bark over so the white side was up. Then she took a small twig of blue oak and chewed the end so that the fibers split small and fine, making a brush.

As she worked, Freefoot and Treewing watched, uncertain what to do. Two-Wolves was curled up in a ball now, not really aware of them, so they left him and went over to see what Rainbow was doing. Her behavior was so bizarre that they hesitated to disturb her, but just looked over her shoulder, and stopped astonished at what they saw. She had made a picture of the two dead wolves, as they had been in life, but drawn so realistically that it was frightening.

Meanwhile Greentwig, in his own den, was putting on some greenish clothes, like Fangslayer's. Elves usually hunted wearing their everyday apparel, as bright as it was, but this hunt was different. Fernhare had already changed into something gray, and Glade, with Fangslayer, was just waiting for Greentwig to finish. As he was lacing up the front, Starbright called to him from the entrance.

"Come on in," Greentwig called back, and she did.

"Are you about ready?"

"Sure," he said with a broad smile. "How do I look?"

"Just fine. How about me?" Her own clothes were a muted brown.

"You'll do just fine," Fernhare said. She had been on this kind of hunt before.

"Has Brightmist come by?" Starbright asked.

"She can't come," Greentwig told her, with a sudden drop in his spirits. "She's sick or something."

"Oh, no," Starbright said. "And we were counting on her, too."

"You're going to have to get along without Two-Wolves as well," Fangslayer told her, and told her why.

Starbright, who had come in full of excitement, slumped against the wall in bitter disappointment. "Why did that have to happen now, of all days."

"Why, Starbright," Fernhare said, "I'm surprised. There's no good time for the sudden loss of your wolf friend."

"I know, I'm sorry. It's just that I've been looking forward to this hunt."

"And so has Two-Wolves," Fernhare said. "And so has Brightmist. And not only are they going to miss out on the hunt, but they have their other problems to deal with too."

"Well, owl pellets," Starbright said. "I'm sorry for Two-Wolves, and for Brightmist, but if they can't go, then there will be only two adults on this hunt, and there's no chance we'll succeed."

"I'm still going," Greentwig said.

"Oh, you don't count." She seemed to be totally unaware of his feelings, or those of his parents. "I guess we might just as well call it off." She stood away from the wall and slouched out of the den.

The day, which had dawned so bright and fair, now seemed to her unpleasant, too hot, uncomfortable. She was intensely disappointed, despite her sympathy for Two-Wolves and Brightmist. She headed down toward the stream without really thinking about it.

Dayshine, as he came up from the stream with Rillwalker, on his way back to their den, saw Starbright, and it was obvious that she was upset. He spoke briefly to his mother, then went to join his friend.

Starbright turned away from him, angling downstream, toward the east, but Dayshine fell into step beside her. He didn't say anything as they walked. But when they got to the big flat stone downstream, the one that hung over the edge of the creek, she told him about her disappointment.

"I'm sorry, Starbright," he said. "That's really too bad."

"It's more than too bad. I was hoping that maybe they would give me my adult name today."

"You want that pretty badly, don't you."

"Sure, don't you?"

"Not as much as you do. It will come. But it's sure not fair that you're missing out on a chance like this."

"That's what I think. And you know, if it weren't for Greentwig, I could probably go ahead and go."

"How do you figure?"

"Don't you see? If Greentwig goes on a hunt, the others have to watch out for him. Fangslayer and Fernhare will be so busy keeping him out of trouble, there'll be no chance for me to do any good hunting at all."

"I guess you're right," Dayshine said.

Greentwig was sitting quietly in his den. He was hurt by Starbright's anger, by her dismissal of him as unimportant to the hunt. Maybe he wasn't as clever as the other elves, but he could feed himself. And he had been looking forward to this hunt too. He knew it took the cooperation of several elves, if it were going to work, and now that Starbright had dropped out, there were only three of them left. "Maybe we should call it off," he said softly.

"Do you want to?" Fernhare said. She was half hoping he would, a hunt like this could kill him, but she and Glade had long since given up trying to protect him from his own ineptitude.

"No," Greentwig said after a pause. It always took him a moment to finish a thought.

"Then we'll go."

"Just the three of us?"

"I don't see why not," Glade said. "It will make it harder, but then what you do accomplish will be all that much greater."

"Will you come along with us?" Greentwig asked him.

"I've thought about it," his father said, "but there's someone else who really needs my help right now."

Greentwig thought for a moment. "Two-Wolves," he said.

"That's right. As many of us as can should spend some time with him. He would appreciate your help too, but he knows how much this hunt means to you, and you can see him when you get back."

"I think you're right," Fangslayer said. "And I think we should start out as soon as possible."

"Okay," Greentwig said. He looked wistfully at his father, then picked up his weapons and supplies. Fernhare and Fangslayer did the same, then the three left the den, and went around the west end of Halfhill and turned north into the forest.

Stringsong saw them go. He was sitting at the top of the bluff, overlooking the holt below, making bowstring from sloth hair. He liked to be by himself on occasion, but still liked to keep an eye on what was going on. He had seen Two-Wolves go out, and come back, had seen Brightmist become entranced with her work, and had seen the various elves go into and come out of Greentwig's den. He wished the hunters luck, knowing it would be hard with only three of them.

He turned his attention back to the work at hand. What he had seen on the lawn below made him guess that there was some trouble, but there were enough people running around so that he didn't feel compelled to come down and add to the confusion. He returned his attention to the bowstring. Occasionally he plucked the string to make sure it was uniformly spun and sufficiently strong, and when he did so it made a kind of music. It was the kind of thing his predecessor, Songshaper, in Prey-Pacer's time had used to do, though Songshaper had used a bow with several strings. Mostly Stringsong used just one string, on a bow he could flex, which gave him all the notes he needed. He felt a kinship with the long dead Songshaper. Their names were similar for a good reason, they both made music.

Stringsong was extremely good at cord making, that was his special talent. He could twist hair, bark, grass, leather, tendon, intestine, almost anything, into the best kind of cord that could be made from that kind of material, and could make whatever kind of cord or string was best for the job. Other elves marveled at his patience, but he enjoyed it. Sometimes he preferred to sit with the others and talk, but sometimes, like today, he preferred to be by himself.

Today, besides a goodly supply of sloth hair, he had some fish guts for fishing line, some deer-entrails that he had cured, some fine deer skin as well, and a large hank of razor grass, which he would turn into a surprisingly soft cord that could be dyed bright colors and woven into cloth.

But even as he worked he started to feel odd, rather distant from himself. The feeling persisted as he finished the bowstring. He began to feel larger than himself, and shrunken at the same time. His arms felt swollen, clumsy, and detached, and he watched his fingers move, fastening the bowstring to the bow, as if of their own accord. He plucked the cord, making the music for which he was named. It sounded strange to his ears, as if there were more to it somehow.

The weirdness increased, and he took a different bow and bound several strings to it, the way Songshaper had done, and began to play, hesitantly at first, but with more confidence as his fingers found the notes. On the lawn below him other elves stopped to listen. He changed the notes by tightening or bending the bow, as he did when it had just one string, but it didn't work the way he wanted it to. It changed all the strings at once, and most of them too much or not enough.

Puckernut, who was still sitting with Brightmist and Shadowflash, heard the music too, and it sent shivers up his spine. He knew it was Stringsong, but he moved back from the steep clay cliff to see for sure. The music stopped for a moment, but he could see that Stringsong was just doing something with more wood and cord. After working a moment, Stringsong held out a different kind of harp, and he started to play again, and Puckernut saw that all those who could hear were both thrilled and disturbed. To Puckernut, the magic of the music was obvious, so he left Brightmist in Shadowflash's care, and went to the upstream end of the cliff, the way the hunting party had gone, which was nearer to him though steeper, to investigate.

He came up the slope, which blocked Stringsong from his sight for a moment, but he still heard the music. It stopped, he hurried on, and when he came through the bushes at the edge to where he could see Stringsong again, the other had rebuilt his harp yet another time. Stringsong started playing again.

Puckernut came up to him. He could feel that the magic was in Stringsong, the same as it was in Brightmist.

He knelt down beside Stringsong and tried to speak with him but, as it had been with Brightmist, there was no response from the entranced elf. Puckernut touched him gently on the shoulder and upper arm. Still there was no response. He even tried to take away the harp, but Stringsong held on firmly, but almost as if he were not aware of what was happening, and continued to play.

Puckernut rocked back on his heels. How did these two have the same magic? It seemed to be getting stronger. Where would it end? He had no answers, so he went down to look for Freefoot.

Meanwhile Starbright and Dayshine were still grumping on the flat rock down by the stream when Feather, Freefoot's younger child, came to join them. He was the same age as they, and their frequent companion. "What's the matter?" he asked when he saw their faces.

With much complaining, interrupting, and laying of blame, they told him.

"Now hold on just a minute," he said. "What are you getting so excited about? The way you're talking, you'd think it was all Greentwig's fault. He hasn't lost his wolf. He's not feeling weird. He's still going on the hunt, so what are you angry at him for?"

"But don't you see?" Starbright said, "Fernhare and Fangslayer will have to spend so much time taking care of Greentwig they won't have time for me."

"But that's not the way it really works, is it?" Feather said. "Greentwig has survived so far without being taken care of."

Starbright turned away from him. She didn't know what to say. She was just angry, and disappointed, and feeling so much sorry for herself that she wasn't really thinking straight. Dayshine was silent too. He recognized the truth of what Feather had said, and he was ashamed of having such bad feelings about the older Greentwig, even if he wasn't very bright or competent.

"I'll tell you what we should do," Feather said. "Let's go find Silverknife, and see what she has to say." Silverknife had been born at about the same time as Feather and Starbright and Dayshine, and up until last summer had been known as Warble. Then one day something had happened, she had changed, and had gone off on a hunt and had come back with her adult name. The four youths were of an age, but Silverknife was an adult.

"I think that's a great idea," Dayshine said. "Come on, Starbright, she might be able to help with your problem."

"I don't have a problem," Starbright said sullenly.

"Is that why you're so cheerful?" Feather asked gently.

"Oh, all right," Starbright said. "Let's go find her."

As the three youths started back toward the holt, Puckernut came down from where Stringsong was still sitting, around the upstream end of the cliff, and saw Freefoot and Treewing as they came out of Rainbow's den. He went over to them, and told them briefly about Stringsong, but even as he spoke he felt the same sense of external magic, coming from inside the den.

"What's the matter?" Freefoot asked.

"Is everything all right in there?" Puckernut asked in turn.

"Rainbow is behaving oddly," Treewing said. "Sort of like the way you say Stringsong and Brightmist are." From where they stood, they could see Brightmist sitting, working her stones, and could hear Stringsong's music.

"Let's go inside," Puckernut said, and entered Rainbow's den, with Freefoot and Treewing behind him. He found Glade and Two-Wolves in the main chamber watching while Rainbow worked. They looked up when he came in, but didn't speak. Puckernut knelt beside Rainbow, watched her for a moment, spoke in her ear, touched her forehead, her arm, her hand.

"It's the same," he said, and looked up at Freefoot. "This is serious."

Freefoot nodded, then went over to sit beside Two-Wolves and told him about the other two entranced elves outside.

Two-Wolves was still distraught — indeed, would continue to grieve for many days — but he knew that his pain must now take second place, until they could find out whether this infection of magic was a threat to the holt, and what they could do about it. "Where were these three all together," he asked, "so that they could all become contaminated in the same way?"

"I don't know," Puckernut said, "but it's fairly obvious, isn't it, that they all became infected at the same time. Otherwise the effect of the High Ones' magic residue would have been different in each case."

"Are they the same?" Freefoot asked. "I mean, each one is doing something different."

"Each one is under the influence of their talent, made stronger somehow, so yes, it is all the same." He bent down to Rainbow. He could feel the magic around her, growing stronger. He thought for a moment, then he whispered the question, loud enough for the others to hear, in her ear. "When were you and Stringsong and Brightmist together? Where were you that was different?"

Perhaps it was that he was not trying to distract her from her painting, but he seemed to get through her focused attention. She kept on painting, but her expression became far away, as if she were thinking, and her brush strokes hesitated once or twice. Then she spoke, in a voice that seemed to come from a long way off. "Stringsong, and Brightmist, and I," she said, "and Greentwig too, we all went on a hunt together."

"Where did you go?" Puckernut asked softly.

"Down by the dry lake, about five days ago ..."

They had been hunting, with their wolves, for red deer, but had started a magnificent black neck buck instead, at the verge of the dry lake. Twice as big as a red deer, the buck was far from its usual range. They decided not to pass up an opportunity like this, and Greentwig was especially eager to pursue the animal, since he had hunted black neck before. So they chased it along the dry rill toward the Great River until they came to a place where the ground was low and damp. The buck sought escape in the boggy ground, and floundered through the dense bushes and bog plants to the center of the soggy area, where a sinkhole opened up.

They all went into the bog after it, though the wolves were strangely reluctant, and the ground gave away some more, pulling the bushes and even some trees down with it. Eventually the sinkhole enlarged to three times its original width before the ground stopped moving and became stable again.

They couldn't see the buck any more, the churned up brush and plants were a dense tangle, but when they listened they could hear it, still moving somewhere ahead of them. They followed the sticky sounds the rest of the way down into the sinkhole, now more than twice as deep as it had been, and at the bottom saw the buck struggling through the soft mud toward what looked like the entrance of a dry cave, which had been revealed by the sinking of the land around it.

The buck heard them coming, and made a great effort to pull itself through the mud and entered the cave. They heard its hooves striking hard stone, and they followed it into the darkness. But they went only a short way, because it too soon got too dark even for elvish eyes, the echoes of their footfalls and the buck's hooves were strange around them, the floor of the cave was uneven, and though they could not see for sure they thought there were side passages in which they might get lost. And besides, they were afraid, so they came back, disappointed.

The wolves were waiting for them, just outside the cave, and would not go in, so they climbed out of the sinkhole and went on with their hunt. They later got the red deer they had originally sought.

"Then that's where it was," Puckernut said when Rainbow had finished. "There was a bit of magic in that cave, left over from the time of the High Ones, and these three became contaminated. And the black neck buck, if it got out, would be affected too."

"But what about Greentwig?" Freefoot asked.

"He, too," Puckernut said. "But how the magic would affect him I couldn't guess. He doesn't have any natural talent as far as I know, and that is what the magic has been working on, and enhancing. Where is he now?"

"He's on the hunt Brightmist and I were supposed to go on," Two-Wolves said. "What will happen to him?"

"Who knows?" Puckernut said.

"But how long will this last?" Two-Wolves went on.

"I don't know," Puckernut said, "but I suspect that it's temporary, just by the way it feels and the way it took so long to come on."

"It seems like it happened rather quickly," Treewing said.

"You mean today. But it's been five days since they were exposed. That's a very long time indeed for even ancient magic to have an effect."

They sat in Rainbow's den while she painted, and listened to Stringsong's music coming in from the top of the cliff outside. "I don't think there's anything we can do," Puckernut said. "It doesn't feel evil. It's their talents that are being enhanced. Let's just hope that something good comes of all this."

Each of the three afflicted did produce something great that day. For Rainbow it was not a painting, but a beading, the bright pieces of shell and stone and wood stitched one by one onto the fur-side of a yellow cat skin, three handspans wide and four high. The beads formed a picture not so much of an object, as of an event, though it wasn't until much later that anybody, especially Rainbow, was able to interpret the radiating lines as antlers, the arched and doubly forked green shape as an elf, the background patterns as indicative of a particular kind of motion. It was the kind of picture that, once you knew what it was about, you saw more and more in it, though the shapes were quite abstract.

Stringsong not only perfected his harp, but perfected certain ways of playing it so that the elves could develop their own singing scale of five tones, which sounded like wolves but like music at the same time. He created a tradition which was incorporated in their howls down through the generations.

And Brightmist, working not with granite or with slate, but with a translucent white stone which was sometimes found in great crystals, made a simple sphere through which the light shone, diffracted and rainbowed, changing according to how it faced the sun.

Each of them finished these marvels shortly after midday, and then their gifts began to fade. Eventually each of them became what they had been before, though Rainbow had a new appreciation of beads, Stringsong remembered how to play his harp, and Brightmist got considerably better with her flint-knapping.

Starbright, Dayshine, and Feather got back to Halfhill long before any of this came to pass. They went to the den nearest the downstream end of the cliff, where they found Silverknife just getting ready for the day. She still lived with her father, Stringsong. After all, though she was an adult, she was still young. Her mother had died long ago, and they were not immediately related to any of the other elves.

Though she was the same age as the other three, she was obviously more mature. She carried herself with a confidence and sureness they didn't have. Her clothes, though bright and fancy, were better suited for hunting in the brush. Her den, and especially her sleeping chamber, was neat and orderly. And there was something in her expression, in her face, that just, somehow, to them, *looked* like a grownup. She greeted them as they came in.

They told her the problem, all three more or less talking at once, but at last Silverknife understood that it was Starbright's perception of the situation that was the real problem. Silverknife thought for a moment, then she said, "I think you should rejoin the hunt."

"But what's the use?" Starbright said.

"Suppose it was just you and Fernhare and Fangslayer," Silverknife said. "Do you think you could do it?"

"Not just the three of us."

"Don't you have confidence in their ability?"

"Yes, but that kind of hunt needs more than just three people."

"Apparently they think that three is enough. And besides, you have Greentwig."

"But he's just a big baby."

"Which never bothered you until now. It's not him that's the problem, it's you."

"But Two-Wolves and Rainbow dropped out," Starbright insisted, "it's their fault."

"You dropped out too, and for no good reason. You didn't lose your wolf, you're not beset by ancient magic, you just got upset. You're not proving the maturity you seek by your be-haviour, and you're letting the other three hunters down — voluntarily, unlike Brightmist and Two-Wolves, who had no choice."

Starbright was upset by this accusation, and wanted to argue about it, but she was somewhat in awe of Silverknife, because Silverknife had "done it," and because she recognized the truth of the accusation. She said, "So you think I should just go running off after them like nothing happened."

"Like nothing had happened, yes, but not just you."

"All three of us?" Dayshine asked.

"All four of us," Silverknife said. "I will go with you, it will help make up for those who couldn't go."

"But we need permission," Starbright said.

"We can't go that far alone," Dayshine added.

"I give you permission," Silverknife said, "and you won't be alone because I will take you. After all, remember, I am an adult, an elder, and I can take the responsibility. Now let people know where you're going." And the three youngsters ran off to do so.

Deerstorm was resting in her den with her boychild Ebony, when she suddenly realized her time had come. The cub in her belly was beginning to drop, and would be born not in three or four days time, but that afternoon. Fangslayer was off on the hunt, so she sent Ebony for her mother.

Ebony went to Dreamsnake's den, but she was not there. He came back by Rainbow's den where he saw Freefoot, with Puckernut, Treewing, Glade, and Two-Wolves, just coming out. "Please come," he said to them. "The cubling is about to be born."

"You go on back to your mother," Freefoot said to him. "I'll get Starflower and send her right over." Ebony ran off. Freefoot turned to his companions. "Will you be all right?" he asked Two-Wolves.

"I will. Glade and I will stay here with Rainbow."

"I'll go sit with Brightmist," Treewing said, which left Puckernut to look after Stringsong.

"All right, then," Freefoot said, and went back to his own den to fetch his lifemate. She quickly gathered up a few things and went with him toward Deerstorm's den.

They met Fire-Eyes on the way, asked her to help, which she agreed to at once, and the three of them got to Deerstorm just as she was starting to labor. Starflower and Fire-Eyes went to her at once, while Freefoot waited in the main chamber just inside the entrance. After a bit Ebony snuck in to see how his mother was doing, and Freefoot decided it was time to leave. He went outside, where he found Treewing talking with Suretrail about what had happened to his son's two wolves. Suretrail was upset, not only by the death of the wolves, but by the fact that Treewing had killed one of them, though there was nothing else she could have done. Freefoot joined his two friends, and was about to go with Suretrail back to Two-Wolves when Ebony came running out of the den behind them.

"Freefoot!" Ebony called. "Come quickly."

Freefoot and Treewing, with Suretrail following behind, hurried back in to Deerstorm. It was not the rule for males to be present at a birthing, but Freefoot had attended several — his presence seemed to have a calming effect when things got tight — and again he assumed a confidence and sureness that was not questioned. Treewing knelt beside Deerstorm, but Suretrail waited out in the main chamber.

A few moments ago the birthing had seemed to be easy, but now Deerstorm was having trouble, and it was all Starflower and Fire-Eyes could do to help, and Fire-Eyes wasn't much help at that. Something about Deerstorm, or the child being born, was making her hysterical. After a moment Freefoot drew her aside so that Treewing could take her place.

Freefoot held Fire-Eyes by the shoulders, then folded her in his arms. "What's the matter," he whispered.

"I don't know," she said. Her voice shook. She took several deep breaths and pushed herself away from him a bit. "I don't know that there's anything *wrong*," she said, "but there's something about that child...."

"Take it easy," Freefoot said. He looked into her face. "What about the child?" Over on the bed, Deerstorm was thrashing and grunting, while Treewing and Starflower did their best to help. "Don't look around," Freefoot told Fire-Eyes. "Just tell me."

She took another deep breath, looked into Freefoot's eyes, and he could see, in hers, the strange light that gave her her name. She could look at an elf and know things about him or her that she shouldn't be able to know. Sometimes she could look back along the line of ancestors, and sometimes bring back stories. "I guess a path just opened up," she said. She took another breath, her eyes fell. "That's all it is, I usually can't feel back unless I've had a lot of dreamberries, but this time, I can feel Fangslayer in the child, and Deerstorm too, of course, and you and Starflower and Grazer and Dreamsnake.... I think that's it, Starflower is helping, but I can feel her through the child's life too. Or something."

"Is Mother going to be all right?" Ebony asked. He was trying to keep his face calm, but the difficulties were making him anxious.

"I think so," Fire-Eyes said. "I'd better go back to her."

"You stay with me," Freefoot told Ebony, while Fire-Eyes did as she said. Then he took Ebony back out to the main chamber.

"I think I'd better be going," Suretrail said. "Two-Wolves has had a hard time, he'll need some help getting over it."

"I agree," Freefoot said.

"Is everything all right here?"

"She's having some trouble, but I think it will be okay."

Suretrail nodded and left.

After a while Starflower came out, looking tired but happy. "It's a boy," she said.

"Is he well?" Freefoot asked his lifemate.

"He is, and so's Deerstorm. The cubling just got a bit turned around."

"How's Fire-Eyes?"

Starflower laughed. "She's really excited. You'd think the baby was hers. He has eyes like hers, they have a special fire, and they were open when he was born. Deerstorm is going to call him Glitter. It seems like he can see everything."

"Will you need me for anything?" Freefoot asked.

"No," Starflower said, but turned to Ebony. "But you can go find Dreamsnake, wherever she is, and bring her back."

"Can I see Glitter first?"

"Of course you can," Starflower said. And while she took young Ebony inside, Freefoot went off to attend to other business.

Greentwig, Fangslayer, and Fernhare had gone north through the forest to the glade, a broad area where no trees had grown in anybody's memory. There were flowers in abundance, and grasses, and some low shrubs, but no briars or brambles, and nothing taller than a elf's shoulder. No one knew why. From there they had gone on north to the clearing at the edge of the prairie, where grasses rippled in the summer breeze. It was an ocean of green. Then they went west along the verge between forest and prairie until they came to where they could see the mesa, then across the prairie, single file through the tall grass, to where the ground began to rise at the foot of the mesa, and around the far side to the easy slope up, between the two halves of this high, steep-sided, flat-topped double hill, and by noon they were on the larger, southern, forested flat. Certain creatures lived here and nowhere else, and it was to hunt one of these that they had come.

Just as the prey which they sought was not an ordinary sort of prey, so the methods of hunting it were not ordinary. When they found what Fangslayer thought was a good spot, among tall trees with high branches near the southern edge of the mesa, the three elves went up, climbing as high as they could. Their clothing blended with the foliage, so that they could hardly see each other, and they moved with utmost caution, so that even Greentwig hardly made any noise. And then Fernhare spotted one of the creatures they sought. It was a ghost ape, kind of large, a white flying monkey that could not walk on the ground, and could only be hunted up in the treetops.

As careful as they were, it was aware of them, and was keeping its distance from them. The sound of its movements was not that much different from the breeze in the leaves, and it carefully kept to shadow, and on the far side of branch and trunk. They pursued it, and it continued to eluded them, for something like an eighth part of the afternoon, climbing ever higher to where the branches were so slender that even an elf had difficulty keeping from falling.

They had maneuvered so that it was moving toward a tree that was cut off from the others on three sides, and since the ghost ape could not really fly but only glide, it would be trapped, and then they would move in. Had there been six of them, as planned, it might not have taken so long, and the certainty of capture would have been greater. A hunt like this was supposed to be a challenge, and it was, more challenging than Fernhare or Fangslayer really liked. Greentwig had more than once almost slipped and fallen. But they went on.

This high off the ground they needed to use ropes, doubled up so they could retrieve them, since the branches tended to be too small to hold their weight, and they swung along the ropes from trunk to trunk. Once they cornered the beast, it would try to defend itself, and though it was smaller than an elf, it had terrible talons and fangs, and absolutely no temper at all.

Their concern at the moment was to keep the beast moving in the direction they wanted, to not let it cut around the side, or climb above or drop below, or run between them — or glide away. Three more hunters would have made a stronger line. But they took their time, and though Greentwig was having trouble, as usual, he was in the middle position, the other two were keeping close, and it was going well, all things considered.

When they finally got the beast where they wanted it, and had identified its most likely escape route, they set Greentwig in place. Then Fangslayer and Fernhare moved out to the sides, closed in, and deliberately frightened the beast. It charged, and when it passed Greentwig he dropped the net which he had been carefully instructed to prepare, and to his immense surprise, caught it. The three of them came together, dragged the net to the ground, and under Fangslayer's instructions, Greentwig drew his knife and dispatched it.

They extricated the ghost ape from the net. Fernhare and Fangslayer praised Greentwig for his part, and he felt good. The beast had good fur, long and soft and very white. It was extremely valuable, though the ghost ape was seldom hunted. It was too dangerous a hunt, and the animal was too rare.

They were about to begin the process of skinning, which had to be done very carefully since the skin could easily tear, when they were interrupted by the sounds of something coming through the forest. They looked up and saw a black neck buck, which seemed to be moving purposefully toward them. When it saw them it paused, and looked from one to the other. It was huge, even for a black neck, and its antlers were gigantic, and its eyes shone with an intelligence and a fury far beyond that which a normal deer could express. Its muscles were bunched, its hooves scored the forest floor. This was not a normal animal, it had been transformed somehow, and it was terrible.

"I've seen that deer before," Greentwig said in surprise. "But it's not the same."

"What do you mean," Fangslayer said as he and Fernhare slowly got to their feet.

"See how that antler has a twist in it? Brightmist and Rainbow and Stringsong and I hunted a black neck just like that five days ago." He told them briefly about the encounter, and losing the deer in the cave at the bottom of the sinkhole.

He, too, was on his feet by now, and and took a step toward the black neck buck, As he did so, he realized, belatedly, just how big it was, far bigger than he had remembered it being. It lowered its head and lunged almost casually forward, and knocked Greentwig to the ground. Greentwig lay there in surprise, not really hurt, and watched with growing terror as the buck backed a step, the better to stomp him with his two huge, sharp, front hooves.

Fernhare felt almost as dull as Greentwig, but at last she broke out of her trance and leaped to the rescue, brandishing one of the climbing ropes as if it were a whip. The buck lurched at her, swung its head to the side, and caught her in the side with the tip of one of its antlers and threw her to the ground. She struck her head as she fell.

Fangslayer was faring no better. It was not like him to be the last to react to danger, and yet today it was all he could do to make himself move. He leaped at the creature, waving the net, which startled the beast and kept it from attacking Fernhare with its antlers. By waving his arms and the net and yelling at the buck, he managed to hold the beast at bay, at least for a moment.

Greentwig got to his feet. He felt guilty and clumsy. He looked around for the wolves, but they were nowhere to be seen. He remembered how they had been afraid of the sinkhole, and the cave.

Movement brought his attention back to the present, and without thinking about it he tried to attack the buck with his ax while Fangslayer had its attention. But it turned too quickly. Greentwig ran, it turned on Fernhare, Fangslayer leapt between them, was himself wounded by the buck's antlers, but he managed to wound the buck in turn with his spear, hitting it high in the shoulder.

Greentwig came to Fangslayer's assistance as the buck staggered off a ways, and they went to Fernhare. Her ribs were scored and her head was bleeding, and as they tried to get her comfortable the buck attacked them from behind and Fangslayer was impaled through both sides of his back on the forward points of the animal's antlers. Greentwig beat at the buck's flank with his ax, which was twisted around so that he hit it with the flat instead of the edge, but it made the buck turn on him, which gave Fangslayer the chance to strike at the buck with the shaft of his spear. Two flank attacks in succession was too much, and the buck turned and ran off into the brush.

Greentwig was about to pursue when Fangslayer fell over. Greentwig went to him. "Are you all right?"

"No, but I'll live." Fangslayer held his arms around his sides. Greentwig then went to his mother. Fernhare was just barely conscious. "You've done well," she said.

"I haven't, Mother." he said.

He did the best he could for them, cleaning their wounds and finding a place, between two large trees at the base of a rock, where they should be safe. When the two wounded adults were as comfortable as they could be, Fangslayer told Greentwig to go back to the holt for help.

Greentwig started back as he had been instructed, though he was not really sure of the way. When he was out of sight of the others he stopped, and tried to remember which way they had come, and then he thought "downhill." He let the slope of the ground guide him, and found the draw between the two halves of the mesa.

As he started down the draw he heard a crashing behind him. It could have been anything, but he knew it was the buck, back by his mother and friend, and he stopped. He had hoped that the buck would not come back. And though he had been told to go to the holt, and was deathly afraid, he couldn't stand the thought of leaving his wounded friend and mother alone with the buck, and so he went back to them instead.

Silverknife had found that getting her three age-mates up to the mesa was perhaps a bit more than she had bargained for,

and that though she was, in fact, an elder, she was not as experienced, as patient, as resourceful, or as strong a leader as one
who had been an elder for even five years or so. Just getting
Starbright, Dayshine, and Feather organized had taken quite
some time, getting them properly dressed, their weapons ready,
the ropes and nets properly coiled and tied.

Then, once on the way, the three juveniles had a strong
tendency to think about other things, such as lunch, bright birds,
what had happened that morning at the holt, and so on, and
they did not make very good progress. By the time they got to
Round Hill, which was just to the west of their route, they were
all getting a bit impatient with each other — Silverknife with the
juveniles for still being so much of what they were, and the
juveniles with her for what they perceived as overbearing
control, though had any elder of their parents' generation
exhibited such control they would not have noticed, let alone
minded.

And then, on the hill, when they were all tired and frustrated
and angry, they happened on a family of gobblers, the huge
birds with the long bronze tail feathers, who yelled and bobbled
through the trees as if they were demented, yet which were
incredibly difficult to shoot, capture, or trap. Remarkably good
eating, even the wolves were interested, and in spite of Silverknife's warnings, that the hunt on the mesa was needing
them, the three youths just had to catch one of the big male
gobblers, and by the time they did it was way past midday. They
ate the bird, saved the best of the tail and wing feathers, and at
last went on their way again.

Silverknife did not talk much, but stalked ahead of them,
and after a while the three youths began to quiet and remember
the purpose of their outing.

"Do you suppose they've caught a ghost yet?" Starbright
wondered.

"If they haven't," Silverknife said, "it's because they needed
our help."

And though by now everybody was rather more tired than
they should have been, and rather sluggish with the meal, they

hurried on until at last they came to the edge of the forest. Ahead of them, to the north, across the prairie was the mesa, the flat hill that rose above the grass, crowned with a miniature forest of its own.

None of them had ever been there before, and the only time they had been on the prairie had been with elders, hunting for antelope. Even Silverknife had to admit that she was just a bit apprehensive, being out of the woods and all. The wolves seemed eager, though, so they started across.

The grass, at this time of year, was just about chest high and very green. It took a while to wade through it, and they had gone no more than an eight of eights of paces when they all began to receive what felt, at first, like a sending, except that it was not directed at any one of them. It was non-verbal, had no other symbolic content, and was just an expression of fear. They paused, feeling the sending.

"That's Greentwig," Feather said at last.

"How do you know?" Starbright started to say, but she recognized the clumsy simplicity of it too. Greentwig had never been a very good sender.

"But where is he?" Dayshine asked.

"Pay attention," Feather said, "what is he sending?"

"Fear," Silverknife said, "what else?"

"Trees," Feather said, "he's among trees, and he's hurrying, and he's afraid."

"So what else is new?" Starbright said.

"Come off it," Silverknife told her. "I've never seen him afraid like this."

"What are we waiting for?" Feather asked.

Shadowflash, attending to Brightmist as she was finishing the crystal, got the same odd kind of sending, remote and concept-less, just fear. He looked at Brightmist, but she seemed to be only minutely disturbed by it. He saw the children, on the lawn and down at the stream. They were paying no attention at all.

But Glade called down from on the top of the cliff, where he was with Puckernut and Stringsong. "Do you feel that?"

"Yes," Shadowflash said. "What is it?"

Puckernut said, "It's Greentwig."

"So it is," Shadowflash said. "I thought he had gone to the mesa."

Freefoot came from upstream, where he had been with Two-Wolves. "He did," he said. "I think the sending is coming from there."

"I didn't know he had such power," Glade said.

"It's not him that has the power," Puckernut said, "it's the magic."

Beside him, Stringsong stood up somewhat unsteadily, plucked a few more notes. "It was that cave," he said. He sounded as if he were recovering from a night of dreamberries.

"It was that," Puckernut said, "but how do you know?"

"I can feel it," Stringsong said, "in the back of my teeth."

"But what about Greentwig?" Glade asked.

They all looked at each other. They were all getting the same thing — fear, determination, woods, movement.

"What do we do?" Shadowflash asked.

Greentwig returned to the "secure" place just as the buck was about to attack Fangslayer, who couldn't even stand. The buck was dancing forward on its hind legs, its front hooves pointed at Fangslayer's chest. The blow would crush the elf, the hooves penetrate all the way through his body and into the soil. Without thinking, Greentwig yelled as loud as he could, so that the buck lost its balance and its front feet came down several handspans from Fangslayer's body. Fangslayer groaned and rolled away, and the black neck buck, startled and frightened, ran off.

Greentwig ran up to Fangslayer. "I'm not going to leave you," he said. Fangslayer just moaned. Greentwig went to his mother. Her eyes were open, and she watched him. "You can't take care of yourself," he told her.

"You should leave," she said, her voice a whisper. "The buck will come back."

"That's why I can't leave," he said. He was terrified, but he was determined. He made sure that their backs were secure, then he took Fangslayer's spear and Fernhare's arrows, and sat down in front of them with his own ax and bow to wait.

He was not aware of his sending, or that Silverknife and her age-mates were receiving his heightened emotions as they hurried across the prairie toward the mesa. Though there was no visual imagery in the sending, they knew through Greentwig's feelings, rather than his thoughts, that Fernhare was wounded, that the other, who must be Fangslayer, was wounded, and that the menace, whatever it was, was out there somewhere, and still a threat. They felt Greentwig's determination, his fear, and what they realized was his courage. All were upset, and hurried as fast as they could through the thick grass, and Starbright was especially ashamed, as a consequence of what she was perceiving, of her earlier thoughts and comments.

At the holt, as Greentwig's projected feeling intensified, Shadowflash, Glade, Stringsong, Puckernut, Freefoot, Brightmist, and Two-Wolves, who had gathered together in front of the cliff, came to realize that it was not a sending as they knew it, but a kind of projected empathy, Greentwig's feelings only, which were now of stronger determination, anxiety for his mother and Fangslayer, apprehension and fear of whatever moved in the forest.

Stringsong had always had the ability to feel an elf-child's potential talents, and through all of Greentwig's life he had recognized nothing in him, just a kind of sluggish dimness. But now that he could feel Greentwig's projected empathy, enhanced as it was by the magic from the cave, he recognized that he had in fact felt this thing in Greentwig all along, he had just never recognized it for what it was, the ability to have others empathize with him, which up until now was all that it took, the tiny bit necessary, for everyone to do just enough to help Greentwig survive, when another elf might have died of ineptitude while still a child. He had a special talent after all, and though it could not be used to anyone else's benefit, it had served Green-twig well, and was what now enabled all the adults to know what was going on in his heart, if not his mind.

They knew that, when the buck came again, Greentwig was terrified. But he held his ground and stood between it and the two wounded elves in their poor shelter between the trees. He expended all his arrows, and those he'd taken from Fernhare. His shots were enough to keep the buck from closing too quickly, but few of them hit, and those that did caused only superficial wounds. Greentwig was just not very good.

When the arrows were gone, he dropped the bow and took Fangslayer's spear. The buck reared, its hooves crashed down on branches and rocks, its antlers glittered.

"Set the butt," Fangslayer shouted.

Greentwig almost turned to ask for clarification, but then he remembered, and set the butt end of the spear against the ground, crouched down to aim the head at the buck, which now attacked. But his aim was poor, and the buck, striking the spear off center, impaled itself through the shoulder. The butt skidded along the ground, knocking Greentwig down. The buck reared back, dragged the spear out of Greentwig's hands, and crashed off into the brush.

All the other adults at Halfhill joined Freefoot and the others on the lawn at the base of the cliff. The cublings watched them curiously, anxiously, but kept their distance.

Everybody who was able to receive the bizarre sending was in full accord with Greentwig's perceptions, and could almost see and hear through him as well as feel, as he climbed to his feet, panting, his hands raw, his body sore. He went to Fernhare and Fangslayer, ashamed of his failure. Fernhare could not talk any more.

"You did as well as you could," Fangslayer said. He seemed to be more comfortable now.

"But it was not good enough," Greentwig said.

"It's not over yet," Fangslayer told him, and handed him his ax.

"I know," Greentwig said, and back at the holt they all witnessed his utter terror and absolute courage as he turned away from Fangslayer and Fernhare, listened to the crashing in the bushes, and stepped forward to meet what was coming.

The buck came back, and with an ax in each hand, Greentwig met its charge, and delivered the killing blows on either side of its skull, right through the eyes, even as its forward horns, the ones that had speared Fangslayer, opened his belly, spilling his guts on the ground. The deer fell. Greentwig staggered back, and went to his knees.

He knelt there, knowing that it was his death he saw before him, gray and red on the ground. He felt no pain yet, an odd kind of pressure, perhaps, an ironic emptiness. Fangslayer crawled up to him, saw that the buck was dead, then saw that, though he still breathed, Greentwig was too.

"You are a hero," Fangslayer said. "You struck with your axes as if they were your own hands. Stonefist, that's who you are."

"How is my mother?" the elf who was now Stonefist asked.

"She's all right," Fangslayer said, "she'll be just fine."

Then Stonefist, who had been Greentwig, closed his eyes and slowly leaned forward into the mess of himself and died, and everywhere, people felt him fade.

The Flood

It had been a rather wet autumn to begin with, and as all but the oaks and sycamores lost their leaves, it became absolutely soggy. There were no bad storms, no lightning and thunder, no strong winds, just an almost constant rain that soaked the ground, the elves, the animals. Hunting was hard in this weather, especially during the last three eights of days, when there had been no let up at all.

But for some reason which she didn't quite understand, Graywing didn't care all that much about it any more. She had been feeling a little peculiar, a little different somehow, for the last few days, and had lost interest in hunts, weather, and the doings of people. She didn't know why.

All she knew was that today she wasn't going to do any work at all. After all, she was the oldest elf, she could take a day off if she wanted to. She didn't have a very clear idea of what she was going to do, but that didn't bother her either.

She stood in the entrance to her den and looked out over the common yard, the clear space between the face of the clay cliff that gave Halfhill its name and the stream that provided them with refreshment, sanitation, and recreation — as well as good fish in certain seasons. The gentle slope of the common yard was muddy, with occasional puddles and little rivulets running down to the stream. There were trees on the banks of the stream, more on the other side than on this, but none in the common yard, which extended to the right and left almost to where the sides of the hill came down to the level of the rest of the ground.

All she wanted to do was sit and watch, but it was awfully wet out there. Graywing went back into her store room, where she rummaged around until she found the things she wanted —

a large pigskin for a waterproof, two poles not quite as tall as she, three small stakes, a bit of gut twine, and a wooden spade. From her bedroom she got a cushion of sheep's wool, skinside out. Then she went outside, with the waterproof draped over her head.

The common yard was not perfectly flat, though it had been trodden on by elves for more hundreds of years than Graywing liked to think about at the moment. Near the cliff, but a dozen or so paces from it, and a bit to the right of the entrance to her den, was a place where the ground was just a bit higher, and thus dryer. That was what Graywing wanted. She went to it and set to work.

It was a bit of a trick keeping dry as she dug a small channel around the uphill side of the mound, and even more of a trick to stake out the back end of her waterproof while still under it, but she managed, and she also managed to keep her sheepskin cushion dry. She set this down on top of the mound, sat on it, then pushed the ends of each pole into the front corners of the waterproof and the bottom ends into the ground, so that the pigskin formed a tiny, personal, lean-to tent.

She settled down and looked out at the gray and dripping world around her. It was morning, and there should have been lots of activity, but the rain was keeping people indoors. Fernhare and Glade came up from the stream and called out a greeting as they hurried back toward their den. They looked at her a little oddly, but Graywing didn't care.

Rain fell. Graywing found the sound of it on her waterproof soothing. It was a warm autumn, if a wet one, and she was comfortable. Silvercub, Ebony, and Dewdrop, almost grown but not quite, came out of their respective dens, wearing almost nothing. They glanced her way curiously, said good morning, then went down to the stream together, where they must have found something interesting to do, because they played there, half concealed by the willows, for quite some time. Sometimes they dug, sometimes they moved rocks, sometimes they just splashed in the rising water. After a while Ebony came back to the dens, and reappeared a moment later with those children and infants who had not gone off hunting with their parents, and took them down to the stream to join in whatever game it was the youths had invented. Graywing felt good just watching them.

After a while she noticed Two-Wolves by his den, watching the youngsters down at the stream. He glanced at her and smiled, then went inside. Later he came out again, with Rainbow this time. Rainbow called Silvercub to her, and when he came running up, she handed him a small bundle like the ones she and Two-Wolves were carrying. Off for a hunt. Graywing wished them luck, and watched as they went upstream and out of sight.

The young elves eventually tired of their game and went elsewhere. Other elves came and went. A few stopped to speak with Graywing, and though she was polite, she did not encourage conversation, so they left her pretty much alone. Midday came, and everybody went in search of lunch, except Fernhare, who was down by the stream where the children had been, pacing up and down and kneeling to look in the water.

Fernhare was unremarkable as an elf, with one exception — she had had four children, by three different fathers, and none of them from recognition. Graywing had once envied her the richness of her life, but now she saw it differently. Fernhare had had to endure the loss of two lifemates — only Glade still lived — and one child. Death was natural, a part of the way, but Graywing had had only one mate in her long years, and only one child, still living, and so had had to suffer less than Fernhare had.

Graywing's thoughts must have taken her quite out of herself, because she was surprised to realized that Fernhare, the object of her contemplations, was kneeling in front of her, staring at her curiously. Water was streaming off her rain-darkened hair, puddling around her bare feet.

"Are you all right?" Fernhare asked.

"Goodness, yes, I was just thinking. I didn't mean to ignore you."

"That's okay. I was just wondering if you wanted something to eat."

"No, I don't think so."

"It's past lunch time."

"I know, but I'm not that hungry. I'll have something later. Could you figure out what the children were doing down at the stream?"

"Not very well, the water has washed away most of what they did. I'm kind of worried, Graywing, the stream has risen nearly two handspans since Glade and I first came out this morning. That's more than twice as much as it has risen in the last three eights of days. It looks like we're in for a flood."

"We could be, I guess," Graywing said, "though it's never happened before."

"There's always a first time," Fernhare said. "I'm going to talk to Freefoot about it. Are you sure I can't get you something to eat?"

"I'll be just fine," Graywing said.

The day went on, elves came and went, the rain continued to fall, gray and thin and not really the kind of rain that brought floods. If the water had risen as high as Fernhare said it had, then it must have come from the uplands to the south.

Graywing spoke when she was spoken to, but initiated no conversations. When at last she felt hungry she had young Dewdrop bring her a piece of meat. The meat was old, and the wet weather meant it had begun to spoil, but she had eaten worse before.

As she sat she thought that it really wasn't a very good day for watching the world go by, and wondered that she hadn't gotten bored by now. She had never been one to enjoy being inactive for very long. But today she seemed to be content, just to sit and think. She wasn't really sure what she was thinking about, but she didn't worry about it.

With the sun always concealed by heavy overcast, it was hard to tell the time, but it was sometime after mid-afternoon when wolf howls came from the forest. In weather like this, the wolves were left to fend for themselves unless elves wanted to go hunting. A party had gone out before sunup, and it sounded now like they were returning. But there was a quality to the howls that boded ill, not howls of victory, but of grief.

For the first time since she'd come out this morning, Graywing found herself interested in something outside herself. The howls had come from downstream, where the hunters had gone, hoping to find some decent prey on Long Ridge. Graywing felt her stomach contract. Other elves came out of their dens, and stood around on the common yard, watching and waiting. The howls came again, and yes, it was the hunting party, Silverknife's wolf loudest of all — and most grief-stricken. Somehow the rain seemed colder and grayer than it had just a few moments ago.

It wasn't long before everyone's worst fears were confirmed. Out of the forest came Talon, Dreamsnake, and Stride, bearing between them a frightful burdon wrapped in their waterskins. Their wolves slunk along beside them, wet, bedraggled, heads and tails down. Silverknife's wolf, Rakejaw, came behind, and howled again.

The three hunters brought their burden up to the common yard.

"Where is Stringsong?" Talon asked.

"He went out," Freefoot said, "shortly after you left."

Suretrail was standing beside Ebony, and turned to the youth and told him to go find Stringsong. Ebony did not need to be told what message to take. He stared for a long moment at the burdon the three hunters still held, gave a deep sigh, and then went toward the stream, and across it on the bridge tree to find Silverknife's father.

The three hunters now took their burden up to the entrance of the den which Stringsong had shared with his daughter since Whiteraven, Silverknife's mother, had died, nearly a hundred years ago, when Silverknife had been just an infant known as Warble. There they put the body down, and the others gathered around.

Graywing's chest hurt, and not, she knew, from the weather. She had seen death many times before, usually violent, but this time it was different somehow. Carefully, so as not to upset the supports of her little tent, she got up from her seat and joined the others.

"What happened," Freefoot asked. The full story would be told when Stringsong got here, but Freefoot was chief, and needed to know.

"We were on the south side of Long Ridge," Dreamsnake said, "just below where the boulders stick out. The rain must have washed a lot of the soil away. Silverknife slipped in the mud, put out a hand to steady herself, and the boulders above her fell."

No predator springing from ambush. No prey defending itself to the death. Just a stupid accident.

No more was said at the moment. The elves waited, and even the children and infants seemed to know that this was not the time to fuss or play.

At last Stringsong came, with Ebony beside him. The youth had told the elder elf the worst, and he was as prepared as he could be. The other elves made way for him as he approached. He knelt by the covered head, Dreamsnake beside him, Talon and Stride on the other side.

Only now did they take the coverings from Silverknife, the brightest and the best of the younger elves. Her body was crushed and broken, smeared with mud and blood. The rain fell on her and began to wash her.

Now Talon, Dreamsnake, and Stride told what happened, and this time they told the full story. By the time they had finished, Silverknife's body was clean. Stringsong, Dreamsnake, and Stride straightened the bent limbs, the crooked body, while Glade, Fairheart, Starflower, and Dewdrop went to the nearest trees and cut, as they would not have done on any other occasion, a few slender branches with which they made a light litter. Then they brought the litter to Silverknife, and put her on it, and carried her into her den. The other elves went too, except for Graywing. She just stood in the rain for a long moment, then went back to her shelter to sit, and think, and watch the rain come down.

Graywing had not discovered what she was thinking about, nor figured out how she felt about Silverknife's death, or why she should feel the way she did, when the elves of the holt came out of Stringsong's den. Had the mourning been that brief? No, the sky was darkening, it was late afternoon. Graywing had just lost track of the time. That was not like her, but she suspected that it would be more typical in the future.

Some of the elves, especially the youths and children and infants, went home to their dens, but others made up a special party. Stringsong took the lead, with his wolf Yellowtooth, and Silverknife's Rakejaw, on either side. He walked slowly toward the upstream end of the common yard, and behind him, carrying Silverknife in her light litter, came Dreamsnake, Talon, Stride, and Freefoot. After them came Suretrail, Starflower, Fairheart, Moonblossom, and Treewing. Slowly they made their way around the western end of Halfhill and northward, into the woods. Every now and then Rakejaw howled softly, and turned as if to drop back to where her mistress was being carried, but Stringsong kept her beside him.

Graywing watched the funeral procession, felt the chill of late afternoon, of autumn, of senseless death. Silverknife would be carried deep into the woods, far from the holt, into places where the elves seldom went, to a private place where she would be left to the care of her wolf and other wolves of the holt. That was The Way. The weak die, and the strong die — oh, and surely Silverknife had been one of the strongest! — and life goes on.

Light faded from the gray sky, and Graywing finally decided it was time to pack up her shelter and go into her den. There she found a bit of something for her supper, and went to her bed, almost surprised at how good it felt to be warm under the furs. She hadn't been aware of being quite so cold out there on the common yard.

She lay in her bed for what seemed like a long time, though she knew that her sense of time was not to be trusted any more. She had lit no lights, so it was dark in her den, and quiet except for the gentle sound of the stream flowing past. That should have been shut out by the skins that covered the entrance. The water was so high, and getting higher. Graywing seemed to remember a couple of other times when the stream had risen, but she didn't care to pursue the thought at the moment.

Maybe she drowsed or maybe she didn't, but she was surprised to hear footsteps squishing through the mud outside her den, and soft voices. Wherever her thoughts had been, they came back to the present, and it took her a moment to realize that she was hearing the funeral party returning from their trek into the woods. It was after sundown then, but not all that late after all. Poor Stringsong, she thought. She knew he would take it hard. Somewhere off in the distance, a wolf howled. She turned over under her furs and went to sleep.

The next day was as rainy as before. Everyone at the holt was getting more and more depressed, especially Catcher. She was the master wood-crafter, and traps were her specialty, and she liked to make them out in the sun. But for too long now she'd had to be content to work just inside the entrance to her den.

Today she was making trigger-drops. Catcher could make a trigger small enough to be hidden by a few leaves, but strong enough to hold a deadweight heaver than an elf; a trigger so stable that you could leave it for eight days, but so sensitive that a mouse could set it off; a trigger that would resist anything smaller than a pig, but that could be set by a child.

She liked to start early, and so she was already up and working when she saw Graywing come out of her den and set up her little skin shelter, as she had done the day before. Her movements were more hesitant today, her face was thinner, and the gray streaks in her hair, from which she got her name, were now white, and more than three fingers broad. The change had begun when the rains had. Catcher didn't understand it, and it frightened her.

Glade and Fernhare came out of their den to wash at the swollen stream, and said a word or two to Graywing on their way back. Then they came over to say good morning to Catcher.

"Is there something wrong with Graywing?" Fernhare asked.

Catcher put down the trigger upright she had been smoothing. "I don't know," she said.

"She's getting old," Glade said.

"I've never seen an elf get old before."

"No one has," Fernhare told her.

Aging was something beyond an elf's experience, though they knew it happened to animals, and the wolves who were their partners sometimes got old. Still, none of them really understood what old age meant.

Glade went off to go hunting with Dreamsnake and Two-Wolves, and Fernhare went back to her own den. Catcher went on working. Several times she thought she ought to go and speak to Graywing but she could never work up the courage. She didn't want to see how much her mother had changed in just the last day.

The rain slackened for a while at midday. The clouds did not thin, the sun did not break through, but for a few moments the rain became just a drizzle. Rainbow, down at the stream with the children, hoped it was a good sign, but even as she sent the youngsters back to their parents and caretakers for lunch, the rain got heavier again.

Rainbow's main fear was flood. The stream was now more than six handspans above its normal level, and still rising, and the face of the cliff was soggy and running with thin steams of mud and dissolved clay. She washed the mud off her hands and went back to her den.

She got a piece of meat and a few white-roots that hadn't started to mold yet, and brought them out to join Rillwalker and Puckernut, who were eating outside, at the upstream end of the common yard, in spite of the weather. They were under the branches of a blackwood tree, an evergreen broadleaf, and not at all common. Puckernut had woven some of the smaller branches together to provide protection from the rain. Catcher joined them a few moments later, bringing some dried red-berries and fuzzy-fruit. Graywing stayed where she was.

They talked about the rain as they sat under the blackwood tree, and about the rising water, and the soggy floors in some of the dens, and the face of the cliff which was being washed away.

"I think we need a drier place to live," Rainbow said at last.

Rillwalker agreed with her, but Puckernut did not. "Rain's rain," he said, "what's to worry about?"

But this was something that Rainbow had been thinking about for some time. Her idea, not clearly formed, was that the elves needed to find a new holt, where they would be safe from the threat of flood, and she urged her companions to help her find such a place.

"We're just fine where we are," Puckernut insisted, and Catcher agreed. Rillwalker did not, and said so quite strongly, as if she, too had been thinking about seeking refuge somewhere.

The conversation got quite loud, and Hornbird, eating alone in her den, heard the ruckus and came out to find out what was going on. She saw the four elves under the blackwood tree and, since she was more than a little bored, she decided to join them, bringing a double handful of dreamberries, slightly wrinkled now, to share.

She didn't think much of Rainbow's plan, however. "There's never been a flood before," she said.

"There could always be a first time," Rillwalker told her.

"I don't believe it."

The two sides were quickly drawn, with Rillwalker and Rainbow advocating the development of a new holt, and Hornbird and Puckernut insisting that their present holt was best even if it was damp. Catcher did not participate in the discussion, though she tended to side with Puckernut.

It was not a serious argument. It was more interesting than sitting in one's den, or trudging through the mud on a futile hunt. Hornbird enjoyed it especially. But her high spirits washed away with the rain when, the others having things to do, she went back to her den alone, and passed Graywing on the way.

Hornbird was, after all, the second oldest elf. Would the changes that were happening to Graywing happen to her someday? She would rather die in a hunt.

Back in her den she gathered up her tools and supplies. Hornbird was the bonesmith of the holt, and kept the elves supplied with needles, hooks, small knives, bird-points, and so on, as well as decorative items. Her depression was not improved when her favorite bone saw broke a tooth and had to be discarded, and it got worse when a slither of mud and gravel came down from the face of the cliff beside her doorway. The holt was old too, and maybe it, like the saw, like Graywing, was worn out.

Hornbird wasn't the only one who felt depressed. Fangslayer had been grumping and fussing all day long, until Deerstorm, after their meager evening meal, finally got tired of it. "If you're so unhappy," she said, "why don't you do something about it?"

"I might as well," he said. "The water's going to get higher before it gets lower. We need to set up a temporary camp somewhere, until the worst is past."

"I think you're right," Deerstorm said. "I'm surprised it took you this long to figure it out."

Fangslayer had seen flash floods before, up in the highlands, and knew that streams and rivers could rise very high with frightening suddenness. He was surprised, now that he thought about it, that such a flood hadn't come already.

In spite of this, he wasn't confident about his decision, but he was determined to carry it out. What made it difficult was that he was afraid of the rising waters, and didn't want others to know that. When they went to bed for the night, the sound of the stream outside was far louder than he'd ever heard it before, and it made him nervous. Would others discover his fear if he proposed a temporary refuge? And what if the water rose no higher after all, would he look silly then, having gone out on a limb?

Best not to think about it until he had to, he thought, and tried to convince himself of that. He might have rested easier had he known how many other elves shared his fear, even some of those who professed the least concern. But they were no more eager than he to reveal what they perceived as a weakness. And so each struggled alone with their thoughts, until at last even the most wakeful elf slept.

It was morning, and it was still raining, and sort of toward the middle of the morning, but the overcast was so thick that Graywing had no idea at all where the sun was.

The youngsters down by the stream were digging in the bank. Graywing thought about joining them, but never quite got up the energy. She could remember what it was like to play, though she hadn't felt that free for years, not since Prey-Pacer's time. Had she really been alive that long?

Her thoughts drifted as far away in time as Prey-Pacer was, and she was badly startled when she realized that someone was staring at her, crouched only a pace or two away. But it was only Fangslayer, who moved back hastily and apologized when he saw her jump.

"Have you had any breakfast?" he asked, as if he had asked the same question before.

"Yes, I have, thank you," Graywing said. She smiled at him, and he smiled back, but he was not really content with her simple answer, and perhaps he had something else in his mind.

"Deerstorm and Ebony and I are going to find a dry place where we can go if the water gets too high," he said. "Would you like to come along?"

"Thank you, no," Graywing said. "I've got too much to think about." Fangslayer looked at her for a moment, then nodded and went away to talk with Freefoot about his plan.

Graywing thought that Fangslayer had a good idea, this weather was unlike anything she had experienced before, either here or at any other place where she'd lived in her long life. And just because it hadn't flooded before didn't mean it wouldn't do it now. In fact, she was rather convinced that it would. But even if it did, she had no interest in leaving.

Stringsong came out and walked halfway to the stream, then stopped, as if he had forgotten what he had come for. Graywing felt sorry for him. He had devoted his life to Silverknife. Graywing had felt before that Stringsong's devotion to his daughter was a bit overdone, for his sake if not for hers, and now she saw that she had been right. There was nothing she or anyone else could do about it. It was something Stringsong would have to work out for himself.

After a bit Catcher came out, and with just a glance at Graywing, went up to Stringsong, put a hand on his shoulder, spoke a quiet word or two to him. Then they went off downstream together, to find something fresh for breakfast.

Graywing tried to remember if she'd had in fact had any breakfast herself. She had told Fangslayer he had, but she was hungry. She'd forgotten whether she had eaten or not.

Fernhare came toward her from the stream. Graywing hadn't noticed her going down.

"The water's not rising so fast today," Fernhare said to her. "Maybe the worst is over."

"I certainly hope so," Graywing said.

"But you don't think it is?"

"It's still raining."

Fernhare looked upstream, then down. She looked across the stream into the forest, which now was getting more than a little boggy, and back at the cliff face which was eroding dangerously.

"What are we going to do?" Fernhare asked.

"I don't know," Graywing said simply, and since she didn't seem inclined to say anything more, Fernhare went away.

The morning passed. Other elves came and went, and some of them even spoke to her, but Graywing stopped paying any attention. Instead she thought about how Freefoot was going to handle this crisis, for crisis it would surely be. She did not know that he had already given his approval to Fangslayer's plan.

Graywing thought back about the other chiefs she had known. What would Freefoot's mother, Huntress Skyfire, have done in this situation? She had never had the potential of floods like this to contend with. Skyfire's brother, Two Spear, hadn't been chief long enough to have been tested like this. And Prey-Pacer, who'd been chief when Graywing had been born, wouldn't have cared.

She could almost remember Prey-Pacer. She tried to conjure up his image in her mind's eye. Funny how sometimes she confused him with her father, Maplebrake, and sometimes with Hawk'sClaw, her lifemate who had died before Freefoot had acquired his adult name.

Why would that be? Prey-Pacer had been nothing like her father, and Hawk'sClaw had been one of a kind. There had never been another romance after him, not even a temporary lover.

She must be getting old, maybe that was it.

Her thoughts came back to the present, and she noticed that there was a trickle of water near her feet. She used her little wooden shovel to adjust the drainage ditch behind her. That loosened her rain shield, so she tightened the stakes until it was just right.

That done, she looked around her at the rainy holt, feeling as if she had just wakened up from a nap. The common yard was soggy, the forest across the stream was swampy. The holt sure did look bedraggled.

Graywing had in fact been more than right about Stringsong, more than even he was aware. Death, after all, was a commonplace. His parents were dead, his mate was dead, her parents and brother were dead, so many others had died. So then, aside from the fact that it was his daughter, why did this one death hit him so hard?

He couldn't help but think what a waste it was. Silverknife had had so much potential. The more he tried to shut the thoughts away, the more he hurt. But if he let himself think, he became confused. He couldn't believe that she was really dead.

He didn't want to bother anybody with his problems, and couldn't see that Silverknife's death was everybody's concern. So he spent the whole morning wrestling with the truth, never winning, never losing, only miring himself down in unexpressed grief.

At last he couldn't stand sitting alone in his den any more, so he went outside to see if anything was going on. The only person on the common yard was Graywing, sitting under her tiny shelter. He went over and, squatting down in the rain, spoke to her. She answered, and for a while they talked, but all he could bring himself to talk about was the weather, the bad hunting, the rising stream. From the way she looked at him, he thought she knew what he was trying to say and was unable to, but he couldn't bring himself to mention death.

Very few animals died of old age, but Stringsong had seen a few, so he had a vague idea of what was involved. The trouble was that Graywing looked like that — grayed, weakened, thinned out, curled up. Death was too close to her, so he rambled on for a while, then felt foolish squatting in the wet like that, so he went back into his den.

He had to keep busy. Stringsong was the cord-maker, the thread spinner, the rope twister. That was what had given him his name, rather than his exceptional hearing, or his ability to sense talents in children.

He went to his shelves, extensive and deep, where he kept his raw materials. Gut wouldn't dry in this weather. Hair was frizzly. Leather was too damp, and rawhide wouldn't dry either. Bark, grass, web-silk, none of them would work while the rain persisted.

It was futile, and a waste of his time, to even try exercising his craft. He went back outside and over to Two-Wolves' den, but the other elf was still out hunting. Stringsong tried talking to Rainbow, but she could think of nothing else than finding someplace else to live, with which idea Stringsong had no patience.

Maybe hunting would be a good idea after all. Even in the rain there was a chance he could run across something. He went back to his den and thought about which way he would go, what would he look for — deer, bear, pig, rabbit, antelope out on the prairie to the north? It had been a while since he'd gone out with Yellowtooth. But even as he decided not to use his bow because the string was slack with the damp, and picked up his spear instead, he lost interest in the project. He didn't feel like making the effort. He didn't want to go alone. It would take too long to get anywhere. He still had some food left.

He went back outside and down to the stream, which was not noticably higher than it had been yesterday, to where the youths and children were playing. He stood for a while and watched as they made mudslides and waterfalls, dug channels in the bank which they blocked up and then opened up again. They'd dug an upper pool, which they filled with water and then let it out through specially prepared grooves and tunnels. They were having a marvelous time.

But after a while their very youth made him sad. Dewdrop and Silvercub were not that much younger than Silverknife was — had been.

He turned away before his emotions could get the better of him and started walking slowly back up the gentle slope of the common yard toward the holt. He saw Catcher, sitting just inside the entranceway to her den, and Hornbird in hers. Both of them were working at their crafts, making themselves useful. Stringsong felt useless, and a burden.

That wasn't true, but he had to talk to somebody about it, about his confusion and how he felt about Silverknife's death. And so he went to Catcher, who smiled at him and gestured to him to sit down beside her. He did so, and thought for a moment, and started to say something, but Catcher wasn't listening. He repeated himself, but her thoughts were elsewhere. After a while he realized that she was staring at her mother.

He silently cursed himself for his insensitivity. If he hadn't felt it appropriate to talk to Graywing about death, how much less appropriate to talk to Catcher. He gripped her shoulder gently to gain her attention, excused himself, and left. Maybe Hornbird would be better after all. She was the second oldest elf, and had helped other elves through times like this before.

But he didn't get very far with his conversation with her. She just wanted him to cheer up, grow up, accept life, accept 'The Way,' and didn't really let him speak his mind.

When he left her, after only a little while, he went toward the downstream end of the holt, so that he wouldn't have to pass Graywing and Catcher again, and climbed up the steeper slope here at the edge of the cliff to the top of Halfhill. He went along the edge of the cliff, treacherous now and almost crumbling, until he came about to the place over his own den, then sat down and let his feet dangle over the side. The rain fell on him, through the leafless branches overhead, but he didn't mind. Somehow it seemed appropriate.

From here he could see just how much of the land was flooded. There was water standing all over the other side of the stream, both up and down. The stream itself was much broader in places than it had been, low places were swamps, and marshy areas were almost lakes.

Maybe Rainbow was right. Stringsong watched as she went down to the stream, then came back with Silvercub. They stopped to speak with Graywing for a moment, too far away for him to hear the words, then went back toward their den. Had he leaned over, he could have seen the entranceway. He didn't bother. And if Rainbow was right, so what? It didn't matter, not to him at least. He just sat on the edge of the cliff, and the rain started coming down harder.

Fangslayer's camp was just up the backside of Halfhill an hour's walk or so, along the ridge to where a stand of small trees grew close together at the crest. The trees provided a framework from which Fangslayer, Deerstorm, and Ebony had stretched skins, forming a kind of wall-less tent. The ground sloped down and away from the tented area in all directions.

The three elves added more to the tent as the day wore on, using a store of skins which had been set aside for clothing. Each skin was hung so that the drip from one fell onto the next, leaving lots of light and space between the skins themselves. The design worked, however, only because there was no wind to blow the rain in under the overhangs.

Ebony, being the lightest, was up in the branches while his parents worked and rigged below. The rain started coming down harder, and they were almost out of skins, but before Ebony could come down he heard someone coming along the crest of the ridge from the direction of the holt. A moment later Suretrail, slickered and carrying a bundle of skins and essential belongings, came toiling through the rain and mud toward them.

He greeted them cheerfully enough. "It's getting far too wet back there," he said. "The floor of my lowest room is getting muddy. I thought I'd come up and stay with you for a while, if that's all right."

"Of course it is," Deerstorm said. "Come in out of the wet."

Fangslayer led Suretrail into an inner part of the camp — it was surprisingly large for the work of just three people. There were fir boughs piled in one corner ready for making beds, and a pile of rocks for a fire pit and a water trough. There he put down everything but the skins, which he carried back to where the others had been working.

Even though it was raining harder now, Deerstorm and Ebony went up into the branches, while Suretrail and Fangslayer worked below. At first it seemed to Suretrail that they were making a bit too much of a camp for four people, but Fangslayer assured him that, if the flood did come, he wanted to be ready for the rest of the people back at the holt. And if the flood didn't come, at least it gave them something to do.

Fernhare also had found something to do, though she was less than sure of what it was, and was completely sure it served no useful purpose. With a skin draped over her head, she was moving some stones by the bank of the stream, upstream from the holt a ways, where the ground was especially low. Her objective was to block off the slowly rising water, to see if she could create an area lower than water level but dry — except for the rain, of course. She had gotten so involved in the project that she was playing like a child, fascinated and frustrated by her inability to control the water.

Graywing, sitting under her tiny shelter, had been watching her for the last couple hours. Fernhare was far enough away, and there were intervening bushes, so that Graywing couldn't see exactly what she was doing. But her movements were the same as the children's had been when they'd been digging in the bank nearer the cliff, so she assumed that Fernhare was doing much the same. Why, she had no idea, and didn't really care. Fernhare was enjoying herself, and that was all that mattered.

A little bit later Glade, Dreamsnake, and Two-Wolves came out of the forest, carrying a deer. As they passed Fernhare she stopped moving her rocks, half embarrassed to be caught playing like a child, but they didn't care. Their wolves, bedraggled but in high spirits, came with the hunters. Two-Wolves was limping, and in some pain, but grinned at Graywing as they came to the holt. He went into his den at once while the other two set the deer down in front of Graywing, to begin the job of butchery.

Two-Wolves had just sprained his knee, but intended to rest for the rest of the afternoon. Fernhare helped with the butchery, as did Rainbow and Hornbird. Graywing just sat and watched as the work went on in front of her. She accepted without comment the bits of liver, marrow, and brains that they gave her.

As they worked, Glade and Dreamsnake told about the woods, how wet and flooded it was already. It was boggy everywhere, except where the land was very much higher or rockier. Even slopes were showing a lot of run-off.

"I wish the holt were a bit higher and drier," Fernhare said.

"There's always Bald Hill," Rainbow told her. "I think we ought to move up there."

"And leave the holt?" Fernhare said. "I couldn't think of it."

"What if it floods?" Rainbow asked.

"I can stick it out, besides, how high could the water get?"

"It can't get much higher," Dreamsnake said. "In fact, it seems to have stopped rising already. I'm going to stay right here, thank you."

"But what if it starts to rise again?" Fernhare asked. "Some of the dens are pretty close to the ground, they could fill up, what then? Maybe we ought to be ready to move out, in an emergency."

"I agree," Glade said, "if there is indeed an emergency. But there's no need to rush off right now, as Fangslayer and Sure-trail have done."

"If we stay here until it's too late," Fernhare said," we might as well stay here altogether, but if we're going to go, maybe we should go right now."

"Well, I'm not going," Hornbird said emphatically. "The holt has never flooded before, and it won't now."

"I don't know," Fernhare said. "The stream has risen a bit today, about four finger-breadths."

"That's not much of a rise," Hornbird snorted.

"Maybe not, but another four, and another four, and another four...."

Glade sighed in resignation. Fernhare just couldn't seem to make up her mind. It was partly to get away from her indecision that he had gone off hunting. His mate's vacillation was causing the others some frustration too, he could see. But Graywing, she just sat and listened.

Catcher woke up the next morning feeling far from cheerful. Her bed was damp. She got up and dragged the furs into another room where the floor was dry, and although she would have liked to sleep in a bit longer there was nothing for it but to start the day. She got dressed and scrounged around in her larder for some breakfast, but there was only a little bit of hopper meat left, and some prickly-pads that were very limp and wrinkly. She would have to go hunting today if she wanted lunch, unless she found something in her traps, which she doubted, since most of them had been set in places which would be flooded by now.

She heard voices outside, so she went to see what was happening. Rainbow, Two-Wolves, their daughter Crystalmoss, and

Silvercub were setting out bundles, as if they were going on a long expedition.

"Going up to Fangslayer's camp?" Catcher asked.

"That's just temporary," Rainbow said. "We're going to Bald Hill. It's dry up there, plenty of shelter."

"Not much drinking water," Catcher said. She glanced curiously at Two-Wolves.

"There's a spring not far away," he said, with a wry smile. He would go along with Rainbow's silly plan, for as long as she cared to try it, but his heart wasn't in it.

"It's not going to rain forever," Catcher said, "and when it stops it will dry up and we'll be comfortable here again."

"I don't believe it," Rainbow said. She hoisted her load on her back. Two-Wolves and Silvercub did the same, but Crystal-moss hesitated.

"I'm not moving up there," she said to Catcher, "I'm just helping them carry stuff."

"Good for you," Catcher said, and started to go down to the stream, but Rillwalker came out of her den just then, carrying a bundle of her own.

"Are you going along with this?" Catcher asked her incredulously.

"The water's going to rise," Rillwalker said. "It's not the rain here, it's the storms in the uplands."

"But that's no reason to abandon Halfhill altogether," Catcher insisted.

But Rillwalker, like Rainbow, had her mind made up, and nothing Catcher could say would change it. At last Catcher gave up trying and let them go off on their way while she went down to the ever deepening stream to wash up. She was more than ready for breakfast when she got back to her den, but her bow-string was limp, so she took two javelines and went out to see if any of her traps were still above water.

Rainbow and her party went north and west toward Bald Hill. When they got there they found their chosen caves still dry, and spent the rest of the day fixing up two dens, one for Rill-walker — and Puckernut when he learned the error of his ways — and the other for Rainbow, Two-Wolves, and Silvercub. As soon as she could, Crystalmoss went back to Halfhill.

There were other elves, however, who held to a middle ground. They had no desire to abandon Halfhill, but were tired of being soggy, and bored into the bargain. So it was that Brightmist, Broadhand, Longoak, and Stride all went up to the ridge crest camp, bringing more tent skins with them.

The camp was becoming quite large by now. Suretrail and Ebony had their own private quarters, curtained off by black-wood branches laced together with willow. There was plenty of room for more, and once the new skins were strung, they would be able to accommodate anybody else who might come up later.

In the middle of the camp was the main fire pit, lined with stones and kept burning day and night. Smoke escaped through the wide windows between layers of skins overhead. At the back of the camp was the water trough, into which the rainwater flowed from the tentskins. The overflow ran down a channel and behind some bushes, which served perfectly well as a sanitary.

It was altogether a satisfactory camp, and what with adding new tent and maintaining old, adding more privacy screens, developing a better fire pit and better sanitary, nobody had a chance to be bored any more.

Those elves left back at the holt were not so lucky. Daytime at the holt was usually spent socializing and working at the various crafts that each elf specialized in. That was hard to do in a constant downpour. The only alternative was to sit around in somebody's den, but the dens were not very large, and after nearly four eights of days of doing that, people were getting desperate.

Hornbird was having an especially hard time of it. For a while she visited Dreamsnake, along with Puckernut and Crys-talmoss, who told them about her mother's strange ideas for making Bald Hill a permanent new holt. Puckernut and Dream-snake were gentle in their ridicule of Rainbow, and Crystalmoss more or less agreed with them, on principle anyway, but Hornbird thought the conversation futile, and after a while excused herself.

Looking for someone else to talk to she went to Freefoot's den, where she also found Starflower, and Bluesky, who was feeling especially lonely. Freefoot and Starflower were convinced that everybody would have to move up to the ridge crest camp eventually, and were glad that Fangslayer and Deerstorm had already done so much work against that time. Bluesky didn't care much one way or another, as long as she had some company, but Hornbird was determined to stick it out at Halfhill, no matter what happened.

When she tired of that conversation, Hornbird went to visit Fairheart and Moonblossom. Talon and Treewing were already there. They, too, were talking about moving to the emergency camp, and Hornbird lost her patience.

"There's no reason to go anywhere," she said. "Nothing is going to happen."

"It's already happening," Treewing said. "Suretrail's den has two fingers of water on the lowest floor, and that's not the only den that's wet."

"They why haven't you already gone up to the ridge?" Hornbird demanded.

"Because our dens are dry, so far," Talon said.

They could see that her bad temper really had to do with something else, and tried to cheer her up, but Hornbird wasn't aware herself of what the true problem was. She was anxious, felt deserted, felt her judgement wasn't being valued — and secretly feared her judgement was wrong. She went back to her den, where she lay on her bed-furs and listened as boulders moved down stream as the flood waters continued to rise.

By midday of the next day, the stream had risen to the base of the cliff in some places. Graywing continued to sit on her cushion under her rain shield, in spite of this. Hers was one of the few 'dry' areas left out on the common yard. The upstream end of the yard had flooded first, oddly enough, but the rest of the yard would soon be under water too.

Catcher had brought her some meat earlier, and had asked her to come in, but Graywing had refused. She appreciated her daughter's concern, and thought she understood what was bothering her, but found it hard to worry about anything other than her own thoughts at the moment. She munched the meat slowly, not really tasting it.

The rain seemed to be letting up a bit but the stream kept on getting higher. Graywing knew she would have to move eventually, but for the moment she was content to sit and watch.

She knew that her presence here was giving the other elves some cause for concern, but apparently they had become accustomed to seeing her sitting under her shelter. When they did speak to her, she had to work either to respond with a smile or a word, or to ignore them. She sympathized with them, but really wished they would leave her alone. Maybe if she went inside they would.

She stepped out from her shelter and stood up and, for a moment she thought she was going to fall. She felt cramped, though she'd been there only half a day. It was hard for her to straighten up.

She pulled up the stakes, took out the poles, dropped the skin over her sheep's wool pad, and picked the whole bundle up and carried it to the entrance to her den. She had to wade through muddy water to get there. There she tossed the skin, shovel, poles, and stakes aside and put the cushion down just inside her doorway. This was at least six handspans above the ground, and her den inside was higher still, so she wouldn't have to worry about the stream, unless it got an awful lot higher. Not like some others, who soon enough would have to seek refuge in the ridge crest camp.

But there was no way Graywing was going to go there, as good an idea as it might be for everybody else. As for Rainbow's silly escape, Graywing hoped it was just a temporary aberration.

Stringsong was another matter. He would have to come to terms with Silverknife's death sooner or later, and the sooner the better. Graywing had known other elves who had mourned too hard but not well enough, and who had followed the deceased into whatever realm the dead called their own. That was something she herself was rather looking forward to finding out about, but Stringsong, he was too young … indeed, as Silverknife had been.

For a while Graywing toyed with the idea of going up to the ridge crest camp, if Stringsong would go with her, but she just couldn't bring herself to take the idea seriously. Stringsong had potentially a long life ahead of him, but her own time was very short indeed, and she had to put her own interest above others now, at the last. Moving to the ridge crest camp would take too much effort, physically and emotionally. She had other, more important things to think about.

She looked out at the muddy, swirling water covering most of the common yard. From the stream she could hear the sounds of boulders and rocks moving with the force of the flow of the flood. From nearer at hand she could hear an occasional splash as some of the cliff face fell off. Water rising wasn't the only problem, the ground above the dens was waterlogged, and only the fact that the clay swelled up when it got wet kept their roofs dry. Even that wouldn't last forever, once water found its way down small cracks and crevices, the way it had coming up along the bottoms of some dens. It was likely that the dens would drown from the bottom rather than from the top.

Graywing sat in her entrance a while longer, and then decided that watching the rain was both too tedious and too distracting. There were a few elves who had gone off on extended hunting expeditions, and whom she didn't expect to return for several days, maybe several eights of days, but that was the way that was. Everybody else, well, she had said what she wanted to say to them. Time to think more about these other things that kept on intruding into the edges of her consciousness, into the background of her dreams. She didn't know exactly what they were, and wanted to find out.

She was surprised at how much energy it took to stand up. She was not at all premature in making this last move. She went into her bedroom, gathered up as many skins and furs as she could carry, and took them into a far, inner chamber, high up in the back of her den. There she made a nest, which she amplified with more furs, as many as she had.

When that was to her satisfaction she went to her larder. She got several gourds of drinking water, and took them back to her nest, and put them in a niche near to hand. She would need no food.

The main chamber of every den has a fire pit, and at this season of the year there was usually a small fire kept in it, for warmth as well as light. Graywing's fire had gone out several days ago, and she saw no reason to start another now. But she did think she'd like some light, so she worked with her drill until she got the tinder to smolder and from it lit a lamp. Then she got a little extra oil, and a twist of wick, and took these, too, into her new nest chamber.

She stood in the doorway, looking at her arrangements, and felt that there was something still missing. It seemed to take her a long time to think of it. At last she wandered back through her den, from room to room, until she found, near the entrance, in its alcove, her spear, and a couple good throwing stones which she'd been saving for a special need. Yes, that was what was missing. She gathered them up and took them to her nest.

And now there was just one more thing. In her bedroom, in the curtained-off alcove where she kept her clothes, under the bottom shelf, was a belt, made and decorated by her mother. It had been repaired many times over the years, until at last it was too fragile to wear any more, and she'd put it away for safe keeping. Now was the time to take it out again. She took off the one she had been wearing — how loose it had become — and put on her mother's belt in its place.

That was all she needed to do. She went back and up into her innermost chamber, to where the tiny light glowed on her deep pile of furs. The spear stood by the door, the stones on the floor beside it, the water gourds and lamp in the niches in the walls. It was good.

She got into her nest and made herself comfortable. It wasn't all that cold, so she didn't have to burrow down in the furs. Or maybe she just couldn't feel the cold any more. She had no idea what time it was, at least by the sun, but she had no illusions about her own time. It was very near. She was going to die, and soon.

She was fascinated by the thought. She had survived every disease, every accident. Not only was she the oldest elf in the holt, she was the oldest elf she had ever known or heard of. But now was the time for it to end, and it would be by simple old age. No other elf had ever experienced that before. Fascinating, she thought, and felt the other thoughts that had been teasing her these last few days gathering around the edges of her mind. Fascinating, she thought, and let those other thoughts come to her, if they would. Death was going to be a very interesting experience indeed.

Stringsong, on the contrary, did not think that death was interesting at all. In fact he found the thought so disturbing, so distasteful, that he had gotten himself involved in a project he would otherwise have avoided had he been more himself.

It had never been Stringsong's pleasure to dig in the dirt. But here he was, digging a trench in front of Dreamsnake's den, along with her and Fernhare. The stream was nearly up to the entrance here, and they were trying to see if they could dig a channel so that the water would run away instead of into the den. The only problem was, there was nowhere for the water in the channel to go, so it just filled up, forming a pool. The deeper they dug, the deeper the pool got, until at last they decided they would be better to stop. Someone might come along and, thinking the muddy water no more than a finger-breadth deep, step in it up to their knees.

"Think we ought to fill it in?" Dreamsnake asked.

"Probably," Fernhare said, kicking at the now runny mud which they had dug from the trench. "It'll be awfully soft."

"Looks like we've made it worse instead of better."

"We should fill it with rocks," Fernhare suggested, "or cover it with strong branches."

"I never thought," Dreamsnake said, "that we'd have to have some place for the water to run to."

"I did," Fernhare said, "and I'm sorry now I didn't say anything before."

Stringsong did not contribute to the discussion as they did their best to repair the damage. He was doing his best not to think at all. But as they filled in the trench and laid a stout section of branch across it, he noticed something missing from the common yard. There was a mound sticking up out of the water.

"Where's Graywing?" he asked at last.

The others looked up and noticed that the old elf was indeed gone from her place.

"I don't know," Dreamsnake said. "Was she there when we came out?"

"I don't think so," Fernhare said, "now that you mention it. Should we see if she's at home?"

But Dreamsnake, though she was Graywing's granddaughter, was reluctant to intrude on the old elf, especially the way she had been these last few days, and suggested they talk to Catcher about it instead.

Catcher was working in front of her own den, by herself, piling rocks in front of the entrance. As the three elves went over to her, they could see that her idea was basically more sound than Dreamsnake's had been. By raising a barrier, well in front of the entrance, some of the water was being kept back. But it was hard to get the rocks to fit close enough together to keep all the water out, and when she tried to pack the spaces between with mud, the water just washed it away. She tried mortaring the rocks with clay, and that seemed to hold for a while, especially if she put down the clay before putting a rock on top. But eventually the water found a crack or hole and started leaking through.

Her main problem was that there weren't a lot of rocks here, and Catcher had had to go far to the upstream end of the cliff to find those big enough to work with but small enough to carry.

The fact of her mother's departure from her accustomed place was news to her, and she had no explanation. Now that it was brought to her attention, she was a bit worried. "She's been getting frailer almost by the hour," she said. "I brought her some meat a little while ago, and she looked like she hadn't eaten anything for eights of days. I hope she hasn't wandered off somewhere."

"More likely she's gone inside," Fernhare said. "Should we go and find out?"

"Well, I'm going to," Catcher said, "whether we should or not," and she put down the rock she'd been holding and went to Graywing's den. The others followed after.

Catcher stepped up into the entrance. It was dark inside, and she could hear no sound. "Graywing," she called, softly at first, then louder.

"Yes, child," she heard the answer at last. "What is it, cubling?"

"Are you all right, Mother?"

"Yes, I'm resting."

"Can I get you anything?"

"No. If I need something, I'll call."

Catcher wasn't sure she believed her mother's reassurances — she couldn't remember the last time Graywing had called her 'cubling.' But she didn't want to intrude, even though she was sure her mother was dying — especially because of that. One did not fondle one's wolf when it came time for it to die. And a wolf was the only model Catcher had, so she sighed and came away to reassure the others that everything was all right.

Fernhare and Dreamsnake went back with Catcher to help her work on her dyke, but Stringsong felt that the whole business was futile. He walked away from the dens, splashing sometimes calf-deep in water, and looked out over the flooded land. Everything looked so different this way. It was hard to believe that this was the home he'd known all his life.

He turned back toward Halfhill. The face of the cliff had changed, scarred by mud-fall, gravel-slide, and running water.

Besides Dreamsnake's den and Catcher's, three others were in obvious danger of flooding — Suretrail's, which was already wet, Fangslayer and Deerstorm's, and Rainbow and Two-Wolves'. And none of them was here to do anything about it.

It was as if those three dens had been abandoned, though Stringsong knew it wasn't true. Other elves, who's dens were better situated, couldn't deal with the problems they had, and those who had worse problems weren't here to do attend to them. Only a few elves seemed to care at all.

Far at the downstream end of the holt was the den where Puckernut and Rillwalker lived. It was far enough away that Stringsong hadn't noticed Puckernut busy working in his own entranceway. Partly that was because Puckernut was completely inside his den, instead of outside. He seemed to have built a wall across the lower part of the entrance. For a moment Stringsong was curious. Then he noticed Fernhare staring at him, and turned away.

Fernhare had been intending to ask Stringsong to come back and help, but he had seemed so intent that she came away from Catcher's den and went to see what he had been looking at. When she saw what Puckernut was doing, she decided it was a good idea, and went to get the others so they could see too.

For his part, Puckernut, as sour as he sometimes was, was glad to show off what he, with the help of Crystalmoss and Hornbird, who were inside, had accomplished. Rather than digging a trench or building a wall, he was carving down the ceiling above his lower chambers and using the dirt to raise the floor altogether.

Stringsong credited the irascible old elf with the only reasonable solution to the problem so far. But what a mess, and how much work, and what would happen if Puckernut scraped up through an impervious later to soggy soil above? His den would fill with mud in a rush, and he'd be lucky to get out alive.

But Stringsong had to admit that his real objection was that his friends all seemed to have something useful to do, or at least were trying, while all he could do was to distract himself from his thoughts, thoughts which every other elf had had before, and had lived with. But Stringsong, for some reason, just couldn't shake off the pain.

He felt useless. He felt tired. He was soaked to the skin, though not muddy any more, and more than a little chilly. It was too cool to just stand around. So he went back to his own den, climbing up to the entrance on the rocks that formed his front steps, and went inside. His home, at least, was high and dry, his floors solid, and there were no leaks in his roof.

He knew he shouldn't go there, but he felt himself drawn to Silverknife's bedroom. Empty, now. Soon, very soon, he would have to give her belongings away, or make use of them himself. It was a waste to just leave them there, good weapons, clothes, tools. But not now, he was not ready for that yet. He sat down on the edge of her bed, and put his head in his hands.

The next morning there was water standing all along the entire length of the cliff of Halfhill, and everybody, except for a few diehards, decided to go up to the ridge crest camp.

Graywing didn't go of course. She didn't even know it was morning, though she was awake, and had been for some time. She had drowsed and waked all night long, totally unconcerned with what time it was, thinking her thoughts, pursuing the images that flickered still around the edges of her mind.

Puckernut didn't go. He might have if Rillwalker had stayed, or had wanted to stay, since he was a contrary fellow, and usually chose the other side in any argument, just for the fun of it. But then he might not have gone either, since he was fairly sure his plan of rebuilding his den's floors would work, and he was enjoying himself, though he might not admit it.

Fernhare stayed behind, in large part because she had not been able to make up her mind whether to go or stay, and since staying was the default decision in a case of acute indecision, she stayed. But she, too, was enjoying herself, though she would have been surprised to have been told that. She spent a lot of time, out in the wet, fiddling around with mud and rocks and

ditches and dykes, not on the common yard any more, of
course, since that was all flooded, but downstream near the base
of the hill, at the edge of the risen stream, where she could
actually experiment with the flow and retardation of water.

Hornbird remained at the holt as well, of course. Her mo-
tives were perfectly obvious, or so she thought. Her belief that
the holt would not flood was not reversed by the present fact.
The last flooding she had experienced had been a long time
ago, and had been nowhere near as bad as this. More important
was the unconscious need to be right, having now committed
herself so strongly, and stated her position so positively. She had
to stay behind if she wasn't to betray her faith in herself.

And Dreamsnake was here, though she had rather gone. She
was fairly convinced that the holt would flood, that the waters
would rise, and her own den was in danger, with muddy floors
and even a dripping ceiling in one storeroom. But her mother
was staying, which in itself shouldn't matter, except for the
concern her mother was obviously showing for Graywing.
Catcher had been inordinately distracted during the last few
days, ever since Graywing had first started showing signs of
advanced age. Dreamsnake understood that, and sympathized.
She was determined to leave Catcher alone, but she wanted to
be near at hand, in case the worst happened, as it had to sooner
or later, to give Catcher the sympathy and support she would
need.

Catcher stood outside her den in the rain, feeling lonely, wet,
and in some strange way frightened. The holt was practically
empty, and those who had remained behind were in their own
dens where it was dry.

Everywhere she looked there was water. Trees standing from
it marked the banks of the stream, now many handspans below
the surface. Further out the water moved, not just over the
stream bed, brown and muddy, littered with leaves and dirty
foam and occasional small drowned animals and twigs and junk.
Still further in the forest the trees were black with wet, leafless

now, even the oaks and sycamores. The sky was a uniform gray, uninteresting, low. Behind her the cliff was a dark beige gray, slick, pocked and grooved by water. Ugly, messy, wet, colorless world. Enough reason for feeling depressed. She didn't need the excuse of her mother's condition.

But that was the true reason of course. Her fear was not because of the flood, or what might happen if the water got higher, but because of what was happening to Graywing. She tried to be rational about it, and it offered no solutions. One was supposed to take death in stride, but if one knew that a friend was about to do something that might kill them, and couldn't stop them, for whatever reason, then one would fear for their life. The fact that Graywing had showed no anxiety herself did not ease the anxiety. She was going to die, and it hurt.

Catcher had tried to leave Graywing alone, but she had felt compelled to take her something to eat last night. She had found Graywing in her nest, all tucked away. She had been trying to deny what she knew was true, telling herself that Graywing was just tired, maybe just sick, anything but dying. But seeing her mother there, in her innermost chamber, with only water, and light, and furs, and her special weapons, wearing her ancient belt — it was too obvious to deny any more.

Death was part of The Way. Graywing wasn't like Silverknife, young and full of potential not yet realized. She was old, so old, and had done everything an elf could hope to do, and more. Her very age made her almost supernatural, though most of the time nobody thought about it. It was time, perhaps, at last, for her to die. So why was Catcher hanging on to her so hard?

Graywing had been surprised when Catcher had brought her her supper, and a bit peeved, as if she would have preferred hunger in privacy. She had thanked Catcher for her consideration, asked her to put the meat down within reach, and without pretense or apology, had said, "Will you please go now? I want to think."

So Catcher had gone, and would leave her alone. She tried not to feel peevish herself about it. It felt strange, unnatural, not to spend some time with Graywing every day. It wasn't right to just go off and leave someone all alone in their den without stopping in now and then to chat and make sure things were all right. But Graywing needed her privacy, Catcher knew that, and understood it, intellectually at least, and so she was determined to stay away from her mother's den, no matter what she felt.

She could see, from where she was, the water standing in the entrance to Suretrail's den. She hoped he'd put things up off the floor before going to the camp. The water was also over the floor of Fangslayer and Deerstorm's den, and of Rainbow's den. Her own entrance was still dry, since it was a bit higher than the others, and taking ideas from both Fernhare and Puckernut, she'd built a solid dyke, very broad at the base, of clay and rock together, and so far it seemed to be holding back what water had come up to it.

Puckernut, of course, was doing very well. He'd raised all his floors until the lowest, at the entrance, was now hip-higher than it had been. He'd taken special care to use only the white clay, that swelled up when it got damp, so that even if water started creeping in from below, its very presence would soon seal the new floor off from further incursions. Catcher could just barely hear him, even now, working away inside. Rillwalker was going to have a big surprise when she got home.

Catcher was feeling decidedly lonely. Fernhare, Hornbird, and Dreamsnake had all gone off looking for something to eat. She couldn't talk to her mother, so that left only Puckernut, not the best of company under most circumstances. Catcher went over to his den and called to him.

He invited her in, and offered her some dreamberries while he showed her how his work was progressing. Catcher tried to be interested, especially since it really was good work, and something she should do a bit of herself, especially where her floor was soggy, but somehow she just didn't have the heart for it. She stayed as long as she could, and then she excused herself, which left Puckernut slightly confused as he'd been in the middle of a sentence, and went back outside.

She was angry with herself for being so indecisive, and was about to call her wolf so they could go out to find something to eat when she heard other calls and howls. Hornbird, Dreamsnake, and Fernhare were coming back. So soon? Had there been more trouble? But no, they had just been lucky, had found a den of hoppers that had been flooded out and had culled their pick. Plenty to eat for all. Catcher called the news to Puckernut, then they all went into Hornbird's den, which was dry, to butcher the kill and eat the dozen or so small animals.

When they had finished there was still plenty left over, and Hornbird suggested taking a share to Graywing.

"I don't think she wants to be disturbed," Catcher said.

"I won't disturb her," Hornbird said, "I'll just take this in and give it to her."

"She didn't like me going in last night," Catcher told her.

"She won't even know I'm there," Hornbird said. She took up three hind legs and went outside. She was confident in her ability to make the gesture. After all, she'd known Graywing far longer than Catcher had, and had seen almost as much of life.

Still, she hesitated by Graywing's door, standing calf-deep in water. Graywing was dying, and it might indeed not be right to intrude on her during these last critical days. On the other hand, what if she lost her strength and needed help? She might be thirsty, if not hungry. Did her bed need to be cleaned?

Catcher would never go in to find out, if Graywing had asked her to stay away. But Hornbird had a bit more of a stake in the situation. She was younger than Graywing by two or three eights of eights of years, but that wasn't very much given the time she had lived so far. If she avoided accident, predators, and disease, Hornbird herself might be facing the same kind of experience some day.

The thought sobered her. She did not, in truth, feel much older than when she'd met her lifemate, now long dead. It was a simple fact that elves, like many animals, grew until they were mature, then showed little change until very late in their life — if they survived at all. But when the time came, when age began to exert its influence, it came on all at once. Hornbird would have liked very much to talk to Graywing about it — when did she first notice a change, what did it feel like, what did she think about?

Hornbird wasn't sure that she wanted to grow old.

She had just made up her mind to go on into Graywing's den, but to just quietly peep in, leave the hopper meat, and leave without speaking when she noticed that the water around her calves was no longer still, but swirling. She looked down and saw the muddy flood rushing past her legs. The broad expanse of water between the cliff and the line of trees where the stream had once flowed was not flat, but agitated, disturbed, twisting, splashing.

There was a change, too, in the subaqueous rumble of rocks being pushed around. It was louder, sharper sometimes, deeper sometimes as if even larger rocks and boulders were being forced from their places and jostled together. It was not all that loud, but it was a most disquieting sound, since it came up through the feet as well as in by the ears.

Rillwalker, had she been here, would have been most fascinated. Rivers and streams were Rillwalker's special interest, and she knew more about the behavior of flowing water than any other elf. It did not help Hornbird's peace of mind any to remember that Rillwalker had gone away because of the rising stream.

There was a change in the quality of sound, not just more rocks, and Hornbird strained to listen. It was coming from far upstream, a complex rushing, splashing sound, a murmur that would have been as loud as a roar had it been nearby.

But it was not nearby, not just upstream where the tree trunks obscured further view, but very far away indeed, a very loud noise to be heard from such a distance. But if it was that far, half an hour's walk perhaps, it surely couldn't be anything to worry about at the moment, and for a moment, Hornbird was reassured.

She was still three or four paces from the entrance to Graywing's den. She took a step toward it, surprised that, in just the tiny moment of time that she had hesitated, the water was now almost to her knees. The rushing sound got louder, and she looked up and saw something odd about the broad expanse of water upstream. It looked like there was a slope to the water, the light reflected off it differently than it did nearer to the holt. There were bushes in the water, swirling around, and logs, rolling, turning end over end. End over end?

Even as she watched, a good sized tree leaned toward her and fell, its roots suddenly above the water's surface for a moment. What she had thought was a slope in the water was exactly that, a sudden rise, who knew how much? coming down at her all at once.

She tried to take a step, against the current, toward Graywing's den, but the water pushed her back, and almost knocked her off her feet. She leaned against the flow, and looked around for somewhere to jump to, something to hold on to, but there was nothing within reach. The water was rising above her knees now, and pushing her down stream, cutting away at the cliff face at the same time, so that clay and mud and rocks fell from the cliff into the rushing flood. There was nothing for Hornbird to do but go back toward her own den.

Time seemed to be standing still, while the water rushed on at full speed. Hornbird turned in place, struggled to keep to her feet. The water rose. She took a step toward her den, the water pushed her along. She stepped on something unstable and slick and fell, to her hands and knees — what had happened to the hopper legs? — and was drenched by water splashing up over her back. She lurched toward the cliff, grabbed the slick and crumbling clay, pulled herself to her feet, the water now well over her knees, and struggled down toward her den. But the cliff face gave way, the mud and clay slid down around her feet and knocked her down. The current was so strong, the flood swept her away, down stream, away from the cliff. Another mass of mud and clay fell, where she had been, and had she stayed there she would have been buried.

She came up against something and was able to get to her feet, waist deep now. She felt small rocks roll past her feet.

Bushes, torn up by the flood, swept past her. The water grabbed her again, threw her down, and she fought to keep her head above the surface. She was spun around, saw a tree trunk splash by, then another, realized the trees were still standing and she was by the stream bed. She passed under a branch, reached up, grabbed hold, and pulled herself up out of the water.

And then for the next few minutes she sat on the branch, and just watched the water rise. Catcher, Puckernut, and Dreamsnake all came out to the entrance of Hornbird's den to watch, and were glad to see her still alive, though her tree of refuge was at the downstream end of the holt.

The flood lasted only a few moments longer, then rose no more, and the water, though it still flowed quickly, became less agitated.

All the dens that had been in danger of flooding, with the exception of Puckernut's, had indeed flooded. Water stood in some of them waist deep, and some of the lower chambers were completely full. It was going to take a lot of work to set things to rights again when the water went down.

Hornbird helped Catcher salvage what she could in her den, and Puckernut was giving Dreamsnake what assistance he could. Fernhare, still undecided about things, sat in the entrance to her den and watched the water. As for Suretrail's den, or Rainbow's, or Fangslayer's, there was nothing to be done until they got back from the ridge crest camp.

Fernhare sat and thought about it. There had been floods before, but nothing like this since the holt was founded, and there might not be another like it for as many years to come. But she wasn't satisfied with that thought.

She watched as another part of the cliff collapsed, saw how tree roots above helped hold the soil, how the grassy areas at the ends of the common yard up and down stream hadn't been disturbed except for the mud, rocks, and branches dumped on top of them. The water was moving more slowly now, was almost still, so Fernhare stepped down from her den to wade around.

The bank of the stream was invisible, marked only by the trees that bordered it. As she walked toward it the water got deeper, and she could feel the scoured and shaped ground under her feet. She didn't go all the way to the trees, some of which were leaning now, but now she remembered how the tree-bridge over the stream had come to be. That had been more than three eights of eights of years ago. The stream had risen to the tops of the banks, and the tree, much smaller then, had been under-cut and had fallen over across the stream. Since then a side branch had grown up while what had been the main trunk had become the stunted branch everyone used as a bridge.

The trees that had rocky bases did better. She looked back at the cliff, saw how it had collapsed where there was sand, how the clay had seemed to hold, how the rocks sometimes held and sometimes didn't.

How about downstream, what if the water could drain away faster? No sense in blocking the water upstream, was there?

The more she thought about it, the more she began to think that something could be done to prevent any future catastrophe. It would take a while, and might not be needed, but it would be a rewarding project, even if nobody else was interested. She started upstream toward where the hill rose up from the waters. She wanted to find out what the flood had done to the slope.

The flood waters remained steady all the next day. Those who had gone to the ridge crest camp knew nothing about it. Those who had stayed at the holt did what they could to clean up the mess, as best they could, under the circumstances and some twenty handspans of water, measuring from the stream's normal level.

Catcher had a rather hard time of it. She had resisted going to check on Graywing after the flood, had refused Hornbird's suggestion to take her mother some supper, had stayed away from Graywing's den all morning, and by midday she could hardly stand it.

She ate her lunch alone in her main chamber. Outside she could hear Fernhare and Puckernut talking about flood control or something while thrashing around in the water. It seemed like a waste of time. Her den had not actually flooded, but the floor of some of the lower chambers, including her bedroom, was soggy, and nothing anybody could dream up could keep the water from rising up through cracks in the ground.

Catcher wished she had gone off with the others, but she knew she couldn't have stayed away, her concern for Graywing would have brought her back sooner or later. But what good was she doing sitting here? She knew her mother's den as well as her own, she could go over there quietly, just take a peek, make sure everything was all right.

But she was afraid. She didn't want to see what changes might have taken place in Graywing's appearance during the last day or so, didn't want to try to understand her change in behavior. The implications of age were not something pleasant to think about. All elves assumed, from comparing themselves to other animals, that baring accident, disease, and predation, they would live forever. Graywing implied something else.

Maybe she was just sick. A disease, yes, perhaps that. But that did not change the fact of her mortality, or postpone the immanence of her death.

Besides, if Catcher tried to sneak in and find out how Graywing was doing, and if Graywing was all right, she'd know Catcher was there, and then there'd be awkward explanations.

Poor excuse, but better than none.

Catcher heard a splopping sound coming from an inner room. She went in and saw that, even though it was higher than her main chamber, the floor was muddy, and there was a trickle of water running across it. Even as she watched, a crack formed in the floor and broadened, and the near wall, from which the water was coming, groaned.

She was suddenly frightened. She backed out of the room and stepped down into water that hadn't there just a moment before. She turned around in surprise, to inspect the chamber, and heard part of a wall collapse where she had just been.

There was a sticky kind of feeling to the whole place, all the walls looked wrong, bits of clay fell down on her head. She hurried toward the entrance as part of the ceiling behind her collapsed and splashed her with muddy water.

From inside now came a flow of water, pouring down toward her entrance. She slipped in the sudden rush and fell, and one wall beside her slumped down, half covering her in mud. She could easily be buried alive.

She forced herself to her feet, and went as quickly as she could the rest of the way to the entrance, just as more roof fell in behind her, layer upon layer. As she reached the entrance the whole den seemed to cave in, and a wave of muddy water washed her out the door.

She floundered around for a moment, then regained her feet and stood, nearly waist deep in water, and looked back at her den. From the outside it looked the same, except for the water coming out. Inside there was water and mud everywhere, but there not as much roof had fallen as she had thought.

Then she heard a call, from Dreamsnake's den, a frightened call that was suddenly cut off. She hurried to her daughter's den as quickly as she could, and when she stepped inside she saw that it was much the same there as at her own home.

"Dreamsnake?" she called. But the response was muffled.

Catcher's mind was paralyzed with thoughts of Dreamsnake being buried under tons of mud and clay, but that did not slow her as she plunged into the mess, and dug frantically around in the direction from which she had heard the sound. It was not long at all before she found where part of a wall and ceiling had slid down, covering a doorway. The mud was loose, and so wet that it was easy to dig the doorway out again, especially when one was as physically charged up as Catcher was. She could hear Dreamsnake digging from the other side, and a moment later they broke through the barrier. Catcher grabbed hold of Dreamsnake's hand and dragged her through the hole, then hurried her outside.

They were both covered with mud, and the shallow lake outside the door was relatively clean compared to what was pouring out through Dreamsnake's entrance. They hugged each other with relief, and then set about checking to make sure that nobody else was trapped. They even called in to Graywing, but she called back that she was fine, and so they left her alone.

Which was just what Graywing wanted. She had to assume that her daughter and granddaughter had had a reason for disturbing her. Maybe it had something to do with that flood. It had been raining rather a lot lately. She could remember other times, some of them very long ago indeed, when it had rained like this. If she thought about it, the images came very clear. As to what yesterday, she wasn't so sure. She had lost track of how long she had been here, snug in her nest. She still had plenty of water, wasn't at all hungry, and her thoughts were all the company she needed. The oil for her lamp was running a bit low, but that hardly mattered, she lay with her eyes closed much of the time anyway.

There was just a bit of light coming in from the room beyond her chamber, which meant it was still day outside — or another day perhaps. That was reassuring, in a way, though she didn't know why. She wasn't completely cut off from the outside world, though she had shut it out.

She drew her attention in again, and lost track of the time. The thoughts that had been flickering around the edges of her mind for the last few days had at last come clear a little while ago. It was the High Ones she had been trying to think about, she didn't know why. All she knew about High Ones were tales she had heard from the elders when she had been a child, tales she had told herself many times to cublings in their turn. If she thought about it now — and she did, oh, yes she did — she realized that the stories she had told most recently were not at all the same as the ones she had heard first. She had thought they had been the same, but they had changed over the years, with other people's tellings, with her 'improvements.' The old stories, how close to the truth were they, if they, too, had evolved with time? What were the High Ones really like? Had there ever been any High Ones at all?

Of course, there had to have been, or people to whom the elves had given that name, their ancestors before the time of memory. No creature came fully developed from nothing, every species had forebears. Her own stories had made the High Ones seem more wonderful than those she had heard, so maybe the people whom the stories had been about had, in fact, not been anything special at all, had just happened to be alive when models were needed.

Or maybe not. She didn't know. All she knew was that it was the High Ones who had been trying to get into her thoughts for some time now, and she could feel them, now that she had identified them, just there, just behind her sight, just beyond her perception …

Her imagination, of course. She was dying, and not suddenly, not by surprise, not in pain, but slowly, with full awareness, and it was special. Her imagination was providing her with images, telling her new stories, to help her during these last days and hours. Of course, that was all it was, nothing more.

Except that death was real, and the High Ones were dead, and wherever their minds had gone, her mind would go there too. And who was she to say that there wasn't some truth to the old tales?

Her thoughts took her on in this way for a long time. She saw, but did not notice, that the light outside her door was dimming, her den growing darker, as afternoon faded into evening. She did not even pay attention when her lamp at last ran dry, and the tiny red and yellow flame burned out. Not until sometime later when she thought that, in darkness as complete and uniform as this, there should be no shadows.

But there were, and their presence roused her from her reverie, and she tried to see them more clearly, but it was, indeed, awfully dark in here, even for elf eyes.

But where was the source of light? Nowhere that she could see. And what was casting the shadows? There, by the door, in her chamber, were several figures, like elves. Had Catcher come to check on her? No, that wasn't it. What if, she thought, it were the High Ones, come to take her away?

If she looked at the shadows in a certain way, she could almost see what made them, and could pretend that they were indeed High Ones. As she built the images in her mind, at first they looked like this, but no, that wasn't right, and obligingly they began to look like that, and then, though it was no thought of her own, they began to look like something else, taller than elves, not as slender but not as strong either. She wished she could make out their faces. She couldn't even tell how many there were.

For a while, trying to see the High Ones was a game, but it stopped being that when it seemed that they were really there. She could not see them clearly, but she couldn't make them go away by just thinking about it. Indeed, they no longer just stood by her door, some of them now sat on the edges of her nest, or stood against the inner walls, and they all were watching her, though she still could not see their faces.

Had her imagination turned into madness? She did not feel sick. How had they gotten here? That didn't seem to matter, all the High Ones were dead, after all, and the dead could go where they wished.

And then it was as if her father were there with them. She could see him so clearly. He introduced the High Ones to her, one by one. They were the parents of the parents of his parents. That wasn't that many generations back. Her own life covered more changes than that.

That's exactly right, her father said. You have done much, it's time for you to go with them now.

Graywing thought she should feel sad about this, but she didn't.

She had seen no source of light before, but there was light now, coming from somewhere, in a direction she couldn't define, but that seemed to be behind her. She turned and there was a passage, opening in the wall at her back, where none had been before.

The image of her father faded, along with that of his parents, and theirs, until only the High Ones were left, a group of people, tall and fair who somehow, without any change in her age, made her seem like a child, so mature were they. They stood in the entrance to the passage, and behind them, in the light, she could see what looked like wonderful caves — or maybe they were trees in a forest — or mountains, they were mountains and valleys ... she couldn't tell, she just knew that, whatever this place was, it was their home — and hers too, now.

Yes, she thought, her home too.

She sat up straight. She felt good, healthy, happy. She stood, and felt strong, rested, content. The bright light of her tomorrow opened before her, and she stepped into it, and followed the High Ones home.

Stringsong was more aware of the passing of that afternoon than Graywing had been, though in a way his mind was more in a turmoil, and his thoughts more distracting. He sat, well back in his den and out of sight, but within view of the entrance, from which he'd withdrawn the curtain, so he could see if anybody passed, anybody with whom he might wish to speak.

People did not pass often. There weren't many elves here, after all, and the water outside was still very deep. Not once did he feel the urge to call out, though he kept watch. What was he waiting for, what did he want?

As the afternoon wore on there was more than the usual amount of activity outside. He could hear voices and splashing, and at the same time the noise of the rush of water and rumble of rocks faded away. The rain was diminishing, too, and as afternoon faded into dusk, it almost stopped.

The worst of the flood seemed to be over, though it would take a long time for the land to recover. Water like that moved a lot of soil, tore up bushes, uprooted trees. Animals that depended on undergrowth for food and shelter would suffer most of all. Those that lived in the ground would be flooded out, drowned, or silted up. It was autumn, and winter was coming on, and it would be a hungry time for everybody. The elves would have to travel far to find food.

But they would survive, as they had before, and they wouldn't have to find a new home. It might be a lean winter, but it was The Way. The weak would fail, the strongest carry on. Of course, a flood like this took many that were strong otherwise. But those who were left were stronger still.

He couldn't help but be aware of the subtle optimism of his thoughts. As the gentle though devastating weather outside improved, so did his state of mind. Had he nearly succumbed to the flood, too, in his own way?

Silverknife had seemed such a promise of greatness. Yet she had failed to observe a treacherous terrain, had failed to react quickly enough to the first signs of danger, and had died. In spite of what had seemed to be strength, there was a hidden and fatal weakness. Had there been no storm, she might not have been tested. What if she had lived, and become chieftess, and then found her flaw exposed when it was not just her life but the life of the holt that was at stake? Had she lived, such a thing might never have happened. The only truth was that, being tested, she had failed.

Her death was tragic, there was no denying that, unlike Greentwig's death. That poor child. He had been a burden on the holt for his entire life, and had never truly become an adult until his death. It had taken his testing to discover the great strength that had been hidden within him. All had regretted his passing. How much more would they regret Silverknife's? But after they were dead, did it matter?

Whiteraven had died while Silverknife was still a child. Stringsong knew, now, that he had never come to terms with that. He had missed her so badly that, even when Silverknife had become an adult, they had continued to share the same den. She should have gone off and dug a home for herself long ago.

He had to live without her now. And as he thought that, he realized that he meant Whiteraven, not Silverknife. He'd carried grief for his lifemate all these years without knowing it. It should have passed as it had for his father, and his mother.

It was getting dark outside. A flood washes away bad as well as good, and brings in new. Stringsong should have given up Whiteraven on her death, and he was sorry that it took Silverknife's death to make him realize that. Such a hard lesson to learn.

Now was the time to let them both go. The best die, and the worst, and those who live must go on, so that others might live too. That was The Way.

Outside, from somewhere, he could hear voices — Hornbird and Puckernut, splashing around, checking out other dens. He got to his feet and went out into the early night. It was already quite dark, though there was just a hint of color to the west, signifying that the clouds were beginning to break up at last.

He listened for voices. Hornbird and Puckernut were over at Suretrail's den, and he went there to join them. "How bad is it?" he called out.

"Not as bad as it might be," Hornbird answered from inside.

"Need any help?"

"Not much to do," Puckernut said as he and Hornbird came out. "Catcher's the one who needs help, and Dreamsnake. Their dens caved in earlier this afternoon."

"Let's go give them a hand," Stringsong said.

The next morning there was an actual sunrise. Hornbird was the first one up to see it, and she also noticed that the water level had begun to fall, though it still lapped the bottom of the cliff.

Which was a mess, with piles of mud and clay and rocks at its base where the face had fallen in. Fortunately none of the dens had been exposed.

Out in the common yard, or where it would be when the water went away, were drifts of gravel and mud, broken branches and torn up bushes, bobbing logs, and boulders that must have come a long way. It was time to start clearing up.

Soon other diehards began to come out of their holes. Catcher and Dreamsnake had spent the night with Puckernut, and were eager to start cleaning out their dens. Fernhare and Stringsong got to work near the base of the cliff, while Puckernut and Hornbird worked further away, taking advantage of the buoyancy of the water to move some of the larger boulders into slightly more suitable places. When the ground finally dried out, it was going to look very strange indeed.

A little later Fangslayer, Deerstorm, and Ebony came back to the holt. Their den had nearly filled up with water, but at least the roof had remained intact. It was going to be a long time before they could sleep dry again. Puckernut showed off what he had done with his own den, and Deerstorm thought it an excellent idea, so they got to work at once, raising the floor by raising the ceiling.

One by one the other elves returned, some of them bringing back their belongings, others leaving them at the camp until their dens were dry. Even Rainbow, Rillwalker, Two-Wolves, and Silvercub got word of the passing of the flood, and decided to come back after all.

The water continued to recede, and by night Stringsong could walk the whole length of the cliff without getting his feet wet. He got his feet plenty muddy, of course. He had been out and about the whole day, still a bit reserved, a bit tender, but he was on the mend, and everybody was glad to see it.

But even Stringsong's recovery couldn't alleviate Catcher's fears. She kept her worries to herself until the evening meal, and then she had to let others know how she felt. It had been two nights ago that she had last seen Graywing, and she was afraid that her mother was dead.

The others agreed that, in spite of Graywing's expressed wishes, they should go find out if she was okay. They all went to her den, and Catcher called in to her. There was no answer.

Catcher was afraid to go inside, afraid of what she might find. The worst would be if her mother had been very ill, or in pain, and had suffered alone. Or maybe her roof had fallen in and she was trapped. The thought made Catcher feel guilty, for not having intruded in spite of Graywing's wishes.

So, as she hesitated at the uncurtained entrance, Dreamsnake came up and put her arm around her shoulder. "Would you like me to go in," she asked.

"Yes, please," Catcher whispered.

Dreamsnake went into the darkness of the familiar den, and felt it somehow strange. Graywing was her grandmother, and more than eight times an eight of eights of years older than she, but Dreamsnake felt as though she were the parent now. She was the child-tender, after all, with only two children of her own, but mother to every child born. Graywing had become a child, and even Catcher seemed a child too, now. Dreamsnake was the adult, it was up to her to do the hard thing and be brave.

Though she had no light, she knew where Graywing's nest was, and had no difficulty finding her way. Much to her surprise, Brownsides, Graywing's wolf, was lying in the doorway to the inner chamber. Brownsides raised his head as Dreamsnake neared, whined softly, then put his head back down again.

Dreamsnake didn't need to go any further, but she did. Carefully, gently, with soft words and a few soft touches, she stepped over the wolf and into Graywing's nest. Only the faintest of light found its way in from the outer door, but it was enough for her to see the pile of furs. She dropped down on her knees at the edge of the nest, and felt out with her hands. There was Graywing, cold. A faint scent of death came to Dreamsnake's nostrils, she'd not noticed it before, not wanted to though she had known it would be there.

"Mother," she called over her shoulder. "Bring a light in here."

Catcher understood, from the term, the tone of voice, what she was going to see, not suffering, not entrapment, just death. Someone — she forgot who — handed her a lamp, already lit, as if they had anticipated its need. She went into Graywing's den and to her nesting place. Brownsides whimpered when he saw her. It would be harder on him than on her.

The two elves grieved their ancestor for a moment, and then they carried her outside to the others. Hornbird came up and touched Graywing's face. "I am the oldest now," she said.

"It is The Way," Stringsong said. "Death for the young, death for the old, and life goes on."

First Born

It was that time of year when the sun was still hot but the air, the wind especially, was decidedly chilly so that, depending on where you were and what you were doing, you could be both warm and cool at the same time. That was the way Freefoot felt now, both inside and out.

He stood, alone, on the prairie far north of the holt, on a low rise of ground barely three times as tall as an elf, but broad, and so gentle in slope that, had he not known it was there, he would not have noticed its ascent as he walked to the top. It was the only undulation of its size in all the vast green and gold grassland, as far as he could see in any direction. And the prairie was so flat that, even from this minute elevation, he could see very far indeed.

Away to the south and somewhat east were the silhouetted figures of two wolfriders, their bodies up to their chests concealed by the ripening grasses, their wolf mounts completely hidden. The sun would march two, maybe three handspans across the sky before they came to where Freefoot was. It was enough time. Beside him, his wolf Shag settled down to doze.

The crest of the low rise was marked not so much by a change in slope as by a change in the texture of the ground. Elsewhere on the prairie the soil between the roots of the grasses was smooth and fine, thickly covered with the thatch of dead grass from countless seasons gone. Here there was gravel — bits of white quartz, gray flint, even some redstone and black slate. Most of it was small, the size of Freefoot's thumb, but occasional pieces were larger, some as big as his two fists pressed together. Many of these larger pieces had, ages ago, been brought together in a long, low, narrow pile in the middle of the area. Freefoot glanced at the pile, then up and away, across the prairie toward the west.

The sun, still rising behind him, warmed his back, the back of his head and arms, his neck. A soft but steady wind from the north blew cold across his face, his chest, through his hair. Thus it was, here, at this time of year, as it had been the few times he had been here before.

Away in the west he could see shadows moving across the prairie, going against the wind. There were no clouds in the sky, the darkness on the long grass was a herd of antelope, the kind with horns like long, curved bows, to judge by their movements. The prong-horns did not travel in so great a number, and the heavier hump-shoulders stayed close together and did not scatter around the edges as this herd was doing.

Freefoot had seen several such herds, and herds of other antelopes, during the two and a half days he'd traveled since leaving the forest, as well as many solitary animals or smaller groups. Indeed, he had feasted this morning on a striped long-leg which he and Shag had brought down just at sun-up. It was a fat year, the first such in many. It made him sad to think that he and his people were going to have to leave it behind.

He could smell other meat on the wind which came down from the cold-lands to the north. With no trees, no hills to disturb the breeze, a good scent could travel farther than the eye could see. The scents were mixed, of course, and thinned by the smell of grasses, a stream too far away to be seen, and all the expanse of air, but among the scents Freefoot could detect the peculiar pungency of a nosehorn, a bit of carrion, and the musky aroma of a long-tooth cat.

Rich hunting now, after four or five eights of seasons of poor fare. It had been a longer lean time than usual, and the returning bounty promised to be greater than usual too, but Freefoot and his people could not stay to enjoy it. Humans were too close, too many in number, too determined to take the land. Freefoot would have to lead his people away, south, deeper into the forest. He hoped that the hunting there would be as good as it was here.

He had hoped, nearly a seven of eights of years ago, when the humans had first come, that they would move on, or that they could be driven away, or would not pose the same threat they had in his mother's time. But that had been just wishful thinking. The wolfriders had been hated and feared by the humans from the start. Though humans lived only a few seasons, five or six of eights, little more than some animals, they had long memories, and told stories, and in this way remembered the time when their ancestors had known elves, and so attacked the wolfriders whenever they saw them. The wolfriders had had to go back to hunting at dusk and dawn, even at night, which was not the way of wolves. They'd had to watch, and move, and even abandon their holt in Halfhill when it was found by a human hunting party. The elves had lived there in peace for almost seven hundred years. It hurt them now, especially the elves who had been among the first born there, to have to move away.

Freefoot looked back to the east. The sun was still rising, though near the top of its climb, and the rippling of the grasses in the north wind shimmered like water. The sun felt good on his face, though it made him squint. At his feet, Shag moaned. Freefoot looked down at his wolf-friend, who stretched his legs into a more comfortable position. His head lay just a hand's breadth from the long, low, narrow pile of rocks.

The mound had been there a long time. The gaps and crevices between the lumps of quartz and flint and slate and redstone had been partially filled in by windblown dust, and even a few grass blades now grew among the rocks. The grass was less dense a cover on the rest of the rise anyway, where the gravel and wind-hardened soil provided little purchase for the roots. The mound of rocks was all but bare.

A shadow passed across the mound, and Freefoot looked up to see one of the great prairie hawks banking high overhead. It must have seen Shag lying there, and thought the wolf dead and hence an easy meal, in spite of the elf's presence. Freefoot spoke to Shag, who raised his head. Above, black and white and russet against the blue sky, the hawk wheeled again. It had seen Shag's movement and was no longer interested. A living antelope, one of the half-grown, would be easier prey. The bird soared off, in

no great hurry for its lunch. Shag put his head down again and
went back to sleep.

Freefoot turned back to the south. He was surprised to see
how much closer the two wolfriders had come. Now, with the
sun higher in the sky, they were no longer silhouettes, but were
still too far away for him to make out their features. Not that he
had any need to.

The situation had been reversed the last time he had been
out there to the rise. That had been a long time ago, though the
memory of the visit was clear and sharp in his mind — if he
chose to remember. He had not thought about those events very
often during the last two hundred years or so, and when the
memories had intruded, he had carefully put them out of his
mind. Except when he had decided that Starflower, his lifemate,
and their two older sons, Fangslayer and Longoak, should know.
He had told that story just one time. It had been painful. It was
painful to think about now. But then, that was why he had come
back here, to think about it, to remember. With the coming of
the humans, the elves would move away, and he might never see
this place again.

Once again he slowly scanned the horizon, pausing at each
shadow, each hint of movement, each sign of life. From here the
world looked so big. In the forest, one could never see the horizon, even if one climbed a tree as high as one dared before the
branches gave way. Here, with nothing to impede the view, the
edge of the world was all too apparent.

It was one of the things that drew Freefoot out here, rather
than down deeper into the woods. Of course, south of the holt
one could climb high ridges, higher plateaus, and far away
many eights of days even mountains. From those elevations,
clear of the horizon-concealing trees, one could see much of the
world indeed. But it was not the same as here on the prairie.

Besides, there were other reasons.

The last time he had been here it had been another who
had stood on the rise, watching, and it had been Freefoot who
rode his wolf out of the south.

———————

He and — Bent-Tail it had been then — had left the woods two days before, and on the morning of the third day had risen early, caught one of the tiny springer antelopes, and continued northward. He was traveling alone, except for his wolf-friend, as he liked to do when he could. The burdens of being chief, even in a peaceful and eventless time such as his, wore him down, tired him out, made him eager to get away, to wander aimlessly in the way that had given him his name.

As he rode northward the small rise became visible in the distance, an imperceptible elevation on the otherwise perfectly flat horizon. The prairie was huge, and in his various wanderings Freefoot had by no means seen all of it, but such irregularities as this were rare, and Freefoot had a memory of once having seen one like it, a long time ago. He rode toward it, there being no reason why he should not. After all, he had nothing better to do.

Around him the tall grass rustled gently. The wind blew steadily down out of the north, bringing with it scents of distant antelope herds, a stinker, and — an elf? yes, at least one. And with it, the pungent tang of the rare prairie goat.

How far away was the source of the scent? He looked straight into the wind, though of course it shifted a bit from moment to moment, so its present direction could give him only an indication of its origin. Still, it was the rise from which the scent seemed to be coming. Bent-Tail could smell it too. He'd had experience with prairie goats, and though still hungry after their meager breakfast, was not eager to challenge the true master of the grasslands.

Freefoot kept his eyes on the rise as he rode toward it. The scent got gradually stronger as he neared, though sometimes it vanished for long moments as the wind shifted slightly. It was not a scent he recognized — any of his own people he would have known by their smell even from this distance — so he guessed the elf to be one of that small band which wandered the grasslands far to the north of the holt. That being the case, he had to assume that whoever was up there was probably watching, advantaged by even that little elevation, concealed by the grasses turning golden with the coming of winter.

Freefoot had met strange elves three times before in his life, and each time it had been difficult. Two of those times it had been prairie elves, and the third time it had been a forest elf, but one who was not a wolfrider and who had no wolf blood. Those experiences had been frightening, and exciting, and not without danger. He had been with other wolfriders each of those three times, but Freefoot was alone now, and thought he would be wise to be cautious.

Even so, he did not slow or change his course and, some while later he heard a tiny sound coming from the now not so distant rise. Unless there were antelope near, there were few things on the prairie that could make noise, except for the wind, which susurrated through the grass with a constancy like, though a sound different from, the noise that a quiet stream makes. Freefoot had seen no signs of antelope in this direction, and such scents of them that came to him were from a long way off, so the noise had to have been made by the goat, no the as yet unseen elf. Prairie goats were a little taller than wolves, so this animal's head would be just below the tops of the grasses at this season. Elsewhere on the prairie their hooves would make no sound on the soil and grass-thatch, but there would be rocks on the rise, resistant of the relentless weathering processes that turned the prairie flat, and what Freefoot had heard was the clunk of a hoof striking stone.

The unseen elf must have realized that Freefoot could hear even that small sound, because a moment later he stood up, just head and shoulders above the grass, staring straight in his direction. Freefoot stopped then, and stared back. The other elf was still too far away for him to make out his features, but Freefoot did not have to see the other's face to know that he was one of the prairie folk. On his head he wore a helmet decorated with prong-horns — something no forest elf would have done, for fear of it getting caught in tree branches or undergrowth.

Neither elf raised a hand, neither elf called out and, after a moment, Freefoot started forward again. Though the smell of goat

got stronger, Bent-Tail did not become excited. Freefoot kept his
eyes on the other elf's face, and though he felt some apprehension,
he kept his outward self calm. He had not seen this elf before, but
he knew his people, and knew that there was no danger — unless
the descendants of banished Two-Spear and his few companions
had changed a lot, as they well could have.

And they had, if this elf was any example. Though partially
of wolfrider blood, all traces of wolf and forest life were long
gone. Instead of a jacket he wore a loose cloak of leather made
soft by chewing. The elf's skin, where it was exposed on chest,
face, and arms, was burned a dark tan by exposure to the sun,
instead of being the ivory of a shadowed forest dweller. His
posture and demeanor were different too, upright and defiant,
without the habit of stealth. His face, as Freefoot drew near
enough to see it, was expressionless, though there was much
behind the eyes that was not being let out. These elves had
indeed changed, and though they were Freefoot's cousins not
that many times removed, they were as different from the forest
dwellers as elves still with wolf blood could be.

Freefoot rode, relaxed in spite of his inner tension, casual
about his glances though he watched the other almost
constantly, with only an occasional sweeping search of the
horizon, first one side, then the other. The other elf stood mo-
tionless, steady, and did not once look away. Even in this small
way they showed their differences.

At last the ground began to rise under Bent-Tail's paws. As
the wolf brought his rider to the top of the rise, Freefoot was
able to see, a few paces behind the other elf, the prairie goat that
served him as his steed.

It was an eminently suitable animal for an elf to ride. It was
a little taller at the shoulder than a wolf, but weighed quite a bit
more, with a deep chest and broad shoulders. Its legs were
sturdy, ending in sharp, cloven hooves. Prairie goats had the
habit, if they knocked an adversary down, of rearing back on
their hind legs, then jumping forward to land with all their
weight concentrated on the two front hooves, held closely to-

gether. The blow was enough to crush a rib-cage, break a spine, or crack a skull.

But a goat's primary attack and defense were its head and horns, the great ribbed horns that curved up and back and out from above its eyes and that, in this case, spiraled full around three times, extending out to the sides a forearm's length from its head. The thickest part of the horns projected forward from the top of the goat's head, and it was with this double curve that the goat, springing forward on strong hind legs, butted its rivals, opponents, and enemies. If pressed closely, it could swing its head from side to side on its strong neck, ripping and tearing with the sharp points of its horns. Faced with a predator, it did not just butt, but gored, slashed, feinted, a violent and furious attack that only a swordfoot or a huge and solitary long-tooth cat could overcome. Even the huge hump-shoulders stayed well clear of a prairie goat.

Bent-Tail stood and watched the goat warily. The goat, head partly lowered, hind legs flexed, watched the wolf in turn. And as warily, Freefoot and the stranger elf watched each other.

They were a different people now, even more than they had been the other times that Freefoot had met them. Life on the prairie posed different threats and problems, required different solutions, exacted a different price in order to survive. In manner, dress, expectations, these two elves were truly strangers, alien to each other. And yet they were kin, both with wolf blood, though the prairie elves had less and rode different mounts now.

Freefoot was not afraid of this elf, younger than he by quite a bit if he could judge. But he was cautious. Freefoot had no taste for fighting, for confrontation, for a contest of wills. He preferred to let his people do what they wanted, in their own way, and those times when he had to exercise his authority as chief were never pleasant for him. So he sat now, watching the other, knowing that the prairie elves were proud, and cautious too, and unfamiliar with his ways, and suspected that this other might in fact be a bit afraid of him, though his deeply tanned face showed no expression. After all, in spite of Freefoot's preferences, he was in many ways very much like his mount, and so might be perceived as a predator.

The moment of mutual regard was not as long as it seemed, but it was long enough. Freefoot, still firmly gripping the thick fur of Bent-Tail's neck with both hands, swung his leg back and over the wolf's hindquarters and dismounted. Bent-Tail, responding to Freefoot's silent sending, sat, then crouched down on the gravelly soil. As he did so, the goat behind the other elf visibly relaxed.

"Good hunting," Freefoot said.

"Good hunting to you," the other answered. "What brings a wolfrider so far out into the tall grass?"

"Nothing important," Freefoot said. "I just wanted to get away from my cares for a while. I like to wander alone when I have the chance."

"As do I," the other said, "though I am not able to do so often."

"This is a most unusual spot," Freefoot said, seeking some topic on which they could converse.

"It is," the other answered. "There is none like it else except where the edge of the prairie can be seen."

It was not a wolfrider's habit to stare too long into another's eyes, and Freefoot felt uncomfortable under the stranger's unbroken gaze. He did not wish to challenge this other, so he glanced around at the prairie, vastly more of which was visible from even this small rise. When he looked back the stranger was still looking at him. The goat, too, had not moved, its large brown eyes staring fixedly at Bent-Tail. This steady gaze was just their habit, and not, as it would have been among wolves, a sign of aggression. And it would appear that the stranger did not take Freefoot's wandering eyes as a sign of cowardice. He had recognized Freefoot as a wolfrider, not just riding a wolf by chance, and so must have met wolfriders or heard of them before. Freefoot thought of Stride, who also liked to get away, alone by herself from time to time, and whom he frequently envied because she was far more free than he to be able to do so. Perhaps she had met this elf or some of his people some time in the past.

Down on the flat of the prairie, even from wolfback, it was not possible to see far when the grass was as tall as it was now. But from the rise the horizon was very far away, and Freefoot could see, toward the east, a disturbance in the grass that he was sure was made by a small herd of antelope, perhaps the small but solid hook-horns. The stranger noted Freefoot's attention, and turned to look the same way.

"Shall we hunt together?" Freefoot asked.

"Yes," the other said, and went to his mount.

It was an act of friendliness, and a test at the same time. Freefoot climbed up onto Bent-Tail's back, and the two elves rode, side by side, down from the small rise into the thicker grass. For this one hunt they would trust each other, while observing each other, to see what each was made of, how they worked, whether they could cooperate, who would dominate and who follow. When the hunt was over they would have a better idea of who they were, and how they would relate to each other. If all went well, they would share mutual respect. But if either showed great weakness, or cowardice, or ignorance, then the other would establish dominance at once, and there could be no friendship. This was as true of goatrider as of wolfrider.

Freefoot could no longer see where the hook-horns were from the bottom of the gentle slope, but the goatrider, far more familiar with the prairie, seemed to know his way, so for the moment Freefoot let him have his lead. They did not speak as they rode at an easy canter, but Freefoot watched the goatrider, and the goatrider watched him.

Freefoot had to trust that the other knew where they were going, though he thought the antelopes had been more to the east and not so much to the south. As it turned out the goatrider was circling around so as to come at the antelopes from down-wind. A wolfrider would have done the same, but in a different fashion.

The antelopes were indeed hook-horns, bodies thick, legs sturdy, their heavy heads just below the top of the waving grass.

Hook-horns moved in small herds of two or three of eights, with one dominant male, several non-breeding or off-males, four to eight females, and as many young and yearlings as might be. The best of these to take would be one of the off-males, an animal least likely to be missed by the rest of the herd.

Freefoot and the stranger slowed their mounts as they approached, still some hundreds of paces away, and looked over the animals upwind of them. There were three off-males to choose from. One was very large, and would most likely take over leadership of the herd when the current bull grew too old or lost a fight. Another was rather small, not much more than a yearling. The third was of middle size, a bit larger than a cow, and not likely ever to breed. Freefoot and the other elf looked at each other without speaking, saw that they agreed on their prey and, at the goatrider's signal, started their attack.

The two elves separated as they urged their mounts into a run, so that when the herd finally noticed them and started to flee, they came at the animals as much from the sides as from the rear, the middle-sized off-male that was their target at the center of their charge. A wolf can run fast, though burdened as Bent-Tail was he was hard pressed to gain on the antelopes, and the prairie goat, too, did little more than keep up, and hook-horns, though slow to start and slow to gain speed, did indeed gain speed, and gradually went faster and faster until it would appear that there would be no chance for the two elves to catch even the slowest of them.

But though Freefoot's favorite weapon was an ax, he also carried a bow, and even as he pursued his quarry, he strung it and fitted an arrow to it. When the hook-horn began to pull away from him, he drew his bow, but movement off to one side made him hesitate. He looked and saw the goatrider, swinging something around and around his head, like stones tied to the end of a long cord. This was something new, and Freefoot held his fire to see just what this strange weapon could do.

The goatrider swung the weighted cord around and around until their chosen prey chanced to lurch aside and was for a moment separated from the nearest of the rest of the herd.

Then the goatrider let loose his weapon, which spun through the air in a flat arc toward the hook-horn's legs. When it hit, the thongs wrapped around the animal's legs, drawn tight by the weighted ends, and the hook-horn crashed to the ground.

The antelope's halt was so sudden that Freefoot and the other elf were past it before they could slow their mounts. The other antelopes sped on their way, unheeded. The goatrider looked at Freefoot, expression on his face for the first time, a grin of triumph. Freefoot grinned back and gave a short, barking howl.

Which perhaps was a mistake, because either the sound, like that of a wolf, or the moment's pause, gave the downed hook-horn a chance to recover. It leaped, struggling, to its feet, disentangling itself from the weighted cord as it did so, and started to run away. And Freefoot and the other elf were at a dead stop. By the time they got up to speed, even though it would take only moments, the hook-horn would have had a chance to regain its own speed, and they would never catch it.

So now it was Freefoot's turn. Even as he observed what was happening, he urged Bent-Tail, not directly after the hook-horn but in an angle. He drew his bow, and as the angle between him and the antelope presented the animal's side, let off one arrow. It sang through the air, aimed just beyond the antelope's nose, and the hook-horn ran into it so that it penetrated just below and behind the shoulder. It ran five or six paces more, and then crashed to the ground. Freefoot glanced at the goatrider long enough to note the other elf's look of admiration, then rode Bent-Tail to the fallen prey.

The two elves arrived at the dead animal at the same time and dismounted. They looked at each other with mutual respect and admiration. "Let me retrieve my tangler," the goatrider said, and turned to walk back to the place where the hook-horn had first fallen. Freefoot knelt and carefully drew his arrow from the antelope's body. The flint head would have to be retied, but the arrow was otherwise sound. He put it away in the quiver at his belt, and waited for the goatrider to return.

They butchered the animal there, Freefoot using his flint knife, the goatrider using a strange knife, as long as his forearm, made from sharpened antelope horn, which every now and then he stroked with a piece of sandstone. This horn knife, when freshly honed, was almost as sharp as flint, but it lost its edge quickly. The advantage was that it had a cutting edge as long as itself, not just a few finger-widths as with a flint knife.

When they were through, Freefoot gave Bent-Tail part of the liver, a kidney, the heart, and a slab of leg-meat. The goatrider, who had been ready to pack the meat up, stopped and waited with Freefoot until the wolf was finished with this small reward. The goat, meanwhile, was munching grass. When Bent-Tail was done they remounted their animals, carrying half the hook-horn each and, with unspoken consent, rode back to the rise.

They got to the middle of the highest part of the ground and cleared away the rocks and sat down to eat. But this time it was Freefoot's turn to wait. The goatrider collected dead grass, dried clumps of grass roots, and still-standing near-hay. With a bit of flint and a piece of shiny yellowish stone, the like of which Freefoot had never seen before, he struck a spark and started a small fire. He gestured to Freefoot to select his meat and, as Freefoot did so, built his fire larger. Then he took several slender sticks, partly darkened by fire but carefully cleaned of bark, from a bundle at his back, under his cloak. He cut some chunks of meat for himself, skewered these on the sticks, then set them over the fire. He added more dried roots and the half-golden hay to the fire, so that it burned hot and smoky.

Freefoot watched with amazement. "Did you learn this from humans?" he asked.

"No," the goatrider said. "Do humans smoke their food too?"

"They call it cooking," Freefoot said, "though I've never seen it done. I haven't seen a human in five hundred seasons or so."

"I've never seen one," the other said, "though I've heard of them from the elders." He turned his meat, so that the bloody raw upper sides could be browned by the smoke and flames, which he had to continually attend.

After a bit the meat was burned to his satisfaction, and he took the skewers from the fire which he now let dwindle down to a few coals and ashes. Then as he bit gingerly at the hot meat, Freefoot gnawed hungrily on his own. Each of them watched the other eating, half fascinated, half disgusted, until they both, and Bent-Tail too, whom Freefoot fed some more, were satisfied.

By this time the sun had started its fall down the far side of the sky. Freefoot and his companion were tired, satiated, and beginning to feel comfortable with each other. As it was now becoming a little chilly, the goatrider rebuilt the fire with more roots and twisted grasses. Then he looked up at Freefoot and said, "My name is Hawkcatcher. I am called this because I can take a hawk from the sky, with a tangler such as this," he touched the now coiled, weighted cords at his waist, "though one more lightly made."

"I'm pleased to meet you," Freefoot said. "My name is Freefoot. My people call me that because I'd rather wander around than be their chief." He smiled as he spoke, but as he spoke he saw Hawkcatcher's face once again become immobile and expressionless. He could not imagine how, but his words had offended the goatrider.

"Tell me," Hawkcatcher said, "are there other wolfriders who bear the same name?"

"No," Freefoot said. Why should his name be so important to this strange elf? For it was that which had made him so suddenly go stiff and formal. "I am the only one."

"Your father, perhaps, or another who no longer lives?"

"No, I am the only one." He watched the other's expressionless face, and for the first time saw that there was something about the shape of the brow, the set of the mouth, that was somehow familiar to him. "I seem to know you," he said. "Are you sure we have not met?"

"We have not," Hawkcatcher said. "I would have remembered it if we had. After all, you are my father."

The wind, at that time of year, blew down steadily from the north, bringing with it the promise of white cold to come. As it blew, it hissed through the tall grass now turning gold with the change of season. Aside from this constant and unchanging susurration, and the single click as the goat shifted a foot and lightly struck a stone, and the sound of Bent-Tail's gentle panting, and the pounding of his own blood in his ears, Freefoot found the whole world to be in utter silence.

"You are Two Shadows' child, then," he said at last. Remarkable, he thought, how loud his voice was in all this emptiness, how swallowed up it was by the grass and the wind and the sky.

"I am," Hawkcatcher said. And now, in the light of the lowering sun, Freefoot could see something of Two Shadows' face in this others', and something of his own as well. And yet Hawkcatcher was so different from Fang-Slayer, Freefoot's eldest son — second eldest, by at least a hundred years — or from Feather, who was still a child. Not only, of course, did Hawkcatcher have a different mother, but his whole life was different, and his way of looking at the world.

"Is your mother well?" Freefoot asked. It had been more than three hundred years since he had seen her — here, he now realized, with a rush of memory that threatened to overcome him, here in this very place. Memories that he had forgotten, pushed aside, hidden away, now came stumbling back.

There had been four of them that time, riding their wolves across the prairie, which stretched as far as they could see in all directions. Freefoot was pleased enough to be away from the holt, little though his responsibilities taxed him, although he rather wished he had been able to come alone. But his companions had insisted that they needed the recreation too, and he had to admit that the hunt had been fun so far.

Beside Freefoot rode Grazer, tallest of elves, on huge Slobber, who was equally large, but was a rather gentle animal for all that. Beyond Grazer rode Sunset, ornamented with brightly colored feathers and beads, her clothing elaborately dyed red and blue and bright yellow. Behind the three rode old Springwillow. She had been Skyfire's friend, and was Freefoot's now, a plain elf and a competent one.

They were hunting antelope, of which there were a wide
variety and a large number out here on the prairie. They had
followed a herd of prong-horns across the long grass, taking the
less fit as opportunity arose, gorging as they went, hunting as
much for sport as for necessity, although they wasted nothing
and took no game in vain. Soon they would tire of this aimless
hunt, but by then they would have identified the big animals
that the herd could best do without, the eldest bucks and does.
When they were ready, they would take out five or six of these
and carry them back to the holt to share with the rest of the
tribe.

At least, that was the plan, and that afternoon seemed like a
good time to put it into action. The herd of antelope, moving
steadily through the tall grass, now turning golden with the
change of seasons, was beginning to get restless. Another kill, or
too hard a push, or too long a pursuit, and they would flee, and
the prong-horns could easily outrun the wolves, burdened as
they were with their elf-friend riders. The sun was hot but the
cool wind blowing down out of the north brought the scent of
long-tooth cats, and that made the antelopes nervous. If the four
wolfriders were going to take their chosen prey — four for the
tribe and one or two for themselves and their wolves to share on
the trip back — they would be wise to do it now.

They studied the movements of the herd as the prong-horns
began to ascend a gentle rise, the only such elevation on the
whole prairie. The slope wasn't very steep and the elves would
not have noticed it if the leading antelopes didn't visibly rise up
above those following. But it was enough of a slope to slow the
prong-horns just a bit, and it gave the wolfriders just the degree
of advantage they wanted. They charged in among them,
taking them by surprise, and so were able to get near to their
chosen prey.

The leading edge of the herd came to the top of the rise
and then suddenly broke to the sides, as if frightened by something they had found on the other side, and started to flee in two
groups, to right and left. The wolfriders were confused and
surprised by this sudden change of motion, but they continued

their attack on the selected antelopes, which were still in the main body of the herd, and still climbing toward the top of the rise. In spite of the gentleness of the slope, the antelopes couldn't get up to full speed, and were further hampered by the milling of their leaders caused by the as yet unseen obstacle, so the elves were easily able to close.

Grazer, with his long lance, charged first and took his chosen antelope just behind the shoulder. It was a clean kill, but as the prong-horn fell, it dragged the point of the lance down with it, and Grazer was forced to let it go lest the shaft break.

Meanwhile Sunset had thrown two darts into the antelope which was her target. These light weapons did not kill it, but made it stumble and turn so that Springwillow, who was riding with her, could finish it with her spear.

Freefoot, a bit apart from the others, had his bow drawn and rode with an extra arrow clenched in his teeth. He shot at his antelope, a good shot that hit the animal well back of the shoulder, but it was not fatal. The prong-horn did not break stride. Freefoot's movements were almost automatic, and without hesitation as he nocked the second arrow, and shot again with a longer lead. This time he hit the prong-horn through the thick part of the neck, which would also have been a non-fatal blow but, combined with the first, was enough to bring the animal down.

Grazer had circled around and recovered his lance and was now racing past Freefoot. There were still two or three antelopes to kill if they wanted this hunt to be successful. Sunset, swinging her throwing ax, was right behind Grazer, but Springwillow had dismounted Snap-Weed, the better to pull her spear from where it had gotten jammed in the spine of the prong-horn.

Freefoot stopped his wolf, Bearbiter, long enough to make sure that his antelope was truly dead, then joined the others just as Springwillow rode past him. He caught up with her quickly, and they came over the top of the rise almost together, and stopped short when they saw what had made the herd act so strangely. On the far side of the rise, riding big-horned goats instead of wolves, were other elves, not of the holt, who were also culling the herd, and who had brought down several of the larger animals. These strangers saw the wolfriders at about the same time, and everything — except the antelopes — came to a sudden halt. Around them the herd of prong-horns scattered. The wolfriders, at the crest of the rise, stared down the gentle slope at the five goatriders who, at the bottom of the slope, stared back.

It was rare to meet strangers of any kind and, except for Springwillow none of Freefoot's companions had had much experience with it. And from the way that the elves on the other side looked up at the wolfriders and fidgeted, it would seem that they were equally inexperienced. They all sat on their mounts for a long time, scattered as they were, while the antelopes ran away and out of sight.

After a bit the five goatriders came together into a group. Two of them were male and three were female, and together they had brought down six prong-horns, which lay in the now-trampled grass nearby.

"What do we do now?" Grazer whispered to Freefoot.

"Maybe we should just back off," Sunset suggested. The goatriders were conferring too.

"Just stand a minute," Freefoot said quietly. Then he slowly walked Bearbiter a little way toward the other group.

With the prong-horns gone, the smell of these goats was now quite pronounced, and all the wolves were a little nervous, and so too were the goats, and all the elves had to work to keep their mounts under control. Freefoot did not go far, but halted Bearbiter just three eights of paces from his companions, and then one of the stranger elves, a tall female with a great mane of golden hair, rode toward him an equal distance and stopped. It was enough to bring them within speaking distance, but just barely.

What does one say to a stranger? Freefoot had never met a strange elf before. Every time he started to speak he thought that the other elf wouldn't understand him and stopped short. Judging by the other's expression, she was having the same difficulty. But at last Freefoot took a deep breath and said loudly, "I hope you have had good hunting."

"We have," the other answered. She glanced around at the antelope bodies lying on the grass. "And yourselves?"

"We have three, on the other side of the rise. We hoped to get two or three more before returning home."

"We cannot carry all we have," the other elf said. "We could let you have one."

"That is very kind of you," Freefoot said. Then he dismounted, and the other elf did the same. The elves behind her hesitated a moment before following suit. Then Freefoot felt a brief, wordless sending from Grazer, and knew that his own companions had gotten off their wolves.

On foot, then, the two hunting parties joined their leaders. The goatriders were all young though mature, slender and darkly tanned. Their clothing, though similar in some ways to that which the wolfriders wore, was distinctly different in other ways, being looser, softer, and, especially when compared with Sunset, far less colorful.

Grazer came up beside Freefoot. He was nervous, had to clear his throat twice, then he said, "Greetings. I am Grazer, the leader of the hunt, and this is my chief, Freefoot."

"Greetings," said the golden haired elf. "I am Goldmane — " she shook her hair — "and leader of my hunt. My chief, Graywolf, could not be with us."

The name of Graywolf was well known to Freefoot and Springwillow, and gave them the knowledge to surmise who these elves must be. "Is Two-Spear no longer your chief then?" Freefoot asked.

"Two-Spear is dead," Goldmane answered, "an eight of eights of years and three ago. How do you know of him?"

"He was once chief of our people," Springwillow explained, "though that was a very long time ago. I knew him then, but I did not know him well."

"Then we are kin," a dark-haired goatrider said, hesitantly, as if she were afraid of how the wolfriders might respond to that.

"If you are of Two-Spear's lineage," Freefoot said, "we are." Two-Spear's departure from the tribe had not been amicable, and Freefoot was somewhat fearful lest the goatriders hate him and his companions for having driven their ancestor away. But even as he thought this he could see that the goatriders were equally apprehensive, and for a moment it seemed as if both sides would be so cautious that nothing further could happen between them.

Then Grazer broke the impasse. "We can find more game to carry back to our holt," he said. "Let's share what meat we have now, and become friends if we can."

Goldmane and another goatrider, a heavily-built male, exchanged glances, then Goldmane said, "We would be honored."

They decided to bring all the game to the center of the rise, and each group went off to recover its own kill. There was some small trouble when first the wolves and goats came together, but this was quickly resolved by the animals themselves, with only a little help from the elves, as both goat and wolf decided that the other was too dangerous to fight and not really a threat and not worth the effort anyway.

There were nine antelopes altogether, more than they could eat, of course, but the elves butchered them all so that they would keep better when both parties, after the feast, went out again to find other herds, so that they could bring sufficient game back to their homes. When the butchery was done the wolves were fed, and the best parts handed out among the elves. There was little conversation while they ate, but as they became satiated they became more sociable.

"Where do you live?" Sunset asked Goldmane.

"Here," Goldmane answered, "in the tall grass."

"Surely there are more than five of you," Grazer said.

"Indeed there are," the stocky elf, Ax-Hand, answered. "Our tribe numbers some three of eights, including kids. How about you?"

"There are five of eight and four of us," Freefoot said. "We live south, in the forest. Where are the rest of your people?"

"North and east of here," the other male, Buckmaster, said. "At least for the most part, at this time of year. We travel the great prairie all year long and, unlike you, have no permanent home."

"How will you find each other," Freefoot asked, "when you want to meet again?"

Two Shadows, a slender and wild-looking female, looked at him, and her expression indicated some confusion. "We always know where we are," she said, "don't you?"

This started a discussion, which took quite some while, made difficult as it was by both caution and unfamiliarity with each other's terms. But at last each group was able to make clear to the other how their respective mental abilities worked.

It turned out that the goatriders could no longer communicate silently as wolfriders did, sending words and thoughts and messages directly from mind to mind, but had instead acquired the ability to always know where others of their kind were, regardless of whatever distance which might separate them. Goldmane and her companions, though they were at the southernmost reach of their hunting area, could "feel" the rest of their people, who were an eight of days ride away to the north and, at this time of year, to the east.

"How many then," Springwillow asked, "of Two-Spear's eight companions still live, besides Graywolf?"

"None besides he," Evensong, the dark-haired goatrider, said, "and no one understands him at all."

"Your ancestors must have been very prolific before they died," Springwillow went on.

"The wolfriders are not alone in the world," Goldmane told her. "Some seasons after leaving the tribe, Two-Spear and his fellow outcasts came on another group of elves, who had wandered down from the far north, and who had no wolf blood in them at all. The two groups joined company, and we have since been joined by a few more elves who came from far to the west, beyond where even wolfriders once lived. Most of our ancestors are now dead, but yes, for a while many kids — or cublings as you would call them — were born, both in recognition and out, especially when the parents were from different tribes. That did not last long, however, and few are born these days, barely enough to make up for those we lose to accident and disease. Our numbers have not changed in many eights of years."

"And yet Graywolf is still your chief," Freefoot said.

"He is," Two Shadows said, "but that is more by courtesy, since he is more wolf than elf in some ways and has no taste for leadership, only dominance. He is far more different from us than you are."

Then the prairie elves told how they had come to ride goats. The wolves that Two-Spear and his fellow outcasts had brought away with them had not prospered on the prairie, and no other wolves had been found to breed with them, and they had died out long since. But the goats were tougher animals than many, and these that the prairie elves rode had been bred up for size, strength, aggression, and ride-ability.

The wolfriders had no concept of breeding animals for desirable features, and it took the prairie elves some time to explain what they meant. The wolfriders didn't like the idea much. The goatriders did this with no other animals, however, and had learned this skill from the relatives of their northern ancestors, who lived in the land of constant snow.

The nomadic life of the goatriders was very strange to Freefoot and his companions, and the wolfriders found the ideas hard to grasp. They, in their turn, told the elves of the prairie something about the holt at Halfhill — which their cousins still knew of, but which was not where they had heard of it being when Two Spear was banished from the tribe — about forests, mountains far to the south, and how this hunt was different from their usual hunts. Freefoot explained how they had come away from the places of men a long time ago and had been free of them ever since. The goatriders, too, had kept clear of men, whom they remembered with great bitterness, as being not only the enemies of their ancestors, but the indirect cause of their banishment.

By now it was getting late in the afternoon. The long conversation at last came to an end. The elves ate some more, and then Ax-Hand, who had been silent most of the time as if trying to work up the courage, finally said what was on his mind. "How is Huntress Skyfire?" he asked.

"She died some two hundred years ago," Freefoot said, "and I became chief in her place. I am her son."

"Are there many who remember Two-Spear?" Ax-Hand asked. "He was my father."

"There are a few," Springwillow said. "I, for one, knew him when I was very young and called Sapling."

"So much has changed," dark Evensong said. "I know these names from stories, though they died before I was born. We are strangers to each other, but we are cousins after all, and we share a common past. We are both a hunting people, but this rise is the only place where we might meet by chance, and so we are not in competition. We might as well be friends."

"Indeed we might," Freefoot said, and all the elves agreed.

They ate more then, and became more relaxed in each other's company, and though both sides remained a bit cautious about the other, they enjoyed being with each other, and decided, as the sun began to go down at the edge of the world, and the sky above became a great cloudless flame, that they would not make two separate camps but spend the night together. The goatriders built a fire, using dry grass, matted thatch, and clumps of thick grass roots which they dug up from the south slope of the rise where the ground was drier. It was a small fire but a welcome one, and more than the wolfriders would have known how to make out here away from the plentiful wood of the forest.

They sat together, and spoke of themselves to their new friends, and after a bit Sunset brought out a bag of dreamberries which she passed around. The goatriders had heard of these, but had never tasted any, they being a fruit of the forest, and found the effects of the berries quite overwhelming. There was an awful lot of giggling and staring into space for a while.

Then the goatriders — those who could still stand — went to their animals and brought back skins of what they called wheatberry wine, made from the fruit of certain of the grasses which grew elsewhere on the prairie. Now it was their turn to laugh as the wolfriders, who were unfamiliar with this form of intoxicant, found it most potent and exhilarating.

Still they were cautious with each other, and though there was much light conversation the two groups of elves each stayed to their side of the fire. The party continued as the two moons rose high in the sky, and when they nearly touched, a glancing kiss, the wolves set up a howl. This surprised and upset the goats, and once again there was some little danger of the animals attacking each other. But the forest elves fed their wolves again, the prairie elves calmed their goats, and now, since all the elves were daypeople after all, they made up their camp for the night.

They were not yet so trusting of each other that they failed to set a watch. Sunset and Buckmaster drew first for each side. They sat more or less together, opposite each other across the tiny bed of coals that was all that was left of the fire, and talked quietly together, as did their reliefs when their turns came.

The night passed uneventfully and the next morning, after a substantial breakfast, they counted up what meat they had left and, given what they would have to eat on the way home, it wasn't enough to bother bringing back.

Both sides agreed that they had to start back home at once, and each invited the other to come with them, at least part way, to share in further hunting. But prairie elf and forest elf alike were far beyond the extreme edges of their normal hunting ranges, and so neither felt they could accept the other's offer, and thus travel even further from their homes. Each group was minded to head back to their own people and catch what they could along the way. And so they agreed, reluctantly, that the best thing to do was part company, with the hope that maybe they or other parties would meet again.

But even as they were saying their goodbyes, Goldmane turned away and looked off into the distance, away to the west.

"We may be able to hunt together after all," she said, and pointed. The others looked too, and sure enough, it was a herd of some kind, hump-shoulders as far as the prairie elves could tell, and they were coming toward the rise.

"There are enough of us," old Springwillow said. The hump-shoulders were huge animals, and the forest elves had hunted them only on occasion, when a herd came far south to within a half a day's ride of the forest.

"Two of them," wild Two Shadows said, "would provide us with plenty of meat for ourselves and our people back home."

The other elves were equally enthusiastic, so they worked out a plan, then mounted their wolves and goats, and set off.

The nine elves split into four groups and circled around to either side of the approaching herd. Tall Grazer was teamed with Goldmane, and Sunset with Buckmaster, while Springwillow rode with stocky Ax-Hand, and Freefoot went with Evensong and Two Shadows.

The hump-shoulders did not pay them much heed — indeed seldom paid anything other than long-teeth much heed — and the hunters had plenty of time to pick out several promising animals. The four elves on one side chose a large young bull, and the five on the other side of the herd selected another which was slightly older and slightly heavier.

The hump-shoulders did not naturally fear elves, were among the few prairie animals that did not fear the goats, and did not know what wolves were, so the two hunting parties were able to maneuver in quite closely to their chosen prey. But both groups of hunters would have to strike at the same time for, once hit, the hump-shoulders would stampede, and there would be no second chance.

On a signal from Goldmane, they struck, each team bracketing its chosen target. And though wolfrider and goatrider had not hunted together before, and could not share a sending, they worked well together, did not get in each other's way, took advantage of their own special weapons, and the two teams brought down their selected prey within moments of each other, leaving the rest of the herd to panic and race off toward the rise.

The two hump-shoulders, separated by some five of eights of paces, lay heavy and huge on the now trampled grass. The elves of both tribes got off their panting mounts. It had been a very short hunt, but a strenuous one, and all the elves were, if truth be known, somewhat surprised at its rather sudden and rapid success. The hump-shoulders were not very far from the rise, but they were far too heavy to move, so the elves began the job of butchery where they were.

First the animals were skinned. Each party would take one of the skins home. But as he worked next to Two Shadows, Freefoot felt an odd confusion come over him, so that his movements were clumsy, his attention wandered, and once or twice he nearly cut himself.

Then each of the hump-shoulders was gutted, and the best of the innards were taken out and eaten on the spot, with the wolves getting their fair share. Still Freefoot felt strange, and though he was self conscious over his inability to concentrate, he noticed that Two Shadows, too, seemed to be having some difficulty.

When they had eaten all they could of the rich, inner meat, the rest of the carcasses were cut up. It was not the way for elves to leave anything edible behind from a hunt, but they still had plenty of antelope left over, and their mounts would be heavily burdened so that the elves would have to walk. The only thing to do was to make up bundles, as large as they could, of what was best, and abandon what was left to the carrion birds.

There was still too much to carry, so they decided to spend a quiet afternoon and evening resting where they were, so that they could eat as much as they could, and then leave for their respective homelands early the next morning. But rather than take everything to the top of the rise they prepared a new camp on the flat of the prairie, just a bit removed from what remained of the hump-shoulder carcasses.

When a wolf or an elf is stuffed full of meat, there is no problem with just sitting back for several hours, or longer if need be, attending to nothing more important than digestion. And so it was now, with little talk, and all of it comfortable, a modest sharing of dreamberries and wheatberry wine, and plenty of dozing under the hot sun, sheltered from the cool breeze by the tall grass which rustled over their heads where they lay. Goats, of course, could much away contentedly forever.

The situation between Freefoot and Two Shadows was becoming impossible. Freefoot couldn't keep his eyes from the other elf, nor she from him, though they both strove to put the rest of the elves between them. After all, though they were closely related and still shared much culture, they had different places to go, different obligations to meet, and had no time for foolishness such as this. But somehow, try though they might, they always managed to find themselves together again and, though they strove to keep their unwanted fascination to themselves, it was impossible to conceal their attraction for each other from the other elves. Goldmane, Sunset, Buckmaster, Grazer, and Evensong watched Freefoot and Two Shadows, with expressions of mixed amusement and concern. Conversation gradually died, and soon the two elves found themselves the center of the unwelcome attention of all their fellows. The other elves did not say the obvious, but watched and waited for Two Shadows or Freefoot to be the first to admit the problem, then shared, with them, their mixed feelings about what it meant.

Springwillow, eldest of the wolfriders, put her hand on Ax-Hand's arm. He was eldest of the goatriders. They exchanged glances, then stood up and went off into the tall grass to confer. Freefoot knew what they were talking about, and Two Shadows did too, as did all the others, but nobody said anything. Freefoot once again tried to move away from Two Shadows, but found when he sat down that he had somehow gotten even nearer to her.

The other elves were not finding it easy either. That which was happening between Freefoot and Two Shadows was usually a cause for rejoicing, but they were strangers to each other, had obligations to other people, and there could be no easy solution to the problems that the consequences of their condition were sure to bring.

The two elder elves did not confer long. When they came back they stood before Freefoot and Two Shadows, who at last got to their feet.

"You are my chief," Springwillow, "but I am your elder. You know what has happened, and what you must do."

Freefoot looked at Two Shadows as Springwillow spoke. If he let himself admit it, he could think of nothing better to look at.

"It is recognition," Ax-Hand said to Two Shadows, who seemed to pay no heed but instead found something of immense interest in Freefoot's eyes. "Our tribes are different, but what of that? You must do what you must, as you truly wish if you let yourselves admit it. As for what happens afterward, that is another thing."

It was what would happen afterward which was of greatest concern to both afflicted elves. Other affectionate attachments would pose no problem, of course, either past, present, or future. But elves who recognize each other not only yearn to mate and produce a child, but also to share that child with each other during its growing years, and to share more of their own lives as they are able.

But they were from different tribes, who lived far from each other. Neither elf could leave their own people to live with the other. Freefoot, after all, was chief of the forest elves, and Two Shadows, as it turned out, was the prairie elves' best night tracker. Neither could be spared.

Recognition was a difficult experience enough, but these two had special problems that none of their companions here or at home could help with. No one knew what to do when two elves from different tribes recognized each other. They could not stay together, nor could they separate. Freefoot didn't want Two Shadows to bear his cub somewhere out of his reach, and Two Shadows didn't want to be alone when her kid was born. But what could they do?

The other elves recognized the difficulty all too well, and discretely gave them room and left them out of their conversation. Freefoot and Two Shadows struggled alone together for a while longer, neither speaking to the other, indeed not really having to, and at last, as the sun began to fall down toward the edge of the world, and the sky began to grow dark, they saw that there was no hope for it. The need of their recognition was painful, so they left the others and climbed, uncertain and anxious, to the top of the rise.

The two moons were nearly full, low in the sky but rising as it grew dark, the Daughter above, the Mother below. Freefoot and Two Shadows stood together in the sparser grass on top of the rise and watched as the two moons came together, kissed and passed, so that now the Daughter was below and the Mother above. But this was one of those rare moments when, instead of separating, the two moons moved together again, kissed and passed again. It was an omen.

"We will meet again," Freefoot said.

"It still isn't fair," Two Shadows told him. "Why do we have to be from different tribes?"

There was no answer for that. Recognition was a fact of life, sometimes hard, though usually a source of great happiness. It happened, and there was no recourse.

They spoke together for a while, trying in a few short moments to learn something about each other, so that they wouldn't feel so much like strangers. Freefoot found himself liking this wild prairie elf, and that almost made it worse. He couldn't be sure but he felt that perhaps Two Shadows liked him too, just a little bit.

Behind them the camp of the elves was quiet. They were as alone as they would ever be. The two moons moved slowly across the sky, drawing farther and farther apart now, but Freefoot and Two Shadows grew closer and closer together.

They were wakened once, when it was still dark, when companions, they didn't know who, drew a warm skin over them to protect them from the chill and damp. Half asleep, they cuddled together, and the two moons went their separate ways down toward the horizon.

Springwillow and Ax-Hand came up the hill together at dawn, talking loudly to announce their approach. Freefoot sat up and stretched. He ached. He was not used to sleeping on the hard ground, and this ground had rocks in it.

"It's time to go," old Springwillow said. Two Shadows rolled over and dragged the skin up over her face, thereby exposing her feet and legs.

"We must get the meat back to our people," solid Ax-Hand said. "Come as quickly as you can."

The two elder elves left them then. For a moment Freefoot and Two Shadows clung to each other. Freefoot sought for something to say, but there were no words that were adequate. He could tell, deep within his body, that the purpose of the recognition had been accomplished, and still he found himself drawn to this stranger. And now they would have to part, and he didn't know if he could keep his regret, his sorrow, his grief under control.

"Is there no way we can stay together?" Two Shadows asked.

"I would go with you if I could," Freefoot said. "I think the life of a nomad would suit me very well indeed. But I am the chief of my tribe, and I can't just walk away from them. I must go back. You are not a chief, you are more free than I. Can you come with me?"

"I see in the night the way none other of my people can. I should be with my tribe even now, instead of here on this hunt, and with the darkness of winter my eyes will become even more needed. I would go with you if I could, but I too must return home."

The sun rose above the edge of the world, and they knew that their friends would be waiting for them. They threw off the skin that covered them and began to dress. They spoke more, quietly, wistfully, but they both knew there was no hope. Freefoot could not live without his wolves, his violent hunting life, and could never be happy in the stoic, formal society of the goatriders, however much he might enjoy their constant wandering.

And Two Shadows could never be comfortable with the violent wolfriders, nor long endure staying in the forest holt, and could not live without the structured society that her people shared. The two tribes might meet now and then without friction, but for either of the elves to go with the other tribe would be a great hardship indeed and, in their cases, a hardship for others besides themselves.

At last they could excuse no more delay. They heard the sounds of voices coming from the common camp, so they walked, slowly, down the gentle slope of the rise to rejoin their friends. They found them eating a light breakfast, tactful but curious about what the two had decided.

"It would be better, of course," Goldmane said, "if you could stay together. Perhaps, Freefoot, you could come and live with us for a while."

"No," Springwillow and Grazer said together, and Sunset just shook her head.

"Freefoot is our chief," Grazer went on. "While he lives, no one else would take his place, and if he went with you it would leave us leaderless."

"Perhaps Two Shadows could come live with us for a while" Sunset suggested.

"No," Ax-Hand said.

"We couldn't spare her," Goldmane said at the same time.

"Two Shadows is too important to us," Buckmaster went on, and told how her night vision served the whole tribe.

"And besides," Evensong said, "our birth rate is now too low, and we know too well the value of a child born in recognition, especially one with more wolf blood, since our wolf blood is growing thin. This child must be born among us."

These arguments were too similar to those which Freefoot and Two Shadows had already answered between themselves, and both were angered and saddened by the repeat. "Enough of this," Freefoot said. "Two Shadows and I have already talked this out, and we can see no solution. We each must go back to our own people." The other elves fell silent.

Freefoot and Two Shadows stood together, with their arms around each other, and paid no attention to the others, who eventually went on about the business of packing up their mounts and getting ready to leave. Though the activity went on around them, it was almost as if they were alone.

"I will come and see you," Freefoot said, "as soon as I can."

"It's a long way," Two Shadows said. "How will you find us?"

"I don't know. When are you farthest south?"

"During the winter, but then we are far east of here. This is the best time of year if you can come."

"It's hard to get away. I try, but I seldom have much time."

"Please come, next year if you can."

"I will try," Freefoot said. "I want to see you again, and see our cubling, our kidling."

"Promise me you will come."

"I promise."

"She is dead," Hawkcatcher said, "a three of eights and three seasons past, trampled by hump-shoulders on a hunt."

Freefoot could not answer for a moment, then, "I am sorry," he said, and he was, truly. He could still remember Two Shadows' face, narrow and tan, though he had known her for so short a time so long ago. He could remember the way she walked in the moonlight, the sound of her low voice, the flash of her hands.

"Why should you be sorry?" Hawkcatcher asked. "You never came back." He stood and turned, then knelt, picked up a fist-sized chunk of quartz, white but streaked with red the color of blood, and flung it away into the tall grass beyond the rise. It was a good throw, farther than Freefoot could have thrown it. Hawkcatcher stood staring after it, long after it fell to earth, his back to Freefoot. "You promised you would come for her," he said.

"I tried," Freefoot said, "many times." It was not easy for him to keep his voice even. "But I was unable to leave my people."

"You promised my mother you would come for her," Hawkcatcher said as he turned to face Freefoot again. His voice, his body, betrayed no anger, though his words hinted at a very great anger indeed.

"I am the chief of my people," Freefoot said, "I cannot just go off as I wish."

"You promised," Hawkcatcher repeated.

"I know, and I'm sorry. But my people were more than five of eights then, against only two of you, however much I cared. It was not a choice I wanted to make."

"Are you sure? Perhaps you were glad to never see my mother again — "

"We were recognized!" Freefoot said as an anger of his own began to heat up in him, pushing aside the shock and wonder and regret. "Neither of us asked for that. But it happened."

And had not happened again. Starflower, his lifemate, had borne him two cubs, but they had never recognized each other. Their fondness for each other could hardly be more than it was, nor their life-long commitment any more profound. But they were not recognized — and Freefoot and Two Shadows had been. . .

Hawkcatcher was staring at him. "I didn't know that." Hawkcatcher's eyes flickered as if he were confused.

"She didn't tell you?" Freefoot asked, astounded.

"No. Though I should have known. A few children are born out of recognition, but not many."

"About half our children come into the world that way," Freefoot said. "All are equally precious to us."

"But not me," Hawkcatcher said, and now the bitter tone in his voice, the anger, the hatred, could not be denied. "If you recognized my mother," he said, and his eyes glittered with ill-concealed emotion, "then you knew a child would be born of that mating. But you didn't care enough to come back and see me."

"I tried," Freefoot said again. "I wanted to come. But I am not as free to leave my holt as I would like to be."

"And yet you are here now."

". . . yes, I am here now."

It had been a long time since he had tried to find Two Shadows. Though he dared not admit it, he had all but forgotten about that one meeting, and the promise. The first year he had tried desperately to break away from his duties, but that had been the year of the sickness. Seven elves had died, and the few who had not caught the fever had all they could do keeping the others alive. The next year he had been on a big hunt far to the south, and by the time they had returned it was full winter, and the chance for all travel that far north had passed.

And so it had been, season after season. There had been times, later, when he had been free to wander, and he had come out, but it would seem that he had not come far enough. This small rise was on the far borders of the goatriders' territory, and was visited by them, if at all, only at certain times of the year. Had he gone further — as in fact he knew how to do — he might have found her, with her people, somewhere, to the far north. But he had not done so.

And the seasons had rolled, and his duties, as minor as they were, had intervened, until at last he stopped trying. And this time, though he dared not admit it, he had come not to find her, but just to get away from the holt for a while, to escape.

"And it is too late now," Hawkcatcher said. "Two Shadows is dead. But I am glad," he said, though he did not sound glad, "to meet you at last."

"I am glad too," Freefoot said, and he truly was, though the emotions inside him were far from comprehensible. That Two Shadows would bear him a cub was the inevitable result of recognition. It was that which had tormented Freefoot most, during those first seasons, when he had been unable to take the time to find Two Shadows as he had promised. Two elves who recognized each other usually mated for life, but not always. Indeed, it was possible, though rare, for recognized elves to not like each other at all. Freefoot had liked Two Shadows well enough and more, but it was the cub he had never met which, then, had drawn his thoughts back to this low rise on the prairie.

Perhaps he should have tried harder. Hawkcatcher was a cub any wolfrider could be proud of. His strength and grace were evident in every movement, his competence proved by his health and presence here, his intelligence obvious in his speech, his wisdom in his bearing and his manner. . . except for that distance which he kept between himself and his father, compounded of strangeness, suspicion, and anger.

"Come back with me to the holt," Freefoot said to his son.

"I will not go anywhere with you," Hawkcatcher said. "I am sorry now that I hunted with you, that I shared meat with you."

The words were like a blow. "But why?" Freefoot asked. He found it hard to breathe.

"Because you are an oath-breaker. You knew my mother would bear a kid, and you were afraid to assume your responsibility. You mated with my mother but you never cared for her, and you certainly never cared for me. You abandoned us — "

"That's not true," Freefoot tried to say.

"And you are a liar," Hawkcatcher said. He stepped up closer to his father so that his face was just a handspan away. "And you are a coward." He pressed forward, and Freefoot was forced to step back. "You dare not fight me," Hawkcatcher said, almost softly, an almost smile on his face.

"I will not fight you," Freefoot said. "You are my son. I wouldn't do anything to hurt you."

"You cannot hurt me. You are a weakling. If it would not shame me, I would strike you down now."

Freefoot backed away. "You don't need to hate me like this. I did come looking for you, many times, but I never found your people. The prairie is large, and it took me four days just to get here. I did not know where to look for you, but look for you I did."

"You did not look very far nor very hard." Slowly, Hawkcatcher drew his long knife. "You just make excuses. My mother tried to make excuses for you too, but I saw her pain, her loneliness, year after year." He took a step toward Freefoot, holding the long horn knife, edge up, out to the side. "She suffered until she died. Now it is your turn. Stand and fight me."

"I will not," Freefoot said. He held his arms away from his body. He had put down his bow and quiver when they had prepared to eat, but his ax still hung from his belt. "I never meant to hurt you, I will not hurt you now."

"You are afraid to try." Hawkcatcher suddenly lunged, slashing across the air with his knife. The movement caught Freefoot by surprise, and the blade of antelope horn sliced through the front of his jacket, and through the skin underneath. Freefoot staggered backward, not so much hurt as shocked.

Hawkcatcher held his long knife out in front of him, waving the point at his father's face. "You will fight me, or I will kill you." Freefoot shook his head and backed away again. "Or run like the coward you are," Hawkcatcher taunted.

And this time Freefoot stood his ground. He knew, he thought he knew, that Hawkcatcher was just trying to provoke him, but an accusation of cowardice is not easy for a wolfrider to bear, and this was the fourth in as many moments, and Freefoot could not pass it off.

"You are mistaken," he said softly, "about this and about many things." Maybe, if he talked to him long enough, the first rush of anger would pass, the shamed surprise at discovering with whom he had shared a hunt and meat would leave Hawkcatcher, and the two could talk more rationally. It hurt Freefoot to think that he could never win his son as a friend, but if he could talk him out of his rage, convince him that, unlike the goatriders, Freefoot had not the ability to find any other member of his tribe, however far away they might be, at least they could part company without violence, and Freefoot *would* come looking for his son again, with his people's approval or not.

And so thinking he was again taken by surprise when Hawkcatcher lunged at him, the point of his knife aimed at Freefoot's heart. Only Freefoot's wolf-like reflexes saved him, making him leap back before he knew what was happening. He realized the seriousness of the assault only when the saw his own red blood dripping from the point of the horn blade.

Perhaps Hawkcatcher was a bit surprised by his own success, for he hesitated just a fraction of a heartbeat before lunging again, and this time Freefoot was able to easily dance out of the way of the stabbing knife. But this only angered the younger elf, who now pressed his attack with vigor. Freefoot was forced back, and back, and tripped on a rock and fell. At once Hawkcatcher was at him, and Freefoot was barely able to roll away in time.

He came to his feet in a crouch, and plucked the flint-headed ax from his belt. Hawkcatcher lunged again, and Freefoot tried to block the blow with the ax, perhaps to break the horn weapon. But Hawkcatcher was too fast, knew too well the fragility of his knife, and pulled his attack so that Freefoot's ax merely whistled through the air.

It was a clumsy if deadly fight. Freefoot was larger, heavier, stronger, but his ax was a heavy weapon, and his swings were therefore slower, and he had to recover after each. Hawkcatcher was quicker, faster, lighter on his feet, and his weapon weighed little and struck quickly, but he dared not let even one blow from the ax strike it or it would shatter. And so they fought, Freefoot trying to keep out of Hawkcatcher's way, and trying to disarm him if he could, while Hawkcatcher tried to catch his father, and at the same time avoid the heavy headed ax that was not aimed at him but only at his weapon.

Freefoot kept his head, and fought purely defensively. In time they would both tire, and then the fight would end perforce. Hawkcatcher, on the other hand, got more and more angry, more and more enraged, but instead of losing control, his attacks became stronger, his lunges longer, his strikes more accurate, until at last he was pricking Freefoot every third time.

If Freefoot was going to survive this fight, he would have to do more than just defend himself. He would have to counter attack, either to wound or to kill.

But he couldn't bring himself to do it. "I would rather die than kill you," he called, panting, to his son.

Hawkcatcher stopped then, suddenly, breathing heavily, his head slightly tilted to one side, his eyes, brilliant and mad, staring as if into Freefoot's soul. "Would you indeed," he said.

"I would." Freefoot lowered his ax. "You are my child after all."

"You have no other children?"

" — I do."

Hawkcatcher smiled, in a strange way. "You would leave them fatherless."

"Rather that than kill you."

"You cannot kill me. You cannot even touch me. And your arm is beginning to tire. Soon I will kill you, whether you yield to me or not. And then your mate will be alone, your children will be orphans, and your people will have no chief." His grin grew broader, and more insane. "It's the easy way out, isn't it?"

Freefoot had never thought of himself as much of a leader, but Hawkcatcher's words stung. He felt guilty about not seeking out his cub before, though his claim of pressing responsibilities had been true. He had said, before, that the needs of the many overrode the needs of the few, and his own desire to find Two Shadows and her cubling. How could he now yield to his distaste for what he must do? Suretrail, the tribe's second in command, was more than capable of leading the elves of the holt, as he had demonstrated many times in Freefoot's absence, but the tribe would be thrown into turmoil during the transition, and if he didn't come back they would come looking for him, and that could only result in more hardship.

Hawkcatcher struck, and Freefoot barely turned aside. He swung his ax backhanded, at Hawkcatcher's shoulder. Maybe he could wound his son so badly that he would have to stop fighting. But Hawkcatcher was even more agile than before, and the blow never struck. Again the younger elf attacked, again the older elf barely avoided death as he sought to disable his opponent, and again he failed.

Then Hawkcatcher feinted at Freefoot's face, and struck instead low down at his belly, not a fatal wound, but a painful one, a long wound, between skin and muscle, a wound that bled copiously.

Freefoot almost didn't feel it. But he knew that the next time, Hawkcatcher would kill him. He knew that there was no way he could disarm his son, no way he could simply wound him. The pain of that knowledge hurt far more than the jagged tear along his body. It was almost more than he could bear.

He was not aware of how long his thoughts wandered. It was not so much an indulgence in memory as a literal return, in his mind at least, to events past. And it was not that, *per se*, which obscured the passage of time so much as the nature of wolf-time, in which there was only "now," no past or future, only a present, whether of objective reality or subjective memory or fantasy. In wolf time there was no time. Whatever one's attention was directed to, that was all of reality, outside in the world or inside in one's thoughts.

And so, though he had not expected to hear the other two wolfriders approach so soon, he was not surprised when they did so since, after all, one moment was the same as another, and just because the sun had moved another handspan across and now down the sky, and the shadows of grass and wolf and himself had turned around from west to east, that was no cause for alarm. This moment, as he looked down the gentlest of slopes toward the two wolfriders now only a few moments away, and the previous moment two hundred seasons before, and the one before that when it had all begun, and the one before that when he had thought that there was still time enough to remember, all were the same moment after all, and as he thought about them now, the moments could not be separated or distinguished, indeed they could not even be ordered.

But as he watched his lifemate and his third and youngest son approach, the threads of time sorted themselves out again. After all, he was not just wolf, but elf too, and the greater part, and as such he had past and future as well as present, especially future.

He couldn't help, as young Oakroot drew near, but search his face, his features, for some resemblance to that other son. But all he could see was himself reflected, and Starflower, a little bit of each in a face that was for the most part Oakroot's own.

Shag sniffed, sat up, sniffed again, recognized the approaching scents, and waited beside his elf-friend. A moment or two later Starflower, riding Snapper, and young Oakroot on Grimjaw — only his third wolf — came to the top of the rise and dismounted. Neither spoke, though Starflower did send a wordless thought of comfort.

Freefoot stepped aside as they neared so that they could stand beside him by the long, low mound of stones. Shag got up and out of the way, and went over to greet the other two wolves on his own terms.

Both Starflower and Oakroot knew the story, though, like Fangslayer and Longoak, they had never been here, and now Fangslayer and Longoak would never get the chance. Freefoot's lifemate and youngest child — nearly full grown, Freefoot thought, just three eights of seasons more — stood quietly, looking at the mound.

At last Oakroot spoke. "Have you visited this place often?"

"Not once since the stones were laid," Freefoot said. "And we won't come here again. The humans are too many and too close. And too dangerous."

"What about his people?" Oakroot asked.

"I cannot believe," Freefoot said, "that the humans would have befriended our prairie cousins, and they almost certainly would have met by now, so Hawkcatcher's people must have been — driven away, at best, or killed, more likely. If they were still alive, I would have expected them to have come to us long before now. We are kin, after all, and they knew where we were, even if we have forgotten them. I'm afraid they have been destroyed."

"We don't know that," Starflower said.

"No, and we never shall. If they escaped alive, the humans are between us and them, and we'll never have the chance to meet them."

"It's strange to think," Oakroot said, "that we lived so near each other, but never visited each other."

"We were too different," Freefoot said. "Even that first time, even then we had become too unlike each other to have easily become friends. And the last time we were all but strangers. They smoked their meat and did not eat it raw. And they put their dead on the ground." He gazed down at the mound.

"Why did you cover him up?" Oakroot asked.

"He asked me to, before he died." He paused for a long moment. "It was the only thing I ever did for him."

Though it was just shortly past midday, the wind from the north began to grow noticeably cooler. Far off on the northern horizon, barely visible, was the first of the huge storm clouds that brought with them the cold weather and the snow. It was the first sign that the season had truly turned, though they would not feel it for some eights of days yet back at the holt.

Except that there was no more holt. The humans who had found it had ravaged the dens, and the elves now lived with their wolf-friends in the woods. And they would all be going further south, away from the coming cold, as well as from the humans.

Freefoot didn't want to go. Since the humans had come, his responsibilities as chief had multiplied. He had more and more often had to exercise his authority, make decisions, assume command — lead. It took more and more of his time, until he was hardly ever able to get away by himself. As it was, of the whole tribe, only his lifemate and his sons had not been angry with him for taking the eight of days it needed to make the trip here and back. But then, only his lifemate and sons knew the whole story, and none was alive now save he who had actually met the cousins of the long grass so long ago.

And with the journey southward, up to the highlands and whatever lay beyond, Freefoot's responsibilities would grow only greater. He wished he could escape all that, go looking for the prairie elves, as he should have done so long ago, far away to the north and east now, to see if they had by some chance escaped the encroaching humans. How long would that take, if they were there at all? Not just an eight of days or two, a season? an eight of seasons?

The wind blew, cool now, and the scent of carrion was gone. Far away were antelopes, moving south from the vast northern prairie, to escape the worst of the cold, some of them to graze right at the edge of the forest. The hissing of the grass grew louder as the wind grew stronger, and a new note crept in as the grass began to move more vigorously, a sound not so much like a stream as like the waves on the lake just north of the forest.

A herd of bow-horns far off to the west made a darkness in the grass. To the east was nothing. North were the storm-clouds, a dark irregular line on the horizon. To the south, invisible, was the forest where Freefoot's people waited for him to return and lead them away. Overhead, a hawk cast its shadow on the mound of stones, and then was gone. And a moment later Freefoot too, with Starflower and Oakroot, were gone, riding their wolves back, to do what they had to do.

Afterword

I became a part of this in 1984. I was attending a convention on the East Coast, possibly SciCon. I had met Robert Lynn Asprin some time before, and we enjoyed our conversations. One time he asked my wife, Diane, how she got along with me being so intense. I guess he wasn't aware of just how intense he was.

This weekend, Saturday night, Bob asked me what I was doing Sunday morning. I said, "Nothing." He said, "Wrong, you're having breakfast with me."

Sigh. Nobody wants to get up Sunday morning at a convention. But I did, went down to the dining room and found Bob and Lynn Abbey, and Richard and Wendy Pini, and other people, all sitting at a large table. I wasn't the last to come. Among these other people were C. J. Cherryh, Janny Wurts, Nancy Springer, and others whom I don't remember right now. They were all far more important writers than I was, so I was prepared to just listen in.

They were discussing a shared-world project, called *Blood of Ten Chiefs*. Bob Asprin and Lynn Abbey had created Thieve's World, a shared world which, while written by a number of people, had internal consistency throughout its many volumes. Each writer had his or her own style, but all the stories linked and tied together. Richard and Wendy wanted to do the same thing, and the writers gathered here were being asked if they wanted to participate. Including me.

Some time later each of us got a contract, and a pile of documents describing the world of two moons, the basics of elf life, a list of the ten chiefs about whom we would be writing (Cutter was the eleventh, hence the blood of ten), and other things.

I had read the comics, collected the compilations, and though I preferred my own worlds, I was pretty sure I could do this. This was going to be fun.

Each of the ten chiefs had a short bio, their parents, children, siblings, special skills, a sketch of their personalities, and so on. I had been assigned Freefoot, and his bio read as follows:

Freefoot.

That was all. Nothing else about him. No history, nothing. I was surprised, and confused, and felt rather left out. Everybody got something they could work with. I got a name. I knew who his predecessor and successor were (father and son), but nothing else.

All right. So. A king has no stories, no history, no adventures and accomplishments. What that usually meant was that he (or she) died shortly after coming to the throne, as it were. (Elves don't have thrones.) There wasn't an awful lot I could do with that.

Or, maybe, that king lived in a time of peace, no wars, no outside enemies, just quiet growth and development. I began to get interested.

What were these elves really like? How did they live? What kind of every-day problems did they have? What kind of problems, the solutions to which made good stories? Hmmm. Since I had been given nothing, I would have a free hand. My story started after everything before hand was resolved, and others when they took up after Freefoot's time wouldn't have to tie in any leftovers. Hmmmm.

I did some research. I found that wolves really hunted mostly in the day time. I found how much area a wolf needed to hunt in without depleting the supply of prey. I added up my elves and their wolves, and created a place large enough that they wouldn't have to migrate. I still have the map.

Then I created the elves. Some I had inherited, there was no helping that, but I still made them my own. Each elf had a name, a wolf, a talent, a personality. I made a card for each, and marked them as adults or youths or children. I did not segregate them by gender. When I needed a character, I drew a card. If I needed a youth or child, I drew from those cards. Sometimes I needed a specific character, such as Freefoot, or the omega-elf, or the eldest elf, but otherwise my characters were chosen at random. I still have the cards.

I wrote the stories for myself. I didn't try to compete with other writers far more experienced than I. If I wasn't good enough, I would be replaced, and I could live with that. I was not replaced, I wrote stories for all six volumes, including the last which, having been accepted and paid for, was cancelled for some reason. I was happy with these stories, I was proud of them. One time Wendy told me that she liked my elves, and you can believe that made me feel good.

———————————

Characters

These are the wolfriders in these stories. Those who lived before and after are described in their own stories, written by others who participated in creating *The Blood of Ten Chiefs*.

Bluesky is an older elf. She is the mother of Rillwalker and Talon. She is the master flint-knapper, with no magic talent whatsoever, just pure skill. She is also a good archer and thrower, and likes to indulge in dreamberries now and then. Her weapons of choice are the bow or javeline, and the ax.

Brightmist is the lifemate of Shadowflash. She is the apprentice knapper. She has a minor rock-shaping ability, which more than compensates for her lack of natural skill. Her weapons of choice are the bow and the spear.

Catcher is Graywing's daughter and Grazer's mother. Her lifemate had died long ago. She is the master wood-crafter and, like Glade, a story-teller, though her stories were more fancies than lessons. She is called Catcher because she made traps, of all kinds, to catch anything that might be caught. It is her preferred way of hunting, though she could use the javelin and the bow well.

Crystalmoss, the daughter of Rainbow and Two-Wolves, is the master thrower, whether with stone or javelin or dart, or whatever else came to hand. She is something of a craftsman, and makes all her own weapons, whether specially for throwing, or the small axes she also sometimes used. She also pays a lot of attention to the cublings, and would take them two or three at a time on expeditions. The process of growing up was very important to her.

Dayshine is the boychild of Puckernut and Rillwalker.

Deerstorm is one of the youngest elders. Her lifemate is Fangslayer, and their boychild is Ebony. Though otherwise unexceptional, she is the healer. Daughter of Grazer and Dreamsnake, she is a good, all-around elf, and prefers to hunt with the bow and the javelin.

Dewdrop is the girlchild of Dreamsnake and Grazer. Small, pretty, pale gold hair. Her adult name is Faun.

Dreamsnake is an archetypal parent. Her main contribution to the clan is the care-taking of the cublings. She likes to do it, and does it well, though she has only two children herself, the girlchild, Dewdrop, and Deerstorm. She is a good teacher, and a good companion, and her presence lends a stability to life at the holt, especially since most of the younger adults had been raised, at least in part, by her. She is called Dreamsnake because she has a gift of dealing with reptiles, and had at one time confronted a giant blacksnake single handed. The huge serpent, which could have swallowed any of the elf cublings whole, had been unable to figure out what to do with her, and she had sent it away. No one else could command reptiles at all. Her preferred weapons are the bow and the thrown stone.

Ebony is the boychild of Fangslayer and Deerstorm. He has black hair.

Fairheart is the lifemate of Moonblossom, the father of Suretrail's dead lifemate, and of Starbright. He is the fire keeper, bow maker, and the wisest elder, on whom all the others depend, even more than Freefoot. Most of the time he makes bows, or hunts with them. His preferred weapon, besides the bow, is simply the thrown stone.

Fangslayer is the son of Freefoot and Starflower, his lifemate is Deerstorm, and he is the father of Ebony. He is the master hunter, and a good tracker. He is good with wolves, is very strong and calm, and is the pacifier when tempers flare. He is not very talkative, though he enjoyed good company. He had killed several of the huge cats they called longtooths, hence his name, and his favored weapons are the ax and the spear.

Faun, child-name Dewdrop, is not quite an adult. She is the daughter of Dreamsnake and Grazer.

Feather is the boychild of Freefoot and Starflower.

Fernhare has outlived two lifemates, and now lives with Glade. She is perhaps the most typical elf, except that she is the most fertile, having four children who survived. Her eldest is Stride, by her first mate. Treewing and Rainbow were fathered by her second lifemate. Glade is the father of Greentwig. None of her children had been born from Recognition. Her preferred weapons are the bow and the thrown stone.

Fire-Eyes, with her lifemate Ironwood, is the mother of Spinner. She is a master archer, with both inborn talent and learned skill. She is also rather long-sighted. She was named for her dreams and visions. The talent that sets her apart is the ability to look inward, nearly as far as she can look outward. She can sometimes talk with her ancestors, and with other elves who had died, and can sometimes, when she has eaten enough dreamberries, tap the ancestral pool that all the elves shared but few could perceive. Her preferred weapons are the bow and ax.

Freefoot is the son of Huntress Skyfire, the chief before him. His lifemate is Starflower, and is the father of Fangslayer of and Feather, who's adult name is Longoak. He is the sixth in the line of chiefs, the symbol of the clan, their leader, arbiter, and judge, their rallying center and the focus of identity. Named because he is something of a wanderer, and exercises his role only when necessary. He likes company is small numbers, and would rather wander the world, perhaps with a friend or two, seeing what was to be seen, rather than to be a chief, making decisions, and bearing responsibilities. Sometimes he feels he is a very bad chief indeed. His preferred weapons are the bow and ax.

Glade is the lifemate of Fernhare, and the father of Green-twig. He is the Keeper of the Way. Graywing knows more lore, but Glade knows what it means, and how to interpret the Way whenever the need arises. He is a special kind of lore-master, a parable-teller, and he is also the most volatile and impetuous, except with his son Greentwig and his lifemate. His preferred weapons are the spear and bow.

Graywing was the eldest elf, and named because she, alone of all the elves, showed a change of color in her long, once-black hair, very rare among elves and supernatural. She was born in Prey-Pacer's time, before Two-Spear and Huntress Sky-Fire, and had several children, but the only one surviving is Catcher. She remembers things, the parentage of all the elves, the major events since she had come of age so long ago, and knows more lore than anyone, though not necessarily its best use. Her preferred weapons are the spear and thrown stone.

Grazer, the son of Catcher, is Dreamsnake's lifemate, and with her is the father of Deerstorm and the girlchild Dewdrop. He is a specialist in herbs and other food plants, and is also the second most reckless hunter. He was at least half a head taller than the next tallest elf, hence his name, tree-top grazer. His preferred weapons are the spear and the bow.

Greentwig is the son of Glade and Fernhare. Though he is fully grown, and has been for many turns of the seasons, he still has his cub-name. He is slow, and simple, and has not grown up.

He is not very good in anything, has no skills, and shows no talents. He is not actually retarded, or he would not have survived so long. His parents love him dearly, though they are unhappy with his inability to mature. They know that someday he will find himself in a situation which any other elf except he could survive. Though he is somewhat of a burden on the other elves, their care of him was exemplary. Had he been a wolf, he would have died long ago, but elves are not wolves, no matter how much they might take after them. His favorite weapons are the ax and the bow, and he is not very good with either.

Hornbird was an orphan, in a way only elves could truly appreciate. She is old enough that her parents died long ago isn't important, but her siblings, her lifemates, and her children are also dead. She is alone, though she was related in some way to every elf at the holt. It is perhaps that aloneness that makes her something of a dreamberry dreamer. She is the second eldest elf after Graywing, and can remember Huntress Skyfire clearly. Her contribution to the clan is being the bonesmith, as well as a decent hunter with bow and javelin.

Ironwood is the son of Talon and Treewing, lifemate of Fire-Eyes, and father of Spinner. He is a typical hunter, but also a Plant Shaper, something of an herbal-loreist, and a woodcrafter. His preferred weapons are the spear and bow.

Lonebriar, later Talon, which see.

Moonblossom is the lifemate Fairheart, mother of Suretrail's dead mate, and of Starbright. Her twin sister is Starflower. She is the number one tracker and the number three hunter. She has the special ability to communicate over long ranges with Starflower. They can reach almost twice as far as even Rillwalker can send. Her preferred weapons are the ax and javelin, and she is an excellent hunting companion.

Puckernut is so-called because his personality was as wry as the nut, as was his tongue. He is the lifemate of Rillwalker, and the father of Quickthorn and Dayshine. He is the tailor for the elves, but his special talent was that he is able to sense magic of any kind, anywhere, and trace it to its source. He can read the other elves to some degree, knowing their health and condition. In spite of his outward nature. His preferred weapons are the spear and ax.

Quickthorn is the elder son of Puckernut and Rillwalker. He has no lifemate. He knows no fear, is a risk-taker, and prone to be reckless, though he is not adventurous or impetuous. His preferred weapons are the long lance and the bow.

Rainbow is Two-Wolves lifemate, and with him the mother of Crystalmoss and Silvercub. She is the artist and the ornament maker, hence her name. She can work as easily in wood or bone or stone or leather, and with any kind of pigment, as long as it was to make a plain thing pretty, or to make some pretty thing. She is also the adventurer, always eager to go off and "do something." Her preferred weapons are the spear and ax.

Rillwalker is the daughter of Bluesky, her lifemate is Puckernut, and her children are Quickthorn and Dayshine. She is the best fisher, and may have an ability with fish. She is quickest of hand, river explorer, and makes needles for Puckernut from fish bones. She is named because she likes to wander up and down rivers and streams, and prefers to be my herself most of the time. She is the strongest sender. Her preferred weapons are the bow and axe, as well as fishhooks and nets.

Shadowflash is the lifemate of Brightmist. He is the clan's mischief maker, and the longest sighted, even more than Fire-eyes. His preferred weapons are the spear and thrown stone.

Silvercub is the boychild of Rainbow and Two-Wolves. His hair is so white it was almost transparent.

Silverknife is the daughter of Stringsong and Whiteraven. She is the strongest and best of the elves, but has a tendency to be reckless.

Smarthand is noted for his girth. His preferred weapons are two axes.

Spinner is the boychild of Ironwood and Fire-Eyes.

Starbright is the girlchild of Fairheart and Moonblossom.

Starflower wis Freefoot's lifemate, and mother with him of Fangslayer and the boychild Feather. She is a leather maker, and the tribe's number two hunter. She shared with her sister Moon-blossom a special ability to communicate over ranges far longer than other elves could, and indeed was almost always aware of her twin, whether either of them was actively sending or not. Her preferred weapons are the spear and javelin.

Stonefist, previously Greentwig, which see.

Stride is the daughter of Fernhare and Treewing's sister. She is especially wolf-like and something of a loner, though wolves are not loners, and she hunts like a wolf. She gets along with the other elves well enough, but she prefers to be by herself. She is an explorer, not only of distant lands but of the forests around the holt, which she knows better than anybody. Her preferred weapons are the javelin and thrown stone.

Stringsong, his deceased lifemate was Whiteraven, and he is the father of the girl-child Warble, who later becomes Sil-verknife. He can make cord from almost anything, from hair, leather, bark, grass, or whatever, and can make it by weaving, plaiting, twisting, or other less common methods. He is a true master. He also makes music with his harp. He has exceptional hearing, and can sense latent talents in children.   An excellent spearman.   Named because he is a sort of 'harpist.'   He is an excellent spearman, and he can also use a bow.

Sunset, named only, died defending the tribe's cublings from a gray bear.

Suretrail is the father of Two-Wolves. He is the second in command after Freefoot, and the number two tracker after Moonblossom, and was named because he could never get lost, and could even find distant places he had never visited, if he knew just one thing about them. His preferred weapons are the javelin and spear.

Talon, previously Lonebriar, is the son of Bluesky, and Treewing's lifemate. He is the father of Ironwood and Whistle. He is an otherwise unexceptional elf, but named because he is the sword-foot 'keeper.'   Does not actually keep the swordfoot, one of those wild and incomprehensible reptiles that only rarely entered the elves' domain. It is the only one in the holt, a 'mysterious stranger', but knows it, can communicate with it, protects it from the others and the others from it. His preferred weapons are the bow and spear.

Treewing is the daughter of Fernhare, the lifemate of Talon, and the mother of Crystalmoss and Whistle. She is a solitary hunter, and an atypical one, who specializes in birds. She was a tree-top climber, even more than the other elves, who all felt at home among the branches, and was especially swift, agile, and quiet. She could talk to birds in a way, which sometimes made her hunting easier, or sometimes harder if she made the mistake of getting to know her prey too well before taking it. Her preferred weapons are the bird-bow and hafted knife.

Two-Wolves is the son of Suretrail, is Rainbow's lifemate, and the father of Crystalmoss and Silvercub. He is a good hunter though otherwise unexceptional, except for his special affinity for wolves. During most of his life he had two at the same time, a most unusual circumstance. He helps the healer, Deerstorm, if she had to attend to wolves, because he could talk to even those who were not his, and even those who were wild. Indeed, he wis on good terms with at least three other wolves in the forest. His preferred weapons are the spear and bow.

Warble, girlchild of Stringsong, later becomes Silverknife.

Whistle, boychild of Talon and Treewing.

Whiteraven, deceased lifemate of Stringsong and mother of Warble.

*****